Tom Keneally was born in 193 ... ...ey. He trained for several years for the C... ... priesthood but did not take Orders.

In a distinguished writing life his work includes *Bring Larks and Heroes*, which won the Miles Franklin Award (1967); *The Chant of Jimmie Blacksmith*, shortlisted for the Booker Prize; *Schindler's Ark*, winner of the 1982 Booker Prize and a major movie.

Tom Keneally is Founding Chair of the Australian Republican Movement. He presently teaches in the graduate writing programme at the University of California, where he holds a Distinguished Professorship. Recently he was made a fellow of the prestigious American Academy of Arts and Sciences.

Other books by Tom Keneally

Thomas Keneally

BRING LARKS AND HEROES

PENGUIN BOOKS

Penguin Books Australia Ltd
487 Maroondah Highway, PO Box 257
Ringwood, Victoria 3134, Australia
Penguin Books Ltd
Harmondsworth, Middlesex, England
Viking Penguin, A Division of Penguin Books USA Inc.
375 Hudson Street, New York, New York 10014, USA
Penguin Books Canada Limited
10 Alcorn Avenue, Toronto, Ontario, Canada M4V 3B2
Penguin Books (N.Z.) Ltd
182-190 Wairau Road, Auckland 10, New Zealand

First published by Cassell, 1967
Published by Penguin Books 1988
2 4 6 8 10 9 7 5 3 1
Copyright © Thomas Keneally, 1967

Made and printed in Australia by Australian Print Group

National Library of Australia
Cataloguing-in-Publication data:

Keneally, Thomas, 1935-
Bring larks and heroes.

ISBN 014 010929 3

I. Title

A823'.3

To Judith
who nursed this poor
herd of chapters
to pasture

AUTHOR'S NOTE

This novel is set in a penal colony in the South Pacific. The time is the late eighteenth century. Though the germ-idea from which the book grew was a passage in Captain Watkin Tench's journal, *Account of Settlement at Port Jackson*, and although many of the administrative details of this fictional station will resemble those of the settlement of which Tench wrote, the members of the administration are all – for better or worse – imaginary.

The geography of the colony suggests that of Sydney, but is not meant to be identified with it.

An example of the liberties I have taken is the use of the word 'felon' in preference to 'convict'. While 'felon' did not, until well into the nineteenth century, become a general term for transported prisoners, it is used generally of prisoners in this story. 'Convict' is a word which possesses pungent tones and colours, a word loaded with distracting evocations, especially for Australian readers. Whereas 'felon' was free to take on the colour of whatever happened in these pages.

Anachronistic idioms have been avoided wherever their use would seem too blatant. But it is hoped that the reader who accepts the claim that the world of this novel is a world of its own will also accept the claim that it is allowed to have an idiom of its own.

I

AT the world's worse end, it is Sunday afternoon in February. Through the edge of the forest a soldier moves without any idea that he's caught in a mesh of sunlight and shade. Corporal Halloran's this fellow's name. He's a lean boy taking long strides through the Sabbath heat. Visibly, he has the illusion of knowing where he's going. Let us say, without conceit, that if any of his ideas on this subject were *not* illusion, there would be no story.

He is not exactly a parade-ground soldier today. His hair isn't slicked into a queue, because the garrison he serves in has no pomade left, and some idle subaltern is trying to convert the goo into candles. Halloran's in his shirt, his forage jacket over his left arm. He wears gaiters over canvas shoes. Anyone who knew firearms would take great interest in the musket he's got in his right hand. It's a rare model that usually hangs in the company commander's office.

The afternoon is hot in this alien forest. The sunlight burrows like a worm in both eye-balls. His jacket looks pallid, the arms are rotted out of his yellowing shirt, and, under the gaiters, worn for the occasion, the canvas shoes are too light for this knobbly land. Yet, as already seen, he takes long strides, he moves with vigour. He's on his way to Mr Commissary Blythe's place, where his secret bride, Ann Rush, runs the kitchen and the house. When he arrives in the Blythes' futile vegetable garden, and comes mooning up to the kitchen door, he will, in fact, call Ann *my secret bride, my bride in Christ*. She *is* his secret bride. If Mrs Blythe knew, she would do her best to crucify him, though that he is a spouse in secret today comes largely as the result of a summons from Mrs Blythe six weeks ago.

One Sunday about New Year, Halloran came to the kitchen door. Ann rushed out to him, and pressed his shoulders with both hands. This economy of endearment was made very spontaneously; and so it's necessary to say that Ann is not always spontaneous with Corporal Halloran. She sometimes suspects his motives; more often, she suspects God's.

'Promise to wait here, Halloran,' she said, pointing at the threshold. She was whispering like a girl today, not like a conspirator; and she was openly exalted to see him. 'Mrs Blythe wants to talk to you. I was to tell her when you came.'

Hence the rapture, he thought. The front parlour is taking *cognizance* of us, as they say in court.

'What does she want?'

Ann squinted and made a gesture of tamping down his voice with both hands.

'I think she wants to make sure you're decent.'

'Decent!' he hissed. He wasn't angry in any honest sense. Anger was futile since Mrs Blythe had the sovereignty over Ann. 'Who's that old Babylonian whore of a heretic to worry whether I'm decent?'

Girlish for once, Ann rocked on her hips, and kept her laughter in with both hands. 'You make me feel I'm ungrateful,' she said.

'To her?' he asked. 'Ungrateful to *her*? I think she might have her eye on your boy Halloran.'

The girl's mouth went haughty at the very idea.

'She's a most sober woman. It's impossible.'

'She wouldn't be the first one who ever wanted to wriggle round the sofa with a well-bred boy like me, who's got no diseases and doesn't look too bad.'

'You make me laugh,' she said.

She bent with her forefingers of one hand in her mouth and laughed over the top of them. The laughter was supple and shivered with colour like a tree. As soon as Halloran was aware that it was beautiful in itself, instead of relishing it, he winced with pity. He winced, visibly or otherwise, any time that her defencelessness was revealed. The poets promised the young some

2

sort of leisure of love, some easeful immunity. Forget the leisure of love! A long acrid pity for an Ann who would weep, bleed and perish in season, possessed him most of his days.

However, he covered up the fact that her mortality had stung him. He lowered his eyes and uttered a few worn-out vows, and she took his hesitancy for a sort of ardour, and hunched her shoulders with delight. Once again, poets and story-tellers had formulated what a courting male should say, had created the counterfeit coinage of love; and a man was stuck with it.

She told him to wait, and he prepared himself to face Mrs Blythe. He laboured into his jacket. One of his elbows caught in its hot sleeve, and he snorted. He flattened his canvas hat and stowed it in against his ribs. He forced the uppers of his shoes, which had come adrift from the bark-thin soles, into trim shape.

Ann was back.

'Be humble now, Phelim,' she whispered.

Humbly, his canvas feet scraped up the few blocks of sandstone that gave into the back parlour.

He followed Ann around the flanks of a pretentious mahogany table where Mr Blythe starved Mrs Blythe twice a day. The Blythes had shipped out such substantial furniture, because the Home Secretary had intended a volume of industry within the new colony that would make a Commissary a substantial figure, doing substantial work. But the industries had been all still-born; and all Blythe did now was to see that everyone was given two and a bit pounds of flour, two and a bit pounds of meat and a few sundries of other food each week. He restricted his own household to this bare ration.

Such moral heroism, rare amongst Commissary officials, had been gingerly praised by His Excellency when the new ration was announced to the garrison. One look into Blythe's household, however, gave a person an indication of Blythe's true motive: that he was trying to starve his wife, short of killing her, until her pious gut cracked. King in the food store, he could at will prise the lid off a barrel of cheeses and filch one from the top. The Portsmouth victuallers would be blamed for such casual losses as went to keep the Commissary robust.

Now Ann and Halloran had come into the hall. It was breathless and dark, seeming full of the grey ashes of that smouldering day.

'Be humble, love,' she repeated, and knocked on a properly-panelled door towards the front of the house.

'Ongtray!' called Mrs Blythe.

'She means go in,' Ann hissed at him.

'I know, I know.'

'Turn the handle!' called Mrs Blythe, as if a door with a turning handle were a specialty to him.

So Halloran turned the handle, and came into the room where Mrs Blythe used all the day on her devotions and her leg ulcers. She sat in a heavy, straight-backed Italianate chair. Her feet rested on a hassock, and there was a rug over her knees. On a table to her left stood all that was needed to rub, anoint, lance, probe, cauterize and dress her leg. A squat stone lamp, the spoons and needles and lancet, the rags and jars of stewing poultice were, all together, the staple of her life. For Mrs Blythe had been blessed with a putrid leg as other women are with children.

On her right, amongst a deal of impassive mahogany, a slender half-circle of walnut, meant to go against a wall but free to wander in view of Mrs Blythe's disorder, attended its mistress on foal's legs. Her books were heaped on it in two tiered pyramids. Halloran had a passion for the leather wholesomeness of books, and the aley smell of book-mould was for him the smell of matured wisdom. So much so that he thought Aquinas must have smelt like that, and Solomon in his chaster days. There was time to read two titles: *Primitive Christianity* by Bishop Cave, *Sermons for Several Occasions* by John Wesley. Then he had to turn to Mrs Blythe.

She had her square owl's face with its baggy jaws fixed on him. All her hair, not a wisp excepted, was swept up into a tight cap, so that eyes predominated and looked perilously alert. Halloran avoided taking her on eye to eye. He gazed at an empty space to the left of her head, and dominated it in a relevantly direct,

4

respectful, staunch and soldierly manner.

'Corporal Halloran,' she muttered speculatively, as if it mightn't be such a bad name for a terrier or a horse.

'Yes, madam.'

'Errh . . . ,' she said by way of a dainty parenthesis, and wriggled her afflicted leg about on the hassock. 'I've asked some of the officers who have visited my husband here, about what sort of young man you are.'

'Yes, Mrs Blythe.'

'I was able to ask Captain Allen also, your company commander, I think. He claims that you are a most temperate and reliable young man.'

'Thank you, madam.'

'No, don't thank me, young man. For this reason, that I find that a soldier's idea, any soldier's idea, of what is temperate and reliable to be very lacking.'

She leant on one buttock as pain diverted her for some seconds. Her narrow mouth opened to the spasm, not altogether humourlessly or ungratefully.

Shuddering, she asked him, 'Do you love Ann?'

Halloran's eyes, having been drawn by the lady's virtuoso agony, returned to the empty space with which he'd earlier chosen to deal. Whatever could the woman mean by the word, when she locked Ann up in the kitchen at night against her predatory husband, while she herself sat here morning and afternoon with pain licking up and down her limbs?

'Yes, Mrs Blythe,' Halloran decided, loath.

'I am not the type of lady who lets her servants go to hell in their free time, Corporal.'

'I'm sure, Mrs Blythe,' Halloran rumbled, out of the deeps of his blushing throat.

No one would go to hell in peace in her household. Not even old Blythe could damn himself at leisure. For Mrs Blythe had confided once to Ann, and Ann had ultimately reconfided to Halloran, the story of how her husband had *walked disorderly* with a domestic in Portsmouth. Even Ann had thought that, in

5

view of what probably passed between Blythe and the girl, *walked disorderly* was a poor choice of terms. Mrs Blythe's father had obtained this expiatory post on the edge of the Southern Ocean for his son-in-law, and bullied him into it. The old man was an august Staffordshire potter, now clawing up the breakneck face of his eighty-sixth European winter; and mad Mrs Blythe wrote to him with ruinous frequency, begging him to exclude herself and indecent Mr Blythe from the inheritance.

'Since the day I had Ann assigned me on the *Castile*,' the lady was grinding on, 'she has been as close to me as a servant can be. I approve her industry, and her standards of behaviour are remarkable in this human sink in which we serve our King, Halloran.'

'Yes, madam.'

Madam took a large, manly handkerchief from her sleeve. She rubbed her neck which grew lividly out of her old lace fichu. Apart from the question of the potter's fortune, had that flawed skin and baggy throat once put furies into Blythe's loins?

'I will not speak indirectly, Halloran,' she said, chin up and the handkerchief rubbing. 'I know how men live in this small parish of hell. I ask you straight. Have you ever lived in concubinage?'

'No,' he said grudgingly. 'No.' Not, he thought, that there would be any concubinage on the earth if all women shared the complexion of Mrs Blythe's flesh and spirit. 'You're not the only one who fears hell, Madam.'

'I do not fear hell, young man. I have a Saviour. And answer me properly!'

'No, I haven't lived in concubinage, Mrs Blythe.' He swallowed. 'I live for Ann.'

'Why don't you marry Ann, then? It is better to marry than to burn.'

As this random lump of St Paul hit him in the eye, he snorted, continuing in mental revolt. Could the woman believe that someone had once burnt for her, and that her dumpy flesh had quenched any fires?

Suffer it to be said that Halloran was doing better with Mrs

6

Blythe than many an Irishman would have. After all, he knew what a large word like concubinage meant, although he claimed to have never practised it; and Mrs Blythe somehow expected, when she used the word, that Halloran would understand it. Although he comes from a tiny place along Wexford Bay, he studied for two years, until he was nineteen, in the Bishop's house in Wexford itself. It was planned that he would be going to the Sulpicians in Paris to be trained and priested. However, he was, there in Mrs Blythe's sitting-room, as he is here in the forest, a corporal of Marines in a different world. Nonetheless, he could remember that in Wexford he read some moral treatises that advocated marriage as a remedy for lust and a cure for the sin of Onan; and he thought, that Sunday when Mrs Blythe quoted scripture, that, in common with such moralists, she wouldn't have recognized love on a fine day, with the sun on its face.

'It is not a matter of burning, Mrs Blythe. We can't marry except before a priest.'

'A papist priest?'

'Yes.'

'And in the meantime, you expose my Ann to temptation. I find your attitude difficult to understand.'

'Mrs Blythe, you know of a district of the soul called the conscience. If Ann married against her conscience, she'd despair. Then, certainly, she'd be open to temptation.'

Mrs Blythe screwed her rigorous nose. Pain was at her again. Her eyes closed delicately. Halloran remembered a time in Wexford, when he himself had been drowning in guilt, and the stairways and the dark corners of rooms had stunk of hell, how a poisoning in his jaw had given him a marvellous repose. He understood Mrs Blythe's indecency as now she groaned for Brother Pain, who had the knack of flushing out of the veins any sense of immensities, of the terrible height of God and the depth of hell; who left you enjoying the uprightness of your chair, the splotch of sun on the floor, the astringent sweatiness of your face, all for their own delicious sakes.

With her mouth partly open and shut eyes, Mrs Blythe enjoyed these things for perhaps fifteen seconds. Then she came back to Halloran; her face wide open for business again, nasty as a hock-shop.

'When I spoke of temptations,' she said, 'I was not referring mainly to temptation from inside Ann herself. I was speaking of temptation from the outside. I was speaking of you, Corporal.'

From the Blythes' garden, doves were mumbling warnings to him. He wondered whether the woman was merely plagued with conscience on Ann's behalf. It was a deadly thing to be conscience-stricken for the sake of others. You needed a leg ulcer for respite. Or was she malicious? He would have to take Ann's advice and be assiduously humble.

'I promise you . . .' he began.

'Your promises won't buy anything in this establishment,' she told him, tipping her right shoulder with the fingers of her right hand. 'The pledges of our men of affairs have given us the appearance of a godly nation, Halloran. The breaking of their pledges has given us an Empire.' She became unexpectedly be-mused, as if, at the back of her mind, she were ruffling through some of the unredeemed pledges she herself had in hand. 'I cannot accept promises.'

'Mrs Blythe, what else can I do?'

Deference came effortlessly to him, now that he was honestly bewildered.

'I am aware you are seeking your brand of salvation. I will accept your oath. On my Bible here.'

She had sovereignty over Ann. All the sovereignty under heaven was in the wrong hands, and as soon as the wrong hands had it, they had you taking oaths.

'Is an oath needed, Madam?'

'Why wouldn't it be, Halloran?'

'I believe my intentions are good, Mrs Blythe.'

'You may believe it. I don't. Your intentions are not good enough for me.'

Down came her fist on the griffin's head in which the chair-arm ended. Poor damned griffin, with its tongue out from being pummelled by such a scourge of a woman. At the same time, her handkerchief fell from her wrist. She allowed Halloran to round the hassock and recapture it for her. It was limp with the heat of the day, and of the day before that too, and rather yellow. He thought, Ann washes her stinking leg rags.

'Thank you, Halloran.'

'I don't think I can take that oath, Mrs Blythe.'

'Listen to me!' She paused to give him time to do so. 'I can arrange your affairs from this room. If I wanted to, I could pester Captain Allen until he gave way. I could have you sent to the Crescent.'

Which was twenty miles up the river. He scratched the side of his neck with crooked, nonplussed fingers.

'How do you dare to argue?' The griffin took another clout. Mrs Blythe held her chin high and shaky; there was some sort of palsy dragging at her far cheek. 'For Ann's sake, I am willing to let you see her once every week. On Sundays, since there isn't any other day; from three o'clock, since there isn't any other time; and on your own, since there is no one to supervise. But I want her virtue more strictly guaranteed than it is. I want you to call God's justice on your head, in the event that you wrong her. There! You have had three times the explanation anyone in your position deserves. I won't have my servant fat with your bastard. Do you understand that? Swear or get out! That's how simple it is.'

Pain, once more. It took her by the corners of the mouth and the corners of the eyes. Oh, it admired her justice and her buttock-rolling straight-talk.

'Then I'll swear the oath for you.' He was pleased to find that sullenness helped him to sound a bumpkin, knowing that what Mrs Blythe wanted for her Ann was an honest bumpkin. 'But I promise as well. And the promise will be just as sacred to me as the oath.'

'A promise cannot be as sacred as an oath, Halloran.'

She lifted the Bible from the table with her left shaky hand. She fluttered it open. It stood on her palm like a bird, its wings spotted with black truth.

'Kneel down!' she commanded.

This afternoon, Halloran is superior to the heat. He isn't dwelling, at the moment, on Ann's defencelessness. He's actually singing, 'Never have I seen a maid oh half as fair as that Spanish lay-dee'. To such an extent is he enjoying the rare wine of self-confidence, that he has even omitted to bring in his shirt today Dean Hannon of Wexford's little book, *De Vera Amoris Disciplina*, a small treatise giving counsels on divine and human love. Written in Latin, printed in Brussels, marked and wise-smelling now from having travelled with dispossessed Halloran through such a range of climates, it, and not his oath to Mrs Blythe, gives him a high authority to see Ann.

He has not told Ann that he's under Mrs Blythe's oath of decency. Some days after the oath-taking, he recalled in a rush the details of a passage towards the back of Dean Hannon's book. With his slow Latin, it took him hours to find the page. When he had found it and read it, it rang in his mind like a mandate.

'The spouses are the true ministers of the marriage sacrament,' it said. 'Does not the Church demonstrate this by one of her laws regulating the sacrament? This is the law which states that two people, moved by mutual affection to contemplate the holy state, yet so placed that they will not, with reasonable certainty, find within a month a priest before whom to exchange their vows, that such people are permitted to administer the sacrament to each other by giving the normal marriage pledges. They are then as truly married as if they had spoken their promises before the Holy Father himself in the Basilica of St Peter.'

'We are castaways,' Halloran told Ann. 'The law is made for us. *They are then as truly married. . . .*'

There was joy in seeing an older, craftier theology triumphing over Mrs Blythe's blunt and callow one. Yet this was not the motive behind Halloran's secret marriage. To penetrate his reasons, Ann's reasons, it has to be explained that in this region were woods and hills and water, yet that they were somehow far too open to a bland, immense and oriental sky. Those who lived here felt that they lived in a desert. In civilized parts, people formed unions for subtle reasons; but in a desert, they united to ward off oblivion. The secret marriage of Ann Rush and Halloran was an attempt at *warding off oblivion*. It was a pledge by each other to each other's survival. It was an attempt to earn pity or leniency from the providence, sultan-wise, sultan-cool, who watched them from the far side of the nightly lattice of stars.

Despite that it is Dean Hannon, Halloran's teacher in the Wexford days, who states the rule on priestless lovers; despite the canon lawyers of the God-binding Curia, who proposed the rule, and the Supreme Pontiff, who ratified it, it is not possible, except on the most sanguine days, for Halloran to believe beyond doubt that he is a husband and has a bride. He is sanguine today. Corporal Halloran, poet and husband; and nobody knows. His poetry is safe in the back pages of Captain Allen's orderly book. His married state is safe in the back pages of Dean Hannon.

2

His elation on what, for the sake of starting the story, we have called *today* and *this afternoon* is buried now beneath a cairn of years. So his *today* is not ours; his *today* is *that day* to us, and we are, after all, the people for whom the story is being told. Keeping sight of him, let us nevertheless say that *that day*, he arrived elated amongst the blighted turnips at the back-door. He had his hand up on the trellis which Mr Blythe's nascent vines had no chance of covering for many a summer.

'It's General Caesar,' he called in a gusty basso, 'come for his Mistress Cleo.'

Ann Rush, the Mistress Cleo, snorted. She was scouring a pot in which the midday beef had been boiled. The pumice grated, and she comforted this or that on-edge tooth with the tip of her tongue.

'Is it time?' she asked slackly.

'It certainly is time. It's just on three.'

He whistled low through his teeth, jigged like a clown or a young animal. He hissed, 'Let your roaring old lover in!'

'If you want me altogether damned . . .' she said.

'Oh, I see, altogether damned?'

What he saw was that she had felt half-damned about their marriage all morning, and that complete damnation would be to lose her place in the Blythes' home and to enter the beggared limbo of women felons, whose little huts grazed on the east bank of Collett's Brook.

'You stay there,' he said gently. 'I'll keep this side of the wall warm for you. That's my especial destiny.'

'Dear God,' Ann called out, 'he's pitying himself now!'

Halloran rolled his eyes. Ann, frightened, would never tell you that she was frightened. She would make ferocious remarks, such as, 'Dear God, he's pitying himself now!' She was still afraid of what he had told her last week about his Wexford studies, and of how they had left him rather in pieces as a lover. In this way. Dean Hannon used to ask, 'What is love?' He could actually write up all the answers in chalk on the wall and stand back unabashed, beaming at all the chaste Latin tags, the names of all the human faculties involved, the geography of the human spirit. Love is a fusing of the mind and will to God, said the Dean, all other loves are good only in so far as they flow from this love. From this source came the love of Jonathan and David, the love of Queen Blanche for her son, King Louis. Of course, there is some sort of dull but steady affection between spouses, aimed at the dull and steady begetting of children. And then, you descend to what is love only in a debased sense of the word, love by analogy only, love execrable in a tipsy ditch with a dirty, racy vagrant woman.

All this, Halloran had tried to explain to Ann the week before. He had said that his aim, whenever he lay with her, was to keep matters as close to God and as far away from the vagrant woman as he could. When Ann showed herself as racy as any vagrant woman, he would be delighted but baffled. His mind would intervene as an arbiter and try to reorganize his motives according to the rules as laid down by Dean Hannon. And his ardour would die, and he would see doubt all over Ann's face.

Last week, she had said plaintively at the end of the afternoon, 'Don't turn into the scholar on me at this stage, Halloran'. She meant, as well, 'Now that you've despoiled me'. He had then soothed her for all he was worth; and, apart from the monstrous aspect of their not seeing each other for another week, she was happy when he left.

Today, he intended to show some wisdom. The trap would be to rant about how he didn't pity himself, but pitied her seven days a week. As if she really wanted to argue about pity! He did not fall into the trap. He did not even glance around the doorway, but stood listening zealously to the clatter of the big pot, and all but seeing her brown tall woman's arms battling it. Thinking of her arms, he came close to the undressed cedar walls, and put his mouth to one of the cracks which they had left in drying.

'My bride in Christ,' he murmured when the pot took a rest. 'My bride in Christ.'

He did indeed suffer a rush of tenderness for her, Ann, overhung by the large brass and copper cruelties of her kitchen.

'I'm dizzy from waiting to see you,' he felt justified in saying.

'I hope so,' she muttered.

She was squinting into the boiler. You could tell that from her voice. And very soon, the big pot clanged with a certain finality, conveying that it had had all the cleaning she meant it to take.

Halloran nuzzled his head against the clammy cedar. The red clay mortar, which tried to fill the wall cracks in this hard climate, rouged his forehead.

'My bride, my bride, my bride. Moriarty, being a real lad, is up and about for you.'

This was the fanciful name he had for the flesh; and he chuckled now, as if Moriarty and all his kin were well-worn friends of his and not the dark strangers they were. Ann was usually diverted by Halloran's fables about this buffoon within his own walls; but she said nothing today. He heard the little rasps of cloth as she rubbed her hands dry, and scrapings of her skirt against furniture. She poured out some water from a kettle. Some spilt, and the querulous old hearth she served snorted savagely back at her.

'Do you think I'm coarse?' asked Halloran, to bring her out.

'Not very much,' she said negligently.

She continued to give three-quarters of her attention to placing utensils and pouring water.

'Forget what I said last week about God and the woman in the ditch!' he persisted. 'It means nothing. It's a minor confusion, that's all, and it's no news to anyone. The damned scholars have been talking about it for thousands of years. They call it the battle between sacred and fleshly love—and the beggars are on to a truth for once. But it doesn't matter. It's commonplace. You're rare, and

14

I'm not so big a fool as not to know it.'

'I have to go and see Mrs Blythe,' Ann told him, coldly ducking the flight of his metaphysics or theology or whatever else it was.

'Hey,' he called at top whisper, 'you do believe, don't you? That you're my bride? Dean Hannon wouldn't be wrong. He had a sharp mind. Too sharp.' He paused, and then, in an attempt to force her into making positive conversation, he talked on. It was a mistake. 'As for me, it isn't likely a man would turn into some kind of church-lawyer to get his desire. Not in a town like this, where you can have nearly anyone for a shirt or a shred of tobacco.'

That's an apish thing to say, he was telling himself before he'd got as far as *shred of tobacco*. He could not believe that he'd said anything so apparently slighting to Ann. However, the words stood, far too barefaced for him to try to tone them down. All he could do was to cock his ear and hope that she was as preoccupied with the kitchen as she pretended to be.

No chance.

She brought her anger close to the wall beyond which Halloran waited.

'You could never have *me* for a draper's full of shirts.'

'I didn't mean you, Ann.'

'What do you want, Halloran? An angel or a whore? Which? You talk about what you learned in Wexford. In what town do they teach men wisdom?'

'I know, I know. I should go there. I'm sorry, Ann. You're all things to me. In my confusion' (he punched his forehead) 'I can say that. You're all things.'

But the dead kitchen creaked. The hearth grunted. She had left him alone in his windiness.

He now had an image of himself as he must seem, flustered amongst the Blythes' decaying vegetables, butting the wall, expounding, jabbing at himself. On the slope behind him stood a leering, entirely disreputable hut. It belonged to the male felon who did the wood-hewing and water-carrying for the house. It stood like a wrecked collier, and the rocks holding on its bark roof seemed the result of a collision rather than of design. In its bay of scabrous timber, it was altogether a poor comment on Halloran's vehemence.

Now, because he was certain of the old lag's ironic presence behind him, he made a late attempt at dissembling. With studied mannishness, he stared through the slaty trees at the very still indigo water. He stared with the patronizing eyes one kept for porpoises or native canoes. Breath on a mirror, a land-breeze stippled the face of the bay, but preluded nothing. In the thin forest behind him, one insect voice burred the edges of afternoon and, without turning to the hillside, Halloran could see, could hear in the noise, the dearth and drought and straggled bark.

As people will when they're embarrassed, he found himself speaking aloud, though covertly. He was thinking, *And what if Ann doesn't come back out to me this afternoon?* 'We had hoped for a more generous spring,' he found himself saying. He spoke in a low throatiness in which he had first heard the ironic sentence spoken by His Excellency on the parade-ground ten weeks before.

'We had hoped for a more generous spring.'

But a disappointing spring had given way to the malign summer in which Halloran, aware of his sweat, no longer sanguine, waited now. December had come rampaging amongst the carnations along Government Road, had trampled on the last blooming of expatriate stocks. It had crushed the title *Advent*, which the two parsons tried to lay upon its back, until every hint of juice and fruitfulness had been ground out. In dutiful vegetable gardens, the leaves of carrots and turnips had tettered and split, shot full of holes by antipodean summer. The grain had already rusted hard beside the little creek called Collett's Brook; and there would be no harvest at Government Farm, where muddied stooks of young corn stood like the camp wreckage of a beaten army.

At the time of his parade-ground speech, the Governor had devoted fifteen minutes to the sentiment that, although nothing but the worm of death seemed to flourish in this obdurate land, it was the duty of those who served the King not to accept things by their seeming, but to out-stubborn the wayward earth. Yet the officers, their regimentals fibrous from three summers' sweat, had squinted at the sky with flat hatred. There was very little assent in their hearts.

And Halloran felt this hatred too, and he was somewhat short of assent. Yet he knew that this was a summer of unequalled promise. He had begun it with such a welter of emotion that, after the torpor of barrack life at Chatham and the dumb pain of shipboard and colonial service, he felt reborn. This was partly because he had no doubt that he was living in a legend, because he underwent all the fervours set down in legends and in poetry. It was as if he actually felt, above himself and Ann, the mercy of a story-teller. However, a French sage asked once, 'How many men would never have loved, if they had never heard of love?' Halloran began to suspect that he was basking in the emotions of other men, and not only that, the emotions of other men as tempered by art and decency, metre and rhyme. By this time, Ann had become the substance of his life.

'Mrs Blythe says you're to take good care of me and remember your obligations.'

She had come into the garden without his hearing. She stood business-like against the skeletal tracery of her master's sick vines. Her dress underlined her thinness; it was abnormally high-waisted and draped all but the toes of Mrs Blythe's cast-off shoes. The dirty green fabric was so very thick that it seemed to be supported by its own hem. It wrapped her hunger round plentifully, to give her the look of one of those Christ-child statues that are enveloped in vast copes and are pink and lost in their kingship. Already, Ann had her hat on, one of those small top-hats which ladies wear to riding; and once more, Mrs Blythe, who had come thirteen thousand miles to stay indoors, had given it to her.

She frowned. But the dull petulance of the kitchen had drained out of her already. Halloran saw this, with gratitude. The next instant, the oblique sun fetched him a clout on the side of the neck. His mouth flew open for a second or two in the terror of fainting. But he didn't fall down. In the freezing sweat of sunstroke, he saw how the dark-green of her dress had imposed itself on her. He felt his soul sliced neatly down the middle by a barbarous desire to be poured out like milk, to flow around her ankles and soften that hard hem of rubbish. Soon, though, he began breathing evenly again.

He came two steps closer to her and laughed. All counterfeit roguishness, he asked, 'Did you tell Mrs Blythe that I'd already taken care of you a few times?'

'No,' she mouthed, and her head went down. Halloran shrugged, softly, you could say. He caressed her elbow. In the shade of the Blythes, he could do no more; but his fingers staggered daft with pity on her arm.

'Halloran,' she said, 'I don't think there's ever been two such hopeless people. You with your confusion and me with mine.'

'Never have I seen a maid,' Halloran recited to soothe her, 'oh half so fair as that Spanish lay-dee. I've been waiting all the week to see your Spanish skin again. Without a lie.'

'Can't we go now?' she asked, without looking up. 'I can't be myself here.'

He collected Captain Allen's miraculous rifle with which he was often sent hunting and hitched it over his shoulder.

'My bride,' he said. 'Come on, then.'

They did not take to the clay road which ribboned up a bunch of officials' homes on the south point. Instead, he led Ann by the elbow up the hill behind the Blythe home, away from the clutter of stale brick cottages. They sidled past the crazy hut. Beyond it, they were aware of being in a sack-cloth forest, in a forest that mad, prophetic, excessive, had heaped dust on its own head.

In no time, the gangling trees had them cut off from the town. Halloran was impressed by the sly antiquity of the place. Glossy shrubs, smelling like a cemetery a week after All Souls, took the spotted light on their tongue and tipped it brassy in his tracks. Rocks smelt of dry age. Here all things went on easily, mercilessly germinating, convinced of their own inevitable survival. For some distance, he was more aware of hostility than he was of Ann. It seemed that in these poor scrubby woods, all his judgements on what a forest should look like were being scarcely tolerated by the whole pantheon of the gods of this, the world's wrong end.

When they were beyond doubt hidden in the forest, Ann stopped. She leaned against a tree-trunk the colour of old iron seamed with vertical corrosion. A honey-coloured ant, one inch from her shoulder, reared up polemically on its abdomen, but seeing that she was, for the moment, invulnerable, it galloped off drunkenly across the gullies of bark. Ann was transmuted by something very close to the pure animal joy of being released from that God-abandoned hutch at the back of Blythes'. Here, in nobody's country, in thin shade and thick heat, she became visibly young again.

Halloran found himself holding on to her head so tightly with both his hands, that he could feel the skull-case, dear and mortal, beneath her hair.

'Do you want to walk, Ann?' he asked her, implying that she probably didn't want to. 'We can find a shady place here and rest, because you need a rest.'

'I need a seabreeze, Halloran darling. It isn't far to the seabreezes.'

Halloran went on to say many trite things for a man who fancied himself as a poet. Just as they separated, he said, 'My bride in Christ'.

But, by the time they had crossed over the hill and come, slipping in the leaf-mould, to a dry stream-bed, Halloran felt again, as he had earlier in the day, that they were patently man and wife. It was about a quarter of a mile behind them that a rather Calvinist deity and the House of Hanover were the names by which contracts and marriages, baptisms and hangings were solemnized. Four hundred yards from the town, on untouched earth, they seemed as much fated, each to each, as two people in a fable.

3

Halloran knew that he would not sight any game. The full-time game-killers, three men chosen from amongst the transported felons, had not brought in anything since New Year. Even so, it was fitting to carry some symbol of your superiority through this knock-kneed forest, every stick of it a sacrament of antiquity and rebuke. Halloran carried not a Bible nor a book of sonnets, but a breech-loading Ferguson, a wonder of its times, capable of downing three men a minute.

They would see no black people, Ann and he. Somewhere between the skirting-board and carpet-edge of the land, the black race, with the secrecy of moths, was dying of smallpox. Or, perhaps, dying out.

One day at the beginning of spring, the disease had struck two people in the town. One of them, the sixteen year old son of Rev. Mr Calverley, died. The boy was an outstanding scholar, and could, as de Quincey later claimed to be able to do, translate news-sheets into Greek at the age of thirteen. Over twenty-five degrees of unredeemed latitude and thirty degrees of longitude that had not bent the knee, his father was parish priest; and lured by this grand and meaningless concept, the boy had been enjoying an empire-building holiday with his parents.

After his death, there were a few other but not-fatal cases within the town. Then, against all the rules which the disease itself had established over centuries in Europe, and in the stewing December heat, it left the settlement. The surgeons were amazed; but it had found a better mark.

All the young subalterns, writing up the occurrence in their journals, felt no gratitude for the exit of the smallpox. They held that here was a stage in the general policy of deceit in which the new land dealt with them, that here was an attempt to subvert their civilized judgments. Some weeks later, they wrote with bitter zest of an incident involving Mr Calverley, which they saw as the summit of the almost personal guile of the land they garrisoned.

It seems that the Calverley boy had died of a bad form of the sickness.

'He must have had some special weakness,' Mr Calverley said numbly in the presence of his son's horrific corpse. For, in the son, the fleshy parts of the body swelled until the Chaplain could see only a pudgy mockery of his formerly trim scholar. The flesh turned purple and suet in streaks, like flesh which has been flogged and flogged but will not, by breaking open, splash out its pain. In the end, panting out a verse from Xenophon, the boy jerked down into his last frozen delirium and choked to death.

It was almost exactly in this way, the Xenophon excluded, that the disease took to the natives.

On the Saturday before Christmas, the Chaplain had gone out with his felon-servant to shoot wild ducks in the reed marshes to which the road past Blythes' finally came to bury itself. The servant went off to wade along the edge of the swamp and start the birds. As Mr Calverley waited, he believed he saw his son, awkwardly at rest, far in under the interlocking branches of three or four acacia trees, embowered as well as you could expect this niggardly place to embower anybody.

He dropped the fowling-piece he carried and fell on his knees. Mumbling at the unforeseen mercy, he scurried under the spiny canopy. He took up the dead head and shoulders of a native lightened to purple by the smallpox. His hands were overcome and awkward, cherishing the head. Waves of contentment rocked him back and forth, and he sang, unaware of the look of what he held.

The wind fell. Slatternly swamp-oaks were arrested by the parson's tragedy, and gaped. So did the servant, coming back into the glade to consult him, having started no birds. Before the servant got to him, however, disbelief set in.

Mr Calverley lifted his head and saw that the light was swarming with gilt beetles, clicking onto bark; and gross flies cropped and bubbled about him. His hands felt too cold, and the face slipped from them. A wide, flared nose was now apparent, with purple death and blowflies ringing it.

Slow panic moved him upright then, through the froth of acacia. Twigs snapped around his waist as he stood tottering in a surf of yellow blossom. The servant reached him and helped him away.

'Come on, sir. It's a dead savage. We don't want nothing to do with him, sir.'

When the transported man spread the story, it was relayed with rare pity and in appalled tones. And so it was recorded by the diarists. But Calverley himself was far from appalled. He rejoiced that his son was feet deep in the soft mercy of the grave, where the big seas of the inverted seasons would wash him down to dust. The Chaplain had catalogues in his head of the mercies and justices of God; and he transferred the truth of man's fitting reduction to dust from its place among the justices, to enrol it high among the mercies.

He refused to be soothed homewards. He wished to stay here and let the sun bite his back through his old broadcloth coat. He wanted to listen to the chirruping of the marshes. There was the fowling-piece, on the mouldy ground. He snatched it up and went his own way, all the while rubbing the florid metal-work of the breech. For a man who had come shooting, it was too early to turn home. In the low fork of a tree with feathery bark, which he picked at a strand at a time, he spent the afternoon.

Only he and Halloran perhaps, in that whole town, did not resent the grotesque land, did not call it evil because it was weird. But the busy compilers of journals called it evil at some length.

4

MEANWHILE, without hindrance, Halloran and his secret bride came to an open space above the sea. It had not been a long walk, but through the settled heat in a lee gully. They huffed and felt greasy.

'Ah,' said Halloran, 'the seas of romance. As they call them.'

Off they went, searching for the edge, half-afraid to find it, wading through a matting of shrubs stripped and cuffed westward by the prevailing wind. Once the green shoals could be seen under the cliff, he sat Ann down on a hump of granite. The cliff-top was sown with partly revealed clods of the rock and was not unlike a half-buried graveyard, with the names and scraps of remembrance having wasted into the crystals of the stones. Ann looked well here; beauty amongst the tombs. Halloran sidled back a step. He watched her take her hat off, shake out her hair, lift her chin to catch the wind beneath it.

Having caught the breeze and jiggled the scalloped top of her chemise before it, she turned her head in time to catch him in his pride of possession.

'Come on, Phelim!' she called, without enthusiasm. 'Come and sit here. None of this adoring from a distance. You make me feel I'm stealing from God.'

There was no mistake; she had gone stale on him again. He had walked her too far.

'I don't know how a poor silly beggar's supposed to know!' he said gently to the ether.

'That's an elegant thought for a lover,' she observed.

'Lovers don't have elegant thoughts,' he said. 'Except in poetry.'

He sat down in a lump, feeling hamstrung that, except for her temporary radiance in the woods, his mood had chased hers downhill for an hour, never catching up.

'Oh dear!' he grinned and gave a long, baffled snort. In fact, he was one of these people who have a talent for expressive breathing. 'Oh dear, oh dear!' he said. His right hand went around and patted her hip. It had to stay there on her glum waist, superfluous as a bird on a tower.

There was something of the settling-in air of playgoers about them as they examined the spacious sea.

'The seas of romance,' said Halloran again.

This was by way of being an invocation. In saying it, he hoped she might recall that into old age their distinction would be that they, with a few others, had punctured the tight horizon and come into an ocean made of the same freakish blue that people see in fevers. That they were brethren of Magellan, no less. But so were all the frayed ladies and soldiery of the colony. So that Ann grunted cursorily.

'I heard you the first time. And if you're talking about waste,' she cried out, as if he had been, 'look at that for waste!'

She pointed to a place just beyond the riot of the shoals. Set in the jelly-blue, a fleet of jew-fish tended slowly north. It *did* make one angry, to see such placid manna a foot or two below the sea-top, passing by the hungry town without a flick of their tails.

Ann wagged her beautiful, house-keeping chin after them.

'You'd think Blythe or somebody else would have a man up here all day,' she said, 'with a trumpet and orders to blow an alarm whenever fish like that go past. Then off we'd go, seine and cutter, and all be less hungry at the end of the day.'

'They're a negligent lot,' he nodded, meaning Blythe or somebody else.

Above all, he was pleased that she was live enough to cherish an opinion. Yet they went on sitting woodenly together. Their ears, drenched by the south wind, tocked like clocks, thumped like sails. At last he took her shoulders, not compellingly enough, and tried to fall with her full-length along the cool rock. She tilted like a buoy but came upright again. Arms up and empty, Halloran ended on his back.

She smiled, in fact. There was a worldly-wise smile on her face before she turned away.

Instantly he was on his feet. Pity for her might occupy him on six days out of seven. Still, he was angry now.

'As if I was after my own comfort,' he mumbled. 'As if I was after your priceless favours....'

A giggling sound came from her, but he couldn't see her face. Her head, at the full stretch of her neck, was turned to, absorbed in the south. Palm in lap, her left arm stood rigid and propped up her concave shoulders. The shoulders quivered.

'They *are* priceless,' he murmured. 'You're not crying, are you? Surely Ann?'

He tried uselessly to turn her face to himself. The barbarous part of him that was saying, *Good, now we can begin to talk*, wished indecently to see the tears on either side of her long nose. After some time, he stood up and walked to the other side of her. Her lids closed. Her nostrils and broad lips cringed.

'Come on, come on,' he said. 'My secret bride.'

He thought that it would be easy to be deft, to reap her head in against his hip.

'Don't call me that silly name,' she said, stiffening herself.

'That true name.'

'That silly, stupid name. Don't call me by it.'

'As you say, Ann.'

He sounded hurt.

'How dare you be hurt!' she called out, standing up. 'You said we would not be alone any more. You said that it would double our chances of coming home. So we gave our vows to each other. In the pagan forest, I might say. In the smell of dust, starlings all round us, scabby trees. We gave our vows, didn't we?'

'Yes.'

'And it wasn't like St Peter's church in Rome, whatever your old Dean might say. And now I'm still alone. Deadly alone. And look at you.'

Which she did, and lost all her anger since he stood so tall, ragged and blank.

'You don't look any less alone yourself,' she said. 'I think the sun will fall on us. Are we truly married Phelim?'

Asking this, she sat down limp. He knew that now he was meant to come up to her, and he did. She put her face against his canvas thigh.

'It's impossible to believe,' she mumbled.

'No, it's not impossible, exactly. I believe it myself most of the day. It's *hard* to believe sometimes. I'll agree to that."

'I don't seem to myself to be a bride, Phelim.'

The hazed wilderness Halloran now faced made him fearful and even pedantic.

'It isn't a matter of what you seem to yourself to be!'

He explained their case to her again, blinking at the charred enamel sun and the woolly forests and black valley seams emitting fogs of heat. The hazards of giving oneself away, to Ann for example, preoccupied him. He felt by instinct that if he and Ann were caught in the fixity of love, they were not, under the gods, halving their danger, but doubling their chances of being buried by this deadly, passive landscape. Two weeks before, and again by instinct, he had felt the opposite. He was a baffled animal indeed.

All the time, though, that he stood there in fear, he gave off a mess of axioms, questionable and otherwise. Her head still lay against him, but in such a way that he saw without warning her comfortless ear, the hair hooked behind it, naked before his palaver. She sat so clearly bereaved and ashamed that she didn't seem to be Ann at all. Helped by all that granite, she seemed a statue to woman in her loss and shame, trapped without any solace but the vapourings of lord-lieutenants and pulpit orators. And, of course, half-literate Corporals of Marines.

'Oh God,' he muttered. He touched her statuesque grief by the shoulder.

'Remember how brides used to be at home, Phelim? Blue coats and long mantles and just a bit of worsted stocking showing. None of them ever looked to me as if they were raging under their decent clothes. Is there something wrong with me?'

'Not to my eye,' he said.

'Do you think under it all they're as shameless as me?'

'They wouldn't be as lucky as all that.'

But she was not to be jollied out of a close look at her shame.

'I was too full of desire. There's something wrong with me. And the whole business, the swapping of vows, I was too full of desire. I don't seem to myself to be a bride, Phelim.'

Then I'm not a bridegroom, Halloran was telling himself. It was an easy thing for the canon lawyers to have a rule for exiles. But even if you were exiles, you still both needed the priest to be the ultimate ratifier of your union. As he was and had been from your babyhood, of all the doorposts, windows, bridal beds and cradles in the gothic town of life.

It seemed to him that Mrs Blythe had prevailed in some way. He felt smothered by events and strongly compelled to bodily violence. At his feet waited a small dome of rock splashed with red oxide. He uprooted it and hurled it out over the sea from above his right shoulder. It hovered like a chicken-hawk, held up by the wind and the hysteria of water. Then, in a split-second that offered him scarcely any relish, it dived under the brow of the land.

'Damn you!' he raved down the chasm at the more practised raving of the sea. His finishing gambit was to kick a footful of rubble into the air, and to pay for it in view of his light canvas shoes.

He limped back, snorting, to the girl and risked holding his hand up to the ear that had been fretting him; the green and blue-rimmed hopeless ear, at large from its place under her hair, naked in the fierce climate. He came very close to toppling when she latched both arms around his hips and hauled at him furiously, burrowing her face into his belly. At last she looked up, spattered eyelids and a long, even smile.

'It doesn't matter, Halloran darling. I think the priests make too much cry altogether about this virginity. I mean that it doesn't last too long, does it, once you settle down to getting rid of it.'

They laughed.

'And except for Mrs Blythe taking me out of the hold, I would have lost it willy-nilly on the *Castile*.'

'I would have liked,' said Halloran, 'to run up against the beggar who tried it. Willy, I would have let him live, but nilly, I'd have dug his tripes out.'

Once more, they both laughed. Life was hearty again and all Dean Hannon's claims beyond dispute.

'Perhaps you think I ranted as I did on behalf of my old mate Moriarty, all prepared to have a luxurious time for himself.'

'I know you better. Of course I don't think it.'

'I was angry,' he said, talking straight at the low sun, 'because I had nothing to tell you except a few bits of moral proverbs I got from the Dean in Wexford. I was angry at the people who say *It is better to marry than to burn*, as if they were saying, *It's better to dig a corner drain than let your field be flooded*.'

In a flash he was angry again.

'They're our vows to make. The marriage vows are ours to make. All the scholars say that. Are they all wrong? Is that likely, Ann? Is it at all likely?'

'It's all right,' said Ann, cancelling the debate. 'It's all gone now. I'm very happy to be your bride. Your *secret* bride.'

She giggled at the stealthy word.

'Have you got your red string, eh?' he said.

He sat down and patted her waist for the red cord she wore under her clothes. It would, she guaranteed, stop her from conceiving before their marriage could be made public.

'You might happen to need it this afternoon,' he said.

They laughed for seconds on end. She laughed partly, though without malice, because of his naïvety. He had no sisters, or rather, they had both died in childhood. To him a woman functioned by laws of pythagorean grandeur and white rules of sortilege. He was willing to be serene on medical grounds about the red cord, that it would protect Ann. But she sensed in him his mannish scepticism towards unaided faith and magic. She did not tell him that the red cord was a sacramental much favoured by women on the east coast. It was called a St Megan's cord. You got an indulgence of four hundred days for wearing it, and all the women of her family had always put their trust in it in matters of female chemistry. So she laughed gently at him, thinking, *And he's a scholar!*

They did not, in fact, need the cord today. Halloran was cubbish; their rare freedom had its chance of going to their heads. But they both knew that they would be freer and more assured for the next seven days if they merely sat together. Perilously, they sat together, placating their destinies.

5

Towards the end of February, His Excellency and the brick-master had, between them, finished plans for a suitable Government House. It was to be a sort of Palladian town house, with a little Ionic portico. They both hoped that when it was finished, it would look like something from Bath.

Although red-brick had been out of fashion at the time His Excellency was last at Bath, red brick it would have to be here, since half the small valley was made of red clay. But no lime-stone for lime mortar could be found anywhere in the country-side around. The town was perilously held together with clay mortar, so that at every gale and equinox a townful of chimneys would be toppled, and walls would split any old day. A viceroy merited lime mortar if his sober cornices and sandstone quoins were not to be a poor joke. The brick-master suggested seashells.

There were middens of shells along the backs of the beaches, where family-trees of natives had eaten their molluscs and dropped the shells, always in the same places. These heaps were shovelled into sacks and crushed and burnt. Still there was not enough lime. Next the idle transported ladies were sent hunting single shells along the coast. Male transports were marched to the beaches at three every afternoon, and off-duty Marines were promised extra pay for joining the search. Halloran himself spent some time, one o'clock to three several afternoons, sifting the beaches, and came back to the company office blinking away the scald of gold they left on his sight.

This lime-hunt became the main civic endeavour, so that on a morning at the end of the month, Halloran was called out of Captain Allen's orderly office to take the Arts by boat to the Crescent. The Arts in that town, on that river, in that fifth of the

30

earth, lived in one man—Thomas Ewers, transported forger, engraver, limner, landscapist. Now he was going to the Crescent to paint some of the birds in Surgeon Daker's aviary. Halloran was handed two Government House letters to the Surgeon, and somebody had written to that queer, stately woman, Mrs Daker.

When Ewers came to the Government Wharf on that particular morning, he was dressed well enough to impart to Halloran and the other four in the boat, two Marine privates, two transport oarsman, that the Arts were not going to allow themselves to row up any little river on the butt-end of any earth. To convey this, he wore a corduroy coat with plenty of nap left on it, though short in the sleeves to show the long, friable forger's wrists and hands. And he had a beaver on his head; mangey, but, beyond argument, a beaver. His equipment was carried in a golden-oak box. He found a space for it beneath the tarpaulin in the stern-sheets. Then he sat, more or less at Halloran's feet.

'You're ready?' asked Halloran, who was hampered by having nearly as much respect for an artist as Ewers himself had.

'Yes. Thank you kindly, Corporal.'

The fellow was a Scot, but somehow uncharacteristic, to Halloran's eyes in any case. His great, horsy nose, broken for him by a Dutch constable at Capetown, predominated and was aimed straight down the boat. His eyes chose to stare down a factitious cleft in the air, whereas Halloran thought an artist would be all observation. Unless the fellow had some inner light. But there went the demure fingers of his right hand, doubling up the palm, caressing their own wrist. Not much inner vision in that type of thing, thought Halloran.

He himself began to call orders like a regular boatswain. The nor-easterly thudded against the back of his head. They were afloat and all the world sounded thereby sharper and more innocent. The ample tide whipped past them with its noises of deep blue regret. Axe-blows and adze-blows and the rant of the cross-saw came to them clean and tonal. Seventy yards out from shore, Halloran was counties away from the timber-pits, where the sun lay kicking like a trapped bull-elephant, and the red dust of cedars lepered the sawyers over.

'Slack on your starb'd,' he yelled.

The boat obeyed him, but once it had straightened out again, the two transports began to hiss like galley-slaves as they rowed. For they were regular boatmen, and Halloran was a company clerk who dimly knew the port and starboard of a desk.

The artist's gaze didn't flicker as they began mocking Halloran. His sight ran aslant their skulls and rested on the olive skyline north of the river. It could have taken in two raw damned little men with sweat in their sternums and hairy navels and nubbly feet gripping the foot-hold either side of his boots. Halloran, who had seen some of the flabbergasting but redeemed ugliness in Leonardo's sketch-book, tended to expect that these two would delight an artist, send him grabbing for his transforming charcoal.

'Fourteen miles to dinner,' said Halloran softly, to show the two and the smirking Privates that they might yet hiss and mean it.

This morning he felt drum-tight, self-contained. He was a victor; he could foretell it. He would have his own house and wife on a sane coast. One day or night, he would drop in front of his fire the story, like a wolf cub that is vicious but manageable by a flick of the boot, of how he took convicts and an artist up a river beyond China, beyond anything.

'Slack on your port,' he sang, 'haul on your starb'd!'

After a time, they came into the main current. The land looked promising from the jolly-boat, the river went west quite royally, spangled with sun, miles wide. Before its massive kindliness, the coves and beaches, cliffs and islands stood back. Halloran sat beside the artist and saw that the man had begun to use his eyes.

'What do you think of it?' he had to ask.

'It's pleasant looking,' Ewers murmured.

'How does it seem to *you*?'

Ewers frowned at him.

'I think it seems the same to me as it seems to you, Corporal. Why do you want to know?'

'I mean, would you feel moved to paint a picture of it?'

Ewers smiled. He had long, very innocent lips.

'Not today. I have no patience with it today.'

'Oh,' said Halloran. An artist was an artist to Halloran, as a poet was a poet; and when an artist said he had no patience with any given square mile of beauty, you didn't argue.

'If I painted this landscape,' Ewers explained, 'those who ever saw it would think that the forests behind the beaches were teeming with fruit and game. They would think that this river led to a kingly town, that Eden lay at the headwaters.'

Eden lay at the head-waters was such a nice phrase that Halloran suspected he was listening to a recitation, perhaps part of the artist's private journal.

'Yet all it serves is to connect the world's worst town to the world's worst village, tyranny to tyranny, slave to slave.'

No doubt about it; here was the starched-up rhetoric with which artists, apparently, treated of their subject-matter.

'Corporal, as you were so kind as to ask me, I find this land a land of broken promises to the artist, as it is to the stomach.'

Ewers' pronounced lips rubbed together, very red, very much in need of each other's fellow-feeling; both elbows went up on his knees, the fingers sought the wrists.

'Of course, it's useless for me to have ideas about the face of the land. I am under command to paint it, which solves the matter.'

'Whose command would that be?'

'Surgeon Partridge's command, and Major Sabian's. I am assigned to Surgeon Partridge, you know. I perform at his demand, and he loans me out to perform on demand for his friends. By God who made me, no wonder I perform badly.'

'Painting's a better business than hauling timber,' Halloran suggested, 'or the clay-pits.'

This made the Scotsman's cheeks go polemically hollow. He squinted at Halloran, trying to discern through precisely which pore of the flesh the barbarian in him had emerged.

'That is not an argument,' said Ewers. 'That is the same proposition as commending patience to a man who's been burgled, on the grounds that he may have been murdered also. Society couldn't stand on the basis of such an argument.'

So says the master-forger, Halloran thought. But he wouldn't risk saying it yet. He had a dread of going into history simply as one of those abounding scoffers who appear in the lives of every artist, philosopher and saint.

'In a civilized city,' went on the master-forger, 'you can hire a sawyer, you can hire a digger. But you cannot hire the Arts. You may patronize them and endow them; but you cannot hire them and have them at your command. Yet Surgeon Partridge is such a Goth that not knowing the Arts from, shall we say, a sow's snout, he thinks that *he* can command them. He will see cloud-banks above mangrove trees, and he'll say, "Paint that, Ewers!" Imagine!'

'I'll give you that in,' murmured Halloran. 'He's the sublimest fool of a man.'

Now the river had narrowed down between high timbered banks. There were some tenuous little beaches, much threatened by forest. Halloran was not at all sure of the way, and there were a number of inlets up which the two transports, if captious enough, could take him. But behold, they were hissing and meaning it! The Marines were reeling at their oars. He called a rest and poured water for the transports from the small cask in the stern. They gaped carefully, shipping their oars, which were of local timber and scarcely floated. One at a time, they drank lingeringly, nose in the mug. Halloran saw Ewers staring at a purple swelling on the shoulder blade of the man diagonally across from him.

'I have something for that,' said the artist.

He leant over backwards to locate his paint-chest. It was under the tarpaulin with shirts, coats, four Phrygian forage caps, which he took upon himself to distribute by the way, three muskets and cartridge pouches. He lifted the box gently out of this alien mess and sat it on his knees. From it, he took a pear-shaped bottle that seemed to be full of claret.

'This, my friend,' he said to the transport with the swelling, 'is the juice of the berry of a spiky shrub very much like the broom.

It grows all around the town. It seems that it's a valuable anti-scorbutic.'

'A what-is-it?'

'It stops you from getting scurvy.'

'If it stops you from getting,' the transport told him, baring his doughy gums for two solid seconds, 'it's a bit late to be dosing me on it.'

The other one started snickering. His mouth wasn't much better. One day soon, the two of them would wake up without the strength to swat themselves.

'You'll poison him, Mr Painter,' the other one said. 'He's had it so long, it's in him. He was bred on it and does a bit of breeding on it himself. His father was a sailor with a terrible hate for lime-juice. You could say, he *is* scurvy.'

'Don't talk rubbish,' Halloran told them.

They laughed together, brother oarsmen. Their peccant gums took too exorbitant a part in it for Halloran to join in.

'You don't want it?' Ewers asked.

'No,' said the man who was scurvy. 'Mr Painter, darling, you only come close to being what I want.'

Halloran felt on his face their moist laughter.

'Take no notice,' he told Ewers. He stood up, beckoning to the two Marines. 'I'm sorry, you'll have to row Mr Ewers. I know it's bad for an artist, but we'll never get there if you don't you see.'

Halloran soon found however, that they'd never get there if Ewers *did*. The artist's style with an oar was to dig it feet-deep into the river. The boat would slew upon itself, the oar would come close to being lost or pulling him off his seat or pushing him flat.

'Send him back to his anti-score-what's-it, Corporal,' one of the scurvy oarsmen begged Halloran humourlessly, as if Ewers by his clumsiness were bringing their day of collapse forward; which, beyond doubt, he was.

Boating was hard work by ten o'clock. The river held them in

35

a cleft amongst rocks, away from the wind. At each bend the woods applied the weight of their numbers and brought within hearing the dementia of summer insects.

Then, on the northern side of the river, stood a beached long-boat. There were five men near it, waist-deep in the river, dabbling after mud-oysters. Four Marines were busy at the boat itself, taking pains to store something, under the supervision of two others. One of these two others was in shirtsleeves, and the second wore an improbably spruce parade uniform of an officer of Marines. A voice from the beach hailed the jolly-boat and ordered it into shore, saying that an officer wanted a letter taken to the Crescent.

Halloran found his coat in the muddle in the stern, and joined battle with it. The sleeves seemed to have melted into one piece with the heat; he mumbled and grabbed for a cartridge belt.

'It's that young Rowley fellow,' he muttered to the artist. 'Look at the silly bugger, ornamental in the wilderness.'

The officer waited for them, dressed like a recruiter, molten at the throat where his gorget took the sun.

'Beside him,' Ewers remarked, aggrieved quite independently of Halloran, 'is the buffoon of the sciences, Surgeon Partridge.'

'Might as well take my weapon to show him I know I've got desperate men aboard.'

'My dear God in heaven, you have a desperate man! My God in heaven you have!'

Carrying a flint-lock, Halloran grunted and stumbled down the middle, through the warm reek of sweat and the leaden smell of half-salt, muddied water. In the shallows, the oyster-gatherers stood up and eyed the boat past as if it bore watching. Lieutenant Rowley eyed it too, waiting in scandalized elegance, back bent as ever with the mere weight of his own grace, above buttocks which seemed opulent enough to support any load.

'Beach it,' called Halloran, running up the sand to report in canvas shoes and no gaiters, but the rest of him regimental enough for the circumstances.

Rowley was nineteen, but he had seventy-year-old grey eyes as a pledge of the Lieutenant-General or chairman of corporation that he would become. He had full lips and jaws born to become the jowls of a dominant old man.

After Halloran had presented himself, the boy said nothing for a wearing time, waiting, with his mouth characteristically pained, for some arcane malaise to leave him be. *Piles*, hoped Halloran. *Angry*, he hoped.

'It is normal,' the boy said at last, 'to answer an officer when you are hailed. When I failed to hear you answer me, Corporal, I thought, perhaps there is a ferryman in charge of that boat. Eh?'

I won't fawn on your ehs, roared a voice in Halloran's belly. 'Yes, sir,' he said.

'You have—how many transports in your boat?'

'Three, sir.'

The lieutenant tapped Halloran's flint-lock with his cane.

'Are you loaded?'

'No, sir.'

The pain of this made Rowley close his eyes and nod.

'Why not?' A small perilous voice. Just the thing to frighten shit out of Irish yokels. But not out of this one.

'Begging your pardon, sir, the quartermaster asked us not to use the cartridges. There are only three rounds for every Marine in the garrison.'

'I know that, Corporal. Yet you have three desperate men and a boat which could, at a pinch, sail to the Dutch East Indies. Sense, Corporal, sense!'

There was no doubt about it. Halloran's lack of sense had brought anguish into the corners of Rowley's eyes, and he would bear it only by calling on his reserves of good-breeding.

'Load now, please!'

The eyes remained close if not closed, as Halloran rigmaroled the butt of the flint-lock to the sand and swung his thin legs apart, trying to achieve the rangy indolence of the good driller, of the soldier never flustered. He allowed himself to be rebellious to the extent of not fumbling. When he'd bitten the cartridge and poured the charge down, he took a moment or two to flick grains of powder from the muzzle, reminding himself inevitably of the priest cleaning the paten before the Purification of the Mass. The ironic image stayed in his mind.

Chins skyward, the men in the opaque river slopped at their industry, but everyone else was quite rapt at the small melo-drama. Attending to the priming pan, Halloran thought, *Sure to go off before we're round the next bend, and cure that boatman of his scurvy.* He followed the rubrics of getting the weapon to his shoulder and himself to attention.

'The surgeon here,' said Rowley immediately, 'wants a message taken to the Crescent.'

He took his elegance back a pace. It was a placid elegance now, his back to a hill-side whose cicada-voice roared its indifference at him. Pointlessly, since only Halloran was aware.

Surgeon Partridge moved in. After Rowley, he seemed studi-ously affable.

'You're carrying some letters to Surgeon Daker, Corporal?' he asked.

Halloran said he was; to deny was not within his duty, though he knew that His Excellency meant to purge Daker from office, while the gentlemen meant to bolster him.

Partridge sent a Marine to get his coat out of the shade at the top of the beach. He took from it a letter marked 'Of Great Importance'. Whatever was a threat in the letters from Govern-ment House, this of Partridge's was the antidote. While brash Rowley, His Excellency's *aide-de-camp*, stood by without blink-ing.

'You'll deliver this one with it. You won't forget?'

The surgeon watched Halloran pocket it, Halloran feeling smeared by the meanness and discontent of all the officers.

'Good!' said the surgeon, and took no more notice of him.

'Ah, Ewers,' Partridge called then. 'Ewers, old fellow. Come up here! I've something amazing to show you.'

Ewers left the boat and came up the beach stooping. Whether it was petulance or humility or petulant humility, no one could have told. He murmured good-mornings and bowed to both gentlemen.

'Ewers, I've done what armed detachments have failed to do.'

'You have, sir?' Ewers paused. 'What particular thing is it which armed detachments have blundered in yet you've brought off?'

'Ha,' said Partridge, clipping Ewers' ear and grinning, 'these gentlemen-convicts, Rowley. They're bastards!' He slapped Ewers a second time. 'Bastards!'

Ewers bowed his head. From where Halloran stood, the forger's nasal, mortified breathing could be heard.

'Come on, Ewers!' The surgeon grabbed the man's coat-sleeve and moved him towards the long-boat. Without a glance from Rowley, Halloran was left ridiculously at attention in the midst of the beach. But even in this barren situation, he knew it would be deadly to dismiss himself or stand easy. He did not enjoy, however, being a monument without import, straight on to nothing, overlooking and flanking nothing, in line only with some mystery of pride and idiocy in that lily of a boy's mind.

Near the boat, Ewers was coughing; for he could tell there was some pungent rot in the bows and dreaded to be brought abruptly upon any monstrosity.

'In the tarpaulin there,' said Partridge.

It seemed that an immense baby had been wrapped in canvas, with a peak for its head. The surgeon pulled the peak aside. Ewers saw two native heads nodding. They were blind with the blind, mouthing purposelessness of snails. Their faces had the same marks as Mr Calverley's savage, and their hair was fibrous with muck and hung in ropes. Days before, before the smallpox found them, they had corded strips of raw fish around their foreheads, and the sun had fried them, and the runnels of fish oil had caked them against insects. Surgeon Partridge now saw fit to lean down and cut these cords away with a pocket-knife, saying, 'It's the sting of death that's the only sting they'll be worried by now.'

'What do you want them for, sir?' asked Ewers. He tried not to voice his numb incomprehension, not wanting to be cuffed again for his sensibilities. The man of talent, if that was what he was, stood and waited for an answer as for a crust.

'I'll attempt to cure the poor fellows,' the surgeon said. 'Then we'll civilize them. His Excellency intends to ship two fully genteel natives home to England when the fleet comes in. These could be the lucky two, Ewers.'

He frowned. The frown was for whether they could be cured. About the civilizing part of the project he was quite blithe.

Halloran, hearing this, wanted to spit and slap his thigh. But his mouth was, of course, dry with heat and conflicts and his own and Ewers' humiliation. Working as orderly of a day made a man soft to humiliation. Still he remained, without making a demonstration, at his skew-whiff sentry post. For comfort, he thought that to educate two savages to the surgeon's level, to teach them to carry their backsides as Rowley carried his, should take the whole of one summer's day.

'There's no doubt they're very sick,' said Ewers complimentarily, over by the long-boat.

'How far now?' said Halloran.

The river had become spacious again, but not in any classic sense. Spits of reeking silt ran out from the bank, peopled with mangroves and harsh birds, cutting the river into zig-zags. The four oars flapped up and down like the legs of a beetle.

'Three miles,' someone grunted.

'It's a grateful thing to live in an age of philosophy,' mumbled Ewers, without consequence, reclining in the stern.

Halloran snorted, implored the sky, held up his left hand and shook it as if it contained a pomegranate. But he said nothing of what he wanted to say, that is, that they had both willingly abased themselves. Which was no disgrace in a relative way, but by the standards of absolute things was an abomination. He felt that they earned their salt meat by servility, but lost the right to deal in ideas. Therefore, Ewers should not mention such a sacred word as philosophy.

'I didn't mean what he thought. He's a hard man for misconstruing,' he had muttered when he came back from watching Partridge's curiosities. He did not see any virtue in having made a small score against Partridge. Instead, he denied having intended to score; he did not seem to believe that it was wrong to be clouted for having an independent wit. But being clouted on suspicion of having an independent wit, that appalled him. So that now he was oblivious that he had forfeited any rights as regards sacred words.

'Rousseau,' he pressed on, recitative again, 'makes a fashionable thing out of cultivating savages. Savages are *us*, it appears, unspoilt. It is the mode to be patient with them, as one is patient with the childishness of a saint. It is a pity that no one has a fashion of patience towards convicted men and women.'

'Why tell us?' asked Halloran over his shoulder. 'We know. There are six of us in this boat, and we've all got a spirit of rebellion, and we'll each of us keep it as big a secret as we can because not one of us wants to be flogged. So if you're feeling rebellious—well, you might as well not talk about it here. It's stale news.'

'Maybe.' Ewers sounded easeful; lolling on his back and looking here and there across the sky through nearly closed eyes, as if he were Michelangelo about to quote a price for illuminating the firmament. 'However, Corporal, listen to this! All these petty men: Partridge, Major Sabian, perhaps even Rowley, are writing their diaries, observing, recording the quirks of this land in the hope that one day a putrescent weed, transplanted hence to Kew Gardens, will bear the name *Flos Perniciosus Partridgensis*.'

Ewers opened his eyes, raised his head, secure that no one had understood his Latin joke.

'I see,' said Halloran impatiently, but kept to his principle of not rebelling in private for some hours after he had grovelled in public.

'Hah, yes. Partridge intends to publish a record of the colony, so too does Sabian, if an editor can be found to spell for them and to stand between them and the mysteries of the comma. And you, Corporal, would not have to be the Prophet Isaiah to tell who

41

will prepare the plates for those sublime works and to foresee whose name will not appear on the title page. Well?'

'I suppose the answer to both is your name, Ewers.'

Ewers' blind skyward face waggled.

'Yes. My name, Ewers!'

The smell of mud affected Halloran with indifference to Partridge's schemes. Mangroves faced him with their lizard-skin front feet in the water. It was all millenia away from the printing presses and polite journals and medals struck by the Royal Society. In the zenith heat, on his way home to the town, Partridge might understand this and, in his lassitude, hurl the two poor blacks overboard.

'You are a blessed man,' Ewers continued, having an option on Halloran's ear despite the mangroves and slow, silty water.

'Do you think so?'

'Yes. You have quick eyes and you respect the Arts. You're the type of man who should be free of the restrictions of the service.'

'Aren't we all?'

'In two years, you will be back amongst your people. If I could say the same . . .'

For half a minute and without warning, Ewers wept, still flat on his back, and his split, navy-style sleeve clamped against his eye-brows. The corners of his long mouth had drawn back prodigiously to show tall, grimacing eye-teeth.

Halloran leant over and nudged his right elbow gently.

'Man, there are pardons you know. I'd imagine you'd be amongst the first to be pardoned.'

'A pardon is useless.' He sat up. 'If I had the decency, I'd die here of shame. Because I'm known as a forger in Dumfries. Even in Edinburgh.'

'Hah!' said Halloran, going gusty and bluff and gesturing over his right shoulder with his thumb. 'There are worse crimes against man and God. Down the river and not so far, there are far worse.'

'I forged four bank-notes on the Bank of Scotland. The Bank's engraver said at my trial in Dumfries that their qualities as forgeries astounded him. I was proud. I can still remember my pride. I was proud, I can remember, and my aunt sat up in the public gallery, and people pointed her out behind her back.'

He turned his face to the north bank and with his hand over his mouth, whimpered or giggled. In that heat it was anybody's guess.

At last, his long face turned back to his brother-boaters. It was stained with grief, not at all its clean-shaven self.

'Let me tell you about my aunt,' he implored.

In common mercy, 'Yes,' sighed Halloran.

This will be as good, he thought, *as one of those fruity sermons on the crucifixion*. On two and a bit pounds of meat every week, he had no emotion to spare for Ewers' aunt in Dumfries.

At this moment Ewers began to doubt himself. As if from a great distance and painfully, he peered at the two transports. He was gratified to find their eyes rolling, their ears full of their own rhythmic exhaustion.

'Her name is Miss Kate Norris. I went to her when I was three years old. I became her life, as you'd expect with a spinster.'

He'll say next that there was never a better woman, thought Halloran.

'There never lived a better woman,' said Ewers. 'Every woman whose company I ever found myself in, I observed closely, to see if she had the qualities of Aunt Norris in however immature a form. None of them ever did reproduce the range of her virtues.'

'I see,' said Halloran. He spoke, not out of enthusiasm for Aunt Norris, but because he felt it within him one day to make Ann's fortune by writing a farce called *The Master-Forger Chooses a Wife*.

'The thought that she rebuffed a number of suitors for my sake is one which I eat with ashes every day.'

There and then, he began to eat it with ashes again and wept for a full minute with most of his face hidden behind his sleeve, his sobbing hidden by the groan of the boat and the slowly plangent river.

'I want you to assure me you'll do a thing for me. For her.'

'That depends,' said Halloran. He said it severely since there was something too unctuous and full-blown about Ewers' misery. Within the system, he had little enough space in which to conspire humanely. Ewers' aunt in Dumfries could ascend into heaven for all he cared; and might, if there wasn't a girl in Scotland to reproduce the range of her virtues.

'No, it's fruitless, soldier,' said the artist. 'It is too much to ask of a stranger. Besides, it could put you in a bad light with your superiors.'

'That would be dangerous,' Halloran glibly assented. In the next seconds, he was shown the benefits of having plenty of skin on your face. Ewers sucked grief in through the right side of his long, peculiar mouth. Then he let the upper lip overlap the lower; and in the end looked immensely more pitiful than a round-faced, tight-featured man ever could.

None the less, he still had much to say.

'What I had intended was to find in you the person who would vindicate me when Sabian and Partridge published their work. I must have someone in Britain to speak out for me, to claim that the plates have been done from the work of a forgotten Scot and to demand that that Scot's aunt should receive justice for her lost nephew's work. If that someone in Britain is importunate enough, not only may the aunt receive a small fortune, but the nephew, grown mildly illustrious, will be pardoned, with an assured future and much to reward his champion with.'

'But you told me a pardon was useless,' Halloran objected.

'I was being excessive.'

Over the river and through the sun, three symbolically large and easeful crows went flapping. They made receding sounds of disbelief, rough as horse-hair, until they became motes in the north-west. Perhaps they were what Ewers merited. For Halloran could all but smell the unreliability of the man. Ewers' grand scheme for his own ransom seemed very chancily put together. It might have occurred to him only in the flush of promise with which the day had begun, or as the result of his humiliation by Partridge.

'I realize now,' the artist nodded, 'that I was beforehand with my request. But perhaps it is not too much to say that you may some day be my champion.'

'I'm afraid it's far too much to say. I've too much to champion as it is,' said Halloran, smartening up the collar of his coat to show what a prosy boy he was, and how unfit for the job. The next time Partridge disciplined Ewers, and the artist exploded into a tantrum, Halloran didn't want his name hurled like some kind of doom in the surgeon's face. God knows, he wasn't a doom. Not with his simple anguish and his simple plans.

'Urrugh!' cried one of the rowers. Because they had come in sight of three open hills. By the standards of summer in the netherworld, they were very green hills. Up one climbed a small white town in column of two. At the top of the town stood a Government House whose thatch roof was being replaced by shingles of blackbutt. Transports moved in and out and about the hole in its distant roof with the effective indolence of maggots in a skull.

There was a hawk above the town, skating the air currents. It hung taut with desire, its eye on minuscule prey in the grass on one of the hills. Halloran pointed to it.

'That's one they'll never get for their aviary,' he said. 'And while we're on the aviary, the word is you'd get a ready ear and no mercy from Mrs Daker. The word is she's a viper.'

But Ewers was looking over the side, deep in specious disappointment.

6

Under the box-trees by the river, Halloran and his two Marines ate their bread. With it, they had their weekly quarter pound of cheese, and drank from their canteens a watered-down Tenerife wine, very laxative, one of Mr Blythe's wise buys. It was perhaps one o'clock, and the shade was very deep.

In sight stood Surgeon Daker's long hospital, clapboard windows propped open, drinking the cool off the river. To Halloran, drowsing in the shade, some minute shift in the air would occasionally bring the thick, excremental smell of the place. The smell and the flies that rode it gave the three of them no rest.

'Let's go and collect our sick man,' he suggested at last.

They approached the doorway with their heads back. 'Hew!' they said constantly in a note of discovery. 'Hew!'

The door was open. Bronze flies sizzled in the daylight on the steps, wavered like the black spots in migraine. Perhaps they too were partially afflicted with disbelief. Faced with one of those things which have to be done quickly, Halloran ducked his head under the lintel and sniffed the dimness. He blinked up the length of the unscreened inside. Somewhere towards the centre, seemingly robust laughter broke out.

The hospital had been fitted out with bedsteads and pallets, but mostly pallets. Men dozed, blankets down, shirts up, legs apart, letting the air to their crutches. An owlish consumptive stared across the room, not to be taken unawares by Halloran or by death. His two stubborn nodules of shoulders were propped against the wall, giving fair promise to remain, stanchion-firm and stanchion-bare, when the rest of the frame had finished wasting from them.

'Good afternoon,' called Halloran. 'Surgeon in?'

The consumptive shook his head, pointing down the hut.

'Orderly,' he suggested, and paid for it with a coughing-fit like axe-blows. The little body jiggled, and Halloran, in decency, waited the spasm out.

There was a clear aisle in Surgeon Daker's hospital, water buckets along the aisle, privies along the walls. All else was random, a melee of bodies and ills. Halloran passed stray charcoal-burners in which something resinous smouldered. A man with lupus face, being a wise monster, stayed close to one to keep off the flies.

'Did you see that, Corporal?' whispered the fool of a Marine behind Halloran.

Then, without warning, they were amongst healthy men. The insanity of the long hospital gained much from these, who stood inert by the windows or rested on their beds in silence. They were watching an acutely craggy woman, shift up around her armpits, on her back on the floor under a small well-fed man. She frowned at the handful the man tried to make of her fruitless little paps. They were people, even separately, ugly beyond telling. A preacher like John Chrysostom would have delighted to have them mate beneath his pulpit as he preached on the viciousness of the flesh, on the death-sweat and -bed of love.

And even there, on the floor, things seemed insanely inert.

Just the same, lust, the size of a hippopotamus, flopped over in the tropic swamps of Halloran's belly. Oh, it alarmed him to have his bowels yearn out towards that sort of oblivion.

'What are you all doing here?' he asked with a severity intended for the hippopotamus. 'Where's the surgeon's orderly?'

They all began to laugh at him. It was the worst type of laughter possible. Their mouths flew open like vents; the laughter came out like a snatch of laughter out of a mine.

They're all possessed, he thought, and went cold.

They pointed at the poverty-stricken woman and her portly burden.

'Don't break him off now,' one of them said. 'You'll never get

47

him started again.'

Halloran could then have kicked the orderly's grey buttocks. They presented themselves, and it would have been befittingly gross to lay his boot to them. But more than that, there came over him a queasy urge to mash both people with his feet and rant against them, text and fury. Yet all of this would have been no more than a device to join himself to them in their sad fever. So he managed to hand his flint-lock to one of the privates, and dragged the orderly upright by the shoulders. As he was hauled up, the man roared and struck at Halloran's waist, and Halloran, exultant, let him go with one hand and knocked him out of the other with a punch flush on the ear.

'Christ, can't do that!' said a satanic Welshman in a shirt.

'Hold hard!' they all said.

But he was not going to be made ashamed before them. He approached the orderly, who looked piteous in his shirt, shaking his little scarified head, blinking.

'I have a warrant for somebody here,' he said. He made a few parade-ground threats, the sort of thing nobody believes in anyhow.

Time to see things straight again was what the orderly needed. He stood shaking his head, making a speech to himself, but couldn't see Halloran. Meanwhile, the woman remained flat on her back, doing nothing about her sad, angular nakedness. The orderly's sweat and her own lay round her throat, on her breasts, in the pit of her navel. There was a peculiar stiff questingness about her raised head which Halloran saw but could not interpret, until one of his Marines said, 'God she's blind!'

'Having a try yourself, General?' called the Welshman when Halloran knelt on one knee beside the woman. She stank, which was no novelty. Over her odious and unwelcoming body he made a poor attempt to pull down the shift. She ground her gums and struck his arm away and laughed drily, as if she had just then got a picture of the proceedings. She was perhaps thirty, utterly desert; her laughter was the dry-leaves laughter of very old women. She had no teeth at all to modulate it. It prolonged itself, regardless of the demands of breathing, until her face was blue. Then she took a great swallow of air and started to laugh again. The others laughed too.

'Whore's got her pride, General,' called the Welshman.

'Get dressed!' Halloran told the orderly.

One of the patients threw the man a pair of trousers, and he throttled them and put them on. But he was still dazed and still had odd-ends of words to say to himself. In the end, he turned to Halloran and said, full of business, 'Who's your warrant for?'

Halloran pulled the warrant out of his pocket and found the peasant name amidst the classic gardens of verbiage.

'Eris Mealey,' he read.

'I thought so,' said the orderly, very gratified about the eyes. 'You can't have him. His back's gone rotten. Daker's left a letter you can take to the Governor.'

'But I'm supposed to hand this to Daker himself.'

'Daker's somewhere out in the hills trapping birds.'

'When will he be back?'

'Tomorrow afternoon.'

'What about the hospital?'

'Hospital looks after itself. You just take this letter and keep your nose out.'

He led Halloran resentfully to the end of the building, to the surgeon's office, an eaves-high partition of wood with a locked door. The orderly opened it with a key which, clearly, he kept tied round his neck no matter what the occasion. Inside was a table and chair and two hospital registers in suede covers bearded with dust. There was a letter also, which said in a tiny hand that it was from Surgeon Daker, Magistrate and Medical Superintendent, the Crescent, To His Excellency the Colonial Governor, concerning the Irish felon, Eris Mealey. Halloran read all this and pocketed it.

'Mealey was flogged?' asked Halloran. 'You said his back was rotten.'

'I said his back was rotten,' the orderly repeated in Halloran's rather moist East coast accent. 'See for yourself!' He pointed to the corner across from the office.

Halloran peered, the other two peered. *What's it like to have death on your back, death triumphant already?* the three of them thought. *Show us, in your face, why you can't will your back unrotten again.*

Naked and stomach-down on a pallet by the wall, with his own water bucket by him, Mealey seemed to have a heavy shadow on his back and buttocks and upper legs. The smell of him, the mass of the smell and its tart edge of dreadful sweetness, stood out above the routine stenches of Daker's infirmary, and once Halloran had linked it with the shadow on Mealey, he stumbled away across the aisle to find a waste-pail and be sick in it.

Hearing him, the man who knelt by Mealey, continually wiping the neck and the side of the face with a wet handkerchief, glanced up.

'Well,' he said, 'there's one pair of sympathetic bowels in the damned place.'

There was no time for him to do more than glance up, because Mealey whimpered in a querulous soprano if the sponging stopped for a second.

Shaking his head, Halloran returned to the enigma of man flogged three-quarters to death. He nodded to the man with the sponge, who was a yeoman type in a grey, high-collared coat only a year or two past its best. The fellow's nose Halloran had seen on other men in Wexford; beaky, pugnacious, it was often found on large, strong, melancholy men. Here, by Mealey, you had a bear-like, strong, melancholy man, who snorted gently but continuously in comment on the patient.

'I was supposed to be taking him back to Partridge's hospital,' Halloran told the yeoman.

'No chance of that.'

The yeoman nodded at Mealey's unspeakable wound. It was so huge an injury that you needed to verify your first sight of it, were compelled towards it, pushing your nose through its solid reek. But it was very dim in the corner, and the putrefaction got in behind the eyes and fogged them. You got an impression though; at least that. Halloran's impression was that from neck to knee Mealey was half-way wrapped round by a fat, black, vampiring slough.

'He has entirely the wrong sort of skin,' the yeoman said. 'One of those blue, girlish skins. Haven't you ever met a boy with that type of skin and neat, straight nose and wished his sister had come with him, she'd be such a beauty?'

The boy gibbered at his pillow. The message came out in slivers of sound, as if the mirror of his mind had smashed; only the urgency was intelligible.

'He has none of the blue skin left here, as you can imagine,' said the yeoman, gesturing with the sponge towards Mealey's back. 'On Sunday, in fact, you could see the shoulder-blades, the white bones themselves. This that's so rotten and stinking is junked muscles and jellies. What's your name?'

'Halloran,' said Halloran, with small patience for anything but Mealey.

'Mine is Robert Hearn.'

'Then why are you preaching anger, Mr Robert Hearn?' Halloran asked shortly. 'What damned difference does it make whether his skin is blue and whether his sister's lovely? Who's going to ever tell anyhow, with his sister across the world and his skin in this state?'

The yeoman acknowledged the point with a lift of the eyebrows.

One of the Marines had gone outside, hiccoughing. Halloran sent the other one now to collect him and take him down to the boat. Then he himself sat on the floor and wept.

'Don't ask me to weep,' said Hearn, dipping his handkerchief into the water-bucket and padding it under the boy's mouth. 'With the first tear, a person starts to forget. I won't ever forget.'

'Hurrah!' said Halloran flippantly through his tears.

Yet there was a force somewhat greater than bombast about the yeoman. Halloran's mockery did not touch him, and he spoke off-handedly, his words incidental to the work of getting moisture into an upside-down man. And without doubt, he was right about

51

tears. Having wept for Mealey, the mind felt justified in reducing him to an anecdote, a parable, a ballad; or something else digestible.

'What was he punished for?'

'Nothing!' said Hearn so lightly but with such finality that Halloran was limited to asking,

'Will he be taken soon?'

'Taken.' Hearn blinked. He despised the timid word and deliberately played upon it. 'He'll have to die first.'

But he swallowed and shook his head then.

'No, I am sorry. I'm not an irreligious man. I cannot see though that when God bears the blame for so much he must bear it for Mealey too. I'll say this. Mealey is burning to death. Surely he'll burn out during the night. Please God.'

'Please God,' said Halloran. 'Did he confess to you?'

'To me? No. I'm a Wicklow Presbyterian. Eris Mealey makes me think there's something to be said for a religion one carries in here,' he punched his own chest, 'as against one which requires ritual even in the hour of death.'

'You understand, I'm not being bitter,' he went on to explain with a certain rueful care, 'but grateful. If a man doesn't happen to be grateful for his religion, where's his good faith?'

'Don't worry yourself,' said Halloran. '*The kingdom of God is within*, even in Mealey's case.'

'I see,' said the yeoman politely.

A solid cheer and a whistle came from the middle of the hut. There someone had achieved something ironic. Perhaps the orderly.

Hearn drenched another cloth in the pail and replaced the one the boy was sucking on. While one was taken away and the other put down, Mealey whimpered, certainly. Yet it was not the whimper of a flayed man but, instead, of a man whose meat has burned or who's been given small beer instead of spirits. It was hardly more than a whine of pretty complaint. The young fellow's mind, wherever it waited, at a place remoter from Halloran than Moscow, did not believe in its own torment. Which was a hint, a genial one, that a person would drown without believing in the gagging waters; go black with typhus and wag his head in disbelief; get the lead in his belly and find it harder than the Trinity to give credence to.

'You'd think the magistrates would have arranged to have him pressed into the army or navy,' said Hearn. 'He'd have been better off. Wouldn't he?'

'Would he?' Halloran asked.

'Ah-ah,' Hearn cautioned, 'your coat's Hanover all over. You are the King's man, as they say.'

'As they say,' said Halloran.

Drowned in the stench, he forgot it for seconds at a time. The long room sizzled with the consequential gluttony of flies, and that too he no longer adverted to. But to see in an instant and by surprise a seam in the boy's purple back and a herd of black flies, whose bite is maggots, drinking from it, *that* made him flee.

He fled fifty yards into the open. Ending under a smooth and tolerant eucalypt and jumping to snatch down some of the leaves from its high branches, he crushed them in his hands and sniffed up their clean astringency. They stung his brain, and he dropped the ones he held and jumped for more.

Hearn had followed him and watched him with sad forbearance.

'Where do you come from, Corporal?'

'Wexford Bay. Erriscombe village,' said Halloran, crumpling and inhaling.

'Ah, Wexford's peaceful. There aren't that many Wexford men serving, army or navy.'

'No. It might be their good fortune, mightn't it?'

There was silence, to fill which Halloran took a further three long sniffs. Then he said:

'I despise that sort of talk.'

'What sort of talk?'

'The sort of talk you're trying to provoke. The sort of talk that will end in my asking what you've done for the ruling powers, since you've got a good coat on and look so well.'

53

'I'm government clerk here at the Crescent. I've had some experience in that type of work. That's how I wear a good coat.'

'Transported, of course?' asked Halloran, meaning the yeoman, not the coat.

'Yes, of course. With less good luck, I could be off in the forest somewhere, dragging timber.'

You could certainly have said that Hearn was honest. But he never laughed with his own honesty, and gave only an occasional half-smile when Halloran said anything sardonic. He failed to smile as he himself leant forward now and whispered.

'Secret Society. Illegal oath.'

Halloran laughed unequivocally. 'Three Christmasses back, I went to a meeting of a body called the Land Tenure Committee. I went with my father and shouldn't have, considering what I was.'

'What was that?'

'A scholar from the bishop's house in Wexford.'

'Amazing! And they got the lot of you?'

Halloran nodded, but said, 'Oh no, not everyone. The father got away by the grace of God. Besides, he's a lucky old beggar. German mercenaries. Ugly big fellows. A boot in the cods was their specialty.'

'Was this in Wexford?'

'The Wexford magistrates were the ones we ended in front of, yes. But I hardly remember Wexford jail. Inside a week an officer of Marines off one of the ships in the Bay came for me.'

While they had been speaking, the aspect of the world had changed. From the unknown south-east hove wet clouds of badly tarnished silver, keeping blockade on the harmless little port. The light was intimidated to thin yellow and gave a luminous fringe to the Irishman's shoulders. A wind had begun blowing, sluicing the hospital reek away. It gave a sharp sense of refreshment to Halloran to see crooked shrubs of yellow and olive on the layered cliff across the river, shaking themselves in the wind.

Of course, it all meant nothing, a show of leniency from the southern ice-regions from which came all that was sufferable in summer. Including this temporary vigour in the air. Halloran savoured it and looked up at the eucalyptus, thinking that now it might endow the yeoman and himself with some of its placidity.

But the yeoman was a hard one.

'And with your young arm,' he said without notice, 'you uphold the system which did for Mealey.'

'No!'

'Yes, oh yes! Indeed!'

'And did you cry out when you recorded Mealey's sentence?'

'He was never sentenced.'

'Never sentenced, my foot!'

'I said that he was never sentenced. He and four other men were heard to have spoken of pikes. The Irishman's cure-all, pikes. After church-parade on Sunday, Daker had them marched out under sergeant's guard. The sergeant couldn't do anything. Not against Daker the Mighty. The landscape was as usual. Empty of officers. Over there, on a hill behind Government House, Daker had them flayed to get evidence. The poisonous thing was that they had none to give, none of the startling stuff that Daker wanted. However, that's apart from our argument. I admit to you, Corporal, that had Mealey been sentenced, I'd have recorded his sentence without a whimper. This is how they have us divided one from another.'

'One from another be damned!' said Halloran. 'And Daker had him flayed. Daker isn't the system I uphold with any young arm of mine.'

'True enough,' said Hearn. 'True enough, in a way.' He paused. 'I don't suppose I have to worry about being reported to the authorities for what I've said this afternoon?'

'What do you think? Do I look like Judas's young brother?'

'No. In that case, you might want to know what Eris Mealey has said to me about the affair.'

The yeoman glanced easefully over his shoulder. Mum as Satan then, he stared into Halloran's eyes.

'He's in a fever, of course, but he claimed that Mrs Daker rubbed poison into his stripes. Came to him where he lay and

55

rubbed rust into his cuts.'

'Gossip!' said Halloran.

'If you think my motives are gossip, so be it. I neither believe nor disbelieve Mealey. But Daker *was* in danger. Now Mealey will die, and the Governor won't be seeing him or hearing his story, and the corps of gallant officers will tell their lies. And Daker will be safe again.'

Above the sound of the wind, Halloran could hear Hearn's bated, interrogative breathing. Hearn went on staring at him from under grey eyelids as big as hearty moustaches. The eyes said what Hearn's yeoman rigorousness would not allow himself to say: *Admit it. You know she looks a poisoner.*

'I have to take the boat home,' said Halloran.

'You have, too.' Hearn stood up straight. 'I was pleased to meet you, Corporal Halloran.'

'And I you, Mr Hearn.'

'Thank you, but I don't think so.'

'What don't you think?'

'That you were glad to meet me.'

'Because *you* were trying to recruit me.' Halloran smiled, and indicted Hearn with his finger. 'I was recruited all the morning by a Scotsman, for his own motives. And now you ...'

'I hope I do a better job,' said Hearn, and blinked. He really did hope it. There was no whimsey in him.

'Oh, I consider you a far more dangerous style of man.'

'Dangerous? I am responsibility itself.' Hearn's disaffected eyes flashed. All that he said now was a recital of disenchantment rather than of pride of class. 'I have held seventy acres at Round-wood, County Wicklow, in the days of my respectability. I was surveyor of roads and hired the gangs who remade the Round-wood to Rathdrum road. As well, I was county Alnegar, a post I held under Sir Andrew Price, Wicklow's Chief Magistrate.'

The final sentence would have been, *And I spit on it all.* But it wasn't spoken—only, once more, conveyed by the eyes.

'It's no use fishing for me,' said Halloran. 'I have such a thing as the soldiers' oath to keep.'

'Oath to whom?' asked Hearn, all deliberate bemusement.
Halloran smiled.

'Oath to whom?' Hearn repeated.

'Oath to God, Mr Hearn.'

'No!' Hearn was just audible. The force of his vision did not make him shout, but reduced him to a pin-point of sound. 'A God conscripted by a realm to give inhuman power to its purposes. A God conscripted, as you were, Halloran, to give binding magic to the links which chain each clod of human dust to its King. That is, no God at all.'

The top of the eucalypt flurried in dissent.

'There is no god-forged chain of power from Daker to His Excellency to George to God. The true God is not coerced into anyone's army, the true God fills no navy's sails. To the true God, the House of Hanover is just a house. Therefore, Corporal Halloran, oath to whom?'

Halloran was mindful of the burning bush. 'To the God of Abraham and Isaac and Jacob, whether that was the God they wanted me to swear to, I don't know. But that's the oath they got from me. So Halloran, like God, is a little beyond recruiting.'

Prophets disgruntled him. He promised himself that the next time Hearn said anything at which some offence could be taken, he would storm away. The chance came immediately.

'Why do you think that the God of Abraham and Isaac and Jacob comes low enough to hear your oath, Corporal?'

Halloran picked up his flint-lock and his disputed vows.

'Who are you to say I live in a pit?' he said with a good show of anger.

Downhill stood a fringe of very dry she-oaks for which he made. He stopped before disappearing amongst them.

'I'll ask about Mealey whenever the boat comes in,' he called. 'I'll sweat on his death, as they say.'

'Corporal,' said Hearn. 'I meant low enough to hear my oath, your oath, anyone's oath.'

Halloran turned his back.

'You won't sweat for long,' said Hearn after him.

As he came down around the corner of the vegetable garden, he wondered to what a degree the true God, the transcendent God, *I am Who am*, was involved in the listless faith he kept with George R. Beside this, Mealey, Daker, the fat orderly, the sick and the hale in Daker's hospital, all were minor puzzles.

7

THE three o'clock drum called Hearn back to his work in the cramped ante-room of Government House. For his rarefied place there, amongst decent, marbled ledgers, he felt improperly grateful. He could remember being grateful in a similar way on the day he'd seen a petrified skeleton found by a slip of the spade in the side of a chalk hill. He could have touched the clean shape of the bones, he came so close to them. They had been no more than the numerals, the ciphers of a man; and this had consoled him, that from them the mountainous frenzies of living and of the last gasp had been eroded.

Similarly rinsed clean of frenzies were the returns he was handed every Tuesday. They came from the Surgeon, the Surgeon as Magistrate, the Commissary clerk, the overseers at the brickfield, quarry, gardens, farm, timber-pits. He recorded these and made skilful abstracts of them; and when he had finished, his masters had something as adequate and as sterile of *human* truth as were those bones in the chalk hill.

For being grateful to deal with the settlement and system in its most innocent form, in numerals, he judged himself. He judged himself unfavourably, because of his diffuse pride. When his patron, a Sir Andrew Price, had shown him how a mere evasion under oath would lead to his acquittal, he was not too conscience-stricken to be evasive. He was too proud. Yet he took no pride now in his pride then. It may have been because he had allowed Sir Andrew to buy him a berth in the bosun's mess, so that he voyaged the thirteen thousand miles as a freeman in his own coat. He had not had to survive the hold and was too proud again not to feel ashamed of being shielded from that testing.

Yet there would have been nothing diffuse about his concern

59

had he known that someone so raw or cumbersomely wily as Ewers had arrived in the Daker household.

A fortnight before, the Commandant, Captain Howard, had warned Hearn that Mrs Daker had applied for an interview, would arrive at half past nine in the morning, and that he himself would be *out* to all other visitors. The following morning, at the given time, Hearn opened the front door on a furnace-breath westerly, and a white town so tenuous amongst the blowing dust that it threatened to vanish if you ceased to believed in it. Hearn believed in it though, too well.

It was a rigorous day for lovers, but there stood Mrs Daker with a slight dew of sweat on her upper lip. She sported a very ripe purple and a fichu of black chiffon, loose enough to show her black chiffon collar, girlish at her neck. There was no subtlety in the meeting of her gipsy skin and deep purple. It took the eye by main assault. The ruffled chiffon was at odds with her, just the same, and needed a woman of a more delicate mouth and reputation.

'This way, Mrs Daker,' Hearn said loudly, calling to the entire hillside of witless little huts to be witnesses of her flagrancy.

Her face was impervious to Hearn as in she came. Somehow her skin had grown smooth over the memory of the Daker of less than four years ago; of Daker on half-pay and drinking most of it, trapped with her in a room above a riotous barber's in Exeter; of the grey tumulus where they two lay all the night, back to belly, in answer to the imperatives of the cold and never of tenderness.

'Through here, Ma'am,' said Hearn, averting his eyes, and took her into the ante-room to find Captain Howard side-on in the doorway of his office. The lady brushed past him, and the door closed on Howard's avid mumblings.

On his way back to his desk, Hearn discovered that between the porch and Howard's Office she had put a sting in his flesh, right enough. He possessed a rugged, monarch will, of the type for which European religions seemed to be tailored. It ruled him under God, it quashed small, futile ructions in the provinces. Yet he was faint from his glimpse of jollied-up Mrs Daker. In conscience, he worked standing, till her raw image faded down the corridors of the blood. When he was next aware of himself, it was of pen-cramp in his wrist. A whole man, a united kingdom, he slid inadvertently into his seat.

A little after ten, Surgeon Daker arrived.

'I have astounding news for the Commandant,' said the little, deathly face as soon as Hearn opened the porch door. Daker's strabismic eye was aimed utterly *un*astounded at the lintel.

'*Astounding* by my standards,' he corrected himself. 'Perhaps only *important* to Howard. Tell him!'

Daker carried a wire bird-trap in his right hand. It was still disguised with wisps of porcupine-grass, and a kingfisher of some kind sat companionably in it. A rich green glorified the bird's back and wings, yet it had hunched itself like a cold navvy and looked sideways at the heat and dust blowing from the west. Red dust had scurfed the shoulders of Daker's blue coat.

'Go on,' said Daker. 'Tell him!'

'He's *out* to all visitors, sir.'

'If he's in at all, he'll be pleased to see me. Go on. Tell him!'

Hearn went indoors, furious with Howard for making him into a farce-figure. There were immense dangers, too, in being hemmed in by an unholy triangle between the front door and the door of Howard's office, when points A, B and C would all see him as smeared with their own guilt or stupidity, and could have him chained or flayed or damned to labour.

When, in the ante-room, he heard male and female laughter indifferently jumbled, he glanced over his shoulder and saw that Daker and the dead-pan kingfisher had followed him down the hall. The back of his neck, the rims of his ears began to burn. Though he refused to hide his eyes from the Surgeon's face, the gesture had no meaning, since Daker's left eye looked through a person, and the right looked at the roof. Brow-to-brow manliness was lost on this little fellow.

What was astounding, however much Hearn expected it, was that nothing happened to Daker's face. Not even the resignation of a practised wittol. The lips didn't curl, the attenuated features of his suet-and-freckle face were quiescent as ever. When he pushed Hearn aside from the office door and left him grasping an empty insult with hands open and chest-high, it was an act of ill-breeding rather than of anger.

So Captain Howard and Mrs Daker saw the surgeon standing ghostly with indifference on the threshold, and Mrs Daker's involuntary yelp and scurry came to Hearn as assurance that the stale comedy had begun. He could not see into the room or tell what state the lovers were in, and he hoped, of course, that they had not got beyond token endearments.

At a loss but respectably shirt-sleeved, Howard came up to the doorway, nodding and alacritous, glowering sideways at his fool of a clerk. *Officer and gentleman, I abominate you*, thought Hearn, word by word, so hard-headed was his enmity.

'This fellow didn't want me to see you,' Daker told Howard. As if all things made a balanced and orderly world, even the fact that his wife couched of a morning at Government House, except for Hearn's disrupting unreasonableness.

Bless you in your maniacy, thought Hearn genially.

'Yes . . .' said Howard, keeping his mouth open, but finding that there was nothing else he could say for the moment, even to the surgeon, without losing some brand of honour.

'I have a matter of no small scientific importance to consult you on.'

'Yes, Surgeon.'

Howard urbanely closed the office door and transformed the ante-room into the seat of government.

'Hearn, you can leave. I shall see you after Mr Daker has gone.'

'Let him stay,' the surgeon contradicted. 'There's no use pretending we have any privacy in this settlement.' He leaned fraternally towards Howard and jabbed his thumb at Hearn. 'They find out everything, you know, Captain.'

The Captain was not in a position to argue. He composed himself and crossed to Hearn's desk.

'Would you care to take a seat, Surgeon Daker?' he said, picking up foolscap. It was easy to tell he was as pleased for the polite formula to fill his mouth as he was for the paper in his hands.

Daker ducked down into the chair, lunatic quick, and put the wire trap, with its sable and green bird, on the desk.

Howard coughed.

'What splendid colour,' he said. 'Is it native?'

'Yes,' said Daker. 'Last summer I had a glimpse of him in flat country five miles beyond.' He thumbed carelessly over his shoulder at the inland. 'There were other kingfishers, too, that had eschewed the river-banks and spent the summer in dry country, but I have been laying the traps all summer long for this one.'

'I see. Congratulations are in order.'

'Thank you, Captain. But I believe I have three other birds in my aviary, all of them captured earlier this summer, which have been hitherto unknown to ornithologists.'

He sat forward and took on more of the look of a feeling organism.

'Two of them are members of the *Cuculidae* family; two of them, this one included, are *Halcyonidae*.'

Howard wagged his head knowingly, as if he were acquainted with *Halcyonidae* from of old.

'This superb fellow I have named *Alcyone viridis*, the Green kingfisher. Provisionally, that is. I hope to hit on a more imaginative name before long. I want that you should be kind enough to to inform His Excellency of all this. It is news which, I feel, deserves a—'

Here Daker shoved his fist hard in under his own cheek-bone, so that the mouth, twisted open in the left corner and showing black rot in the back teeth, laboured for the right word.

'—a *vice-regal* letter.'

On an undemanding blank page, Howard, the vice-roy's viceroy, wrote with fraudulent energy, *Daker. Aviary. Four birds unknown hitherto.*

He pulled his eyes from the page to utter, with immense

63

fervour,

'I'm sure His Excellency will be most gratified to receive news of the results of your work, sir.'

Results of your work. Hearn thought of the complicated horrors of the hospital which was, under G III R, Daker's work.

'Yes, well, in the—vice-regal letter, I would like you to request His Excellency's permission for me to name this kingfisher after himself.'

The bird waited unblinking within its green coat. That it might have His Excellency tacked adjectively to its plumage didn't seem to touch it in its essence.

Request H. E. permission to name one after H. E., the officer wrote, wondering, as Hearn wondered also, how a man like Daker had come by the technical knowledge to discover a new animal and name it rightly, so that men of science would call it by that name until the sun fell. There was no doubt that Daker was capable of this small, immortalizing trick, for he had performed it more than two years earlier, and sent embalmed creatures off to England. Nine months past, the last transport had brought a letter of praise from the Royal Society.

'These are the names which, subject to His Excellency's approval, I intend to give the new species.'

He took a list from his waistcoat pocket and handed it to Howard, who received it almost as heartily as, an hour previously, he had received Mrs Daker.

'I'll draft the letter immediately,' promised Howard.

If there were a smile, bitter or otherwise, stored up in Daker, now would have been the time to bring it forth.

But 'Thank you,' said Daker; and left.

The solid enigma of the man remained, and Howard was, of course, disturbed by it. He roared threats at Hearn, promises of things which would result to Hearn's backbone, shoulders, liver, tripes. Hearn kept a straight head, pricking with fury just the same. At last, Howard felt a fool and abated; so that Hearn was able to speak reasonably and save the backbone and whatever other parts of him were in jeopardy.

'If this ever becomes known . . .' said Howard, white in the face, red in the neck.

But refuse profane and old wives' fables, thought Hearn from I. Timothy. He could have said it aloud, had he been free.

Howard returned dazed to the lady, knowing now that love in the morning shows too much contempt, even for obtuse cuckolds like Daker. Against the mid-morning shabbiness of his position, the Captain made no progress apparently; for after a very short time, he opened his door again, and with convinced, neutral politeness, guided the lady to the front porch. Hearn could have turned in his seat and watched her going down the hill. But, of course, he would not. If he had, he would have been surprised to see with what an air of solid rectitude she plodded through the ferment of orange dust.

8

Ewers had never painted for an ornithologist before. He had thought that such work was done from embalmed specimens. But Daker would not risk embalming the creatures of his fame yet; not until winter, anyhow.

He showed Ewers the kingfisher, which drowsed in a wicker cage.

'*Alcyone Beryllus* is his name,' the surgeon explained. (His Excellency had foregone the pleasure of being the creature's godparent.) Daker spelt out the name three times. 'Paint him first! He is a gem. You must get his colours absolutely accurate, and as for his stance and the line of his head and body, they must all be exact. Have him on a branch. A branch of peppermint or cedar would look excellent. Show him from the front, but slightly to the left. It doesn't matter to me how long you take, so long as you carry my breath away, as he did.'

How do you carry the breath away from a Lazarus-like man?

For a start, you take a close view of the subject—or Ewers did, anyhow. He worked standing, with charcoal and cartridge-paper, about eight feet back, and, despite the intervening slats, tried for perfection of line. When the bird fidgeted or turned his back on him, as kingfishers will in a small cage of cane, he chased it until he saw it from the front and to the left again. He stared at the line he wanted and carried it like a cup of brimming vitriol, that is, perilously, back to the easel.

At first, he had a sense of working well. The day was not intolerably hot, and he had shade from a box-brush. Only feet away, a cageful of finches extolled him, Caledonia's sublimest limner in the nether-world.

But, as was fated to happen, Mrs Daker came walking in her

garden by mid-morning. Like a decent mother of some parish, she wore a dissonant yellow and a straw hat and carried a parasol.

'Ah,' she said, seeing the number of very fine sketches Ewers had done, 'when do you mean to start using your colours?'

'Almost immediately, Madam.'

He became occupied then with a bogus coughing fit. For women alarmed him proportionately as their bearing and manners departed from Aunt Norris's. It behoved a woman to bear her womanhood as a curse, as Aunt Norris bore it. The nausea, the pallor, the pains in the head, the loutish insolence of nature. She was an incarnate, indelible, unsearchable, valiant smile, sitting above an arrant obscenity. Therefore he froze before a woman into whose face the fust of her desires had worked, the fust, if you like, of all the closed rooms and open secrets of her career. He could not find her desirable in any way. Because of a peculiar bemused squeamishness, he could not look at her. He could talk with her, but not anything like adequately.

'Does he behave himself, this bird? Does he sit still?'

'Yes, he's quite passable, Madam,' said Ewers.

But at that moment the kingfisher turned its back on him, making sharp, indolent notes with its throat. Ewers rushed to the bird's new front.

'Why don't you simply turn the cage whenever that troublesome thing turns his back?' Mrs Daker wanted to know. The voice was edged with laughter. On Ewers' account, she thought artists such endearingly silly people.

The artist's prerogative was not to answer, even not to answer ladies. He went on frowning at the green shape.

'Well, why don't you?'

'It would make me come in too close to the bird, Madam. It would confuse my sight.'

His sight was clear now, but though he began to tread back to the easel, he knew she was about to nudge the corner of his mind, to make him spill his vision.

'Don't you think it's an indifferent bird, Ewers?' asked Mrs Daker, between pouting twice at the cage.

'You know my name, Madam?'

How it disturbed him that she had approached him as a person with a name which she knew. It impressed him, rightly or wrongly, in the same way that a lightning manoeuvre impresses an old-fashioned general—more or less as an unfair trick.

'Don't you think it's a very poor bird?' she asked.

They both looked at its hunched back. Ewers wished it to turn. It wouldn't be wished into turning.

'It's far too stocky a bird to bear the grand name, kingfisher. Its stance is not handsome at all. It's hardly a true green at all, is it? Except by the standards of this country.'

He felt infallibly that the lady would applaud him if he said, 'They tell us, Madam, that an ugly stance and a greenness of complexion are not altogether unknown amongst kings.' To take offence at slighting remarks about the monarch was almost certainly not within the perimeter of her vices.

So he said, 'They tell us, Madam . . .'

The lady applauded him, and he blushed and darted away to take another sight on the bird.

'I had an uncle,' the lady remarked at last, under the general topic of art, 'who was a famous draughtsman. He worked at a shipwright's in Portsmouth. He was marvellous with ships. Of course, that is far more just a matter of lines.'

Coming back to his easel, Ewers thought that so was this a matter of lines, if only people wouldn't blur the lines with talk.

'Madam,' he realized all at once, 'would you care to sit in the shade?'

'Thank you.'

Her faded yellow whispered as he let her down into the chair he had not been using.

So positioned, they must have seemed a caricature of the Pastoral landscape. The sky was so enamel, so hard, so high, so bald. Well within this firmament, brown hills rose, worn teeth in an old jaw, perhaps a dead jaw. There was no deep, moist shade, and the leaves on the evergreens flapped rather than rustled, flapped brown side, grey side, brown side, grey, fruitlessness showing both its faces. And amongst half a dozen poor coops of wire and a few wicker cages like lobster traps, Mrs Daker and himself, both vestiges of the northern world, centred their attention in a chunky member of the *Halcyonidae* family.

'Uck!' muttered the kingfisher, and sidled along his perch like a parrot. 'Uck!'

'He can't sing, either. Neither can these others. There is hardly a good note between all of them. What sort of a song is *Uck* for a royal bird?'

'Once more, Madam, it has been known for kings to be guttural as well as a sick shade of green.'

Mrs Daker reeled.

'Oh, what a waste of good wit,' she cried, 'to have you here, Ewers.'

Her amazingly cordial giggles warned him it was time to let his yea be yea, his nay be nay, and to add few words to either.

'What are you Ewers? I mean, what was your crime?'

'Forgery, Mrs Daker.'

In the ensuing silence, he wondered was she disturbed by his frankness.

'What an interesting crime,' she said at last. 'Anyone can steal a beast or write a threatening letter. But forgery must take such skill.'

'That I'm here, Madam, is an indication that I didn't have quite the necessary skill.'

Hand clenched on her forehead, Mrs Daker swayed. Ewers saw her amusement out of the corner of his eye, saw the yellow form doubling.

'*Droll* is the word for you, Ewers. Yes, definitely! *Droll*.'

'Uck! Uck!' said the kingfisher. It had a talent for supplying affirmatives for Ewers, which was an admirable courtesy he had found in none of the birds of the northern world.

At the midday drum, she left him alone. He had been painting and enjoying it, and had managed to mix exactly the right green, so that he didn't stop work now. There was only short shade across the passive dust, however, and he felt bound in mercy to break some branches off the box-brush, one of the more tree-like trees of the region, and lace them through the top of the cage. As he worked at this the bird jigged up one of the uprights and struck at him with its beak. He stepped back frowning at a neat pit of blood in the heel of his hand. Back on its perch, the bird had adopted an air of perfect repose and inculpability.

'You'll get blood on your own silly portrait,' Ewers told it.

For it had pecked out a deep sliver of flesh, and Ewers' good blood, sedulously free of scurvy, flowed too well. He bandaged the wound with a handkerchief and returned to the easel.

During that noon hour, Daker visited him. The surgeon frowned at the bandage, was full of concern if not commiseration; and again ordered him not to rush the work.

Ewers, not accustomed to such consideration, and feeling that the Arts were perhaps beginning to come into their inheritance in this colonial back-garden, smiled shyly at Mrs Daker when she returned later in the afternoon. She carried two blue tumblers, and a carafe whose contents were a secret inside raffia binding.

'I have some lime cordial here, have had it since the last transport came in. I have had the bottle cooling in the river since I left you this morning. You must surely like a glass, Ewers.'

Ewers surely did. He had been gaping at his work with his mouth open, since his shattered nose did not function. A westerly wind had come up and dried him right down into the pit of his throat; and as Mrs Daker placed the glasses on the chair and poured out the lime, he moved his tongue clumsily around his palate, feeling out the lay of his thirst now that it was about to be quenched.

He had very nearly finished an excellent water-colour of the surgeon's gem. But he lingered on it for Daker's sake, to flatter Daker's idea that here was so distinctive a shape, so individual a green and a sable hardly less so, that any artist would be indefinitely extended by them. Between sips from the glass which Mrs Daker kept for him, he pencilled in Daker's fond name for this kingfisher somewhat far from being exactly beryl.

Mrs Daker asked him questions, which he could scarcely refuse to answer in view of her kindnesses. She had never been to Scotland, she had never been beyond Winchester. Did they get great storms in Dumfries? No, she had never heard of Solway Firth. Could you see to Ireland on sunny days? What was Dumfries market like? Was he a Jacobite?

'How is it possible,' she asked, 'that people will not tend to admire a forger, when the essence of his crime is his craftsmanship? In his art, the forger is superior to his judge.'

'As I've said, Mrs Daker,' Ewers amended, 'not too superior; otherwise I would have remained free, though guilty.'

Certainly, as he'd said before. Yet now he said it from motives of companionship, and because the lady was so canny. The officials of Dumfries Circuit Court though were not so canny. He'd been herded in with sheep-thieves, suffered the arrogance of the court to the same extent as sheep-thieves.

By half-past four, he found himself about to look evenly at molten Mrs Daker and her running, molten laughter and her dusk-blue skin. Here was an incontrovertible friendship. *Look, I cannot desire her*, he told himself delightedly, flexing the muscles of whatever appetites he possessed. The piquancy of friendship with someone so distinctive, with what you could call a perceptive harlot, excited him, so that half that night he was to lie awake and think of areas of conversation for their meeting the next day. Now he was willing to put the full weight of his wit into the encounter and he felt a vigorous desire to expose Mrs Daker to Aunt Norris, a Madonna propitious even at a hemisphere's remove.

When she went away then, with her almost empty carafe, Ewers saw calmly her flecked brown eyes and their pouches grey from the heat of the afternoon watch the two of them had kept. He experienced a unique quality of gratitude, but all he used, however warmly, were the accustomed words. For, still, he found her awesome.

The painting was finished. It behoved him to sit tautly, however, on his chair, as if *Alcyone Beryllus* still taxed him. By concentrating on the scalding sun through almost closed eyes, he was able to terrify himself in a titillating way. He saw the hills list upwards into the bottom of his vision, he became aware of the movement of the earth like a lost child in the groves of heavenly darkness—an awareness which takes the gloss off the ermine of kings but exalts the lowly.

It has also been known to give the lowly headaches.

When Daker arrived, Ewers was rubbing his forehead and had his eyes fully closed. Against the reedy boredom of his birds' voices, the little surgeon made his entry soundlessly.

'Just what I wanted, Ewers,' he said with, if anything, a hint of querulousness. 'Just what I wanted.'

He unfastened the painting and bore it and the wicker cage away.

Ewers, despite the movements of the heavens and all the larger sanities, felt bereaved, being left at dusk without pay or praise. He had worked all day to demand, and now his work was appropriated, and even his subject was locked away. He shared the sunset with starlings, wheeling in to sift the futile dust for grass seed. He frowned at the raucous yearnings of the caged birds.

Yet, incontrovertibly, he had a friend.

'Let us attempt yet another one of our friend, *Beryllus*,' the surgeon decided in the morning. 'Take a higher view of him from the right, to show the solidity of his head.'

The solidity of his head was no problem, Ewers wanted to tell Daker. Solidity, even the solidity of *Halcyonidaes'* heads, happened to be the stock in trade of the artist. The lines of Daker's creature bored him this morning: he had spent so long learning them yesterday. He settled down to make a number of sketches for Mrs Daker's delight, if she should come that morning.

She came. She had no parasol, the day being cloudy, promising neither rain nor glare. She had the carafe again, since there lay such a weight of hot cloud over the village.

'Artists mystify me,' she sighed, staring at his preparatory work.

But she moved about in a desultory way and spoke fitfully. Her eyes never looked at him and she maundered around the birdcages making effete noises at the captives. This mood of hers gave Ewers leisure to study her without any danger of misunderstanding.

Her face had become intense to the point of pain, *her* pain. She impressed him, against his will, as being far beyond the limits of his understanding, and, therefore, of his talent.

'Are you feeling ill, Mrs Daker?' he felt bound to ask.

He, master forger, hemisphere's light of art, felt confounded by a face so shut in upon itself. The eyes had no meaning as eyes; that is, they did not look to have been made for seeing. In the shade they seemed anthracite; in the open they held no image and threatened to consume themselves.

'Are you feeling ill, Mrs Daker?' Ewers called again, giving the alarm before her tinder face should go up in flame and singe *Beryllus's* feathers.

A small, sluggish fly was on her nose. She shook her head enough to be rid of it. Then she could see again, and seeing covered her face with astonishment.

It could, of course, have all been merely a disorder of the eyes. So Ewers hoped.

'What were you saying?' she asked.

'Nothing very much, Madam. Perhaps Mrs Daker might want to go home? To rest.'

'Why would I?'

She eyed the dust and gave a private, bitter laugh, which meant that Ewers had presumed.

'What were you saying?' she insisted.

'Nothing very much, Mrs Daker.'

'Then tell me something.'

'Yes, Mrs Daker?'

'Tell me something. Something, anything. Tell me about your school of art in Dumfries.'

'Not exactly a school of art, Madam. It aspired to be a . . .'

'Damn you, stupid Ewers!' She clouted her own thigh. 'Don't hedge. Tell me straight!'

'If you wish, Mrs Daker.'

'Not if I wish, Ewers. You are a transported felon and my husband's servant. I order you. Tell me something!'

Ewers swallowed, despising frowsy womankind. *Vivat* Aunt Norris!

'I made an engraving and printed five hundred oval cards on linen-faced paper. I distributed the cards throughout Dumfries, and even took three out to Lord Dunscore's house in the Nithsdale. He had a daughter and two nieces, you see, who came to Dumfries at least once a fortnight.'

It was such a heavy morning to take out those old hopes, and the dream of patronage from the feckless daughters of the gentry. The surgeon's poor birds emitting their marrow-sucking squeaks made poor music to his nostalgia. So, too, did Mrs Daker.

'Continue please, Ewers!' she said, unaccountably sweet.

'It is not hard to understand how, if even one of these girls had taken my classes, I would have been flooded with pupils. I waited until I knew how many young applicants I had before I hired rooms. I was wise. I had three applicants.'

'How much was the charge, Ewers?'

'A guinea, Madam, for two classes.'

'My word, you were no cheapjack, were you Ewers?'

'I was trying to attract a certain type of young lady, Mrs Daker.'

'Ohhhh . . . !' said Mrs Daker, prurient as a playgoer. 'So?'

'So I used Aunt Norris's pleasant front parlour for the classes.'

'Aunt Norris?' asked Mrs Daker.

Aunt Norris! Where were the words to tell this despicable woman and her mean hills of the heights and depths of Aunt Norris? He did what he could with workaday oratory and a few quotations from the Book of Proverbs. As he spoke, he dabbed indolently at his second portrait of that wearying kingfisher.

The brush jerked with the awareness of a presence at his elbow. It was, of course, Mrs. Daker. She had stood there for an undisclosed time, observing his paean from close quarters, no more than eighteen inches. His head felt quite tight with frightened blood. In mid-virtue, Aunt Norris faded on his lips.

'I have guineas,' babbled Mrs Daker. 'I have pearls, silly

Ewers.'

And she spoke on. Her mouth stood open, her whoredom spoke out quite automatically from its dwelling. What was said had for Mrs Daker a validity like that of an established text of prayer for the devout. And like the accomplished worshipper's, Mrs. Daker's face had once more become blind and closed upon itself.

Ewers ran away from her, holding his head which swelled to splitting with disgust. His neck he carried stiffly, solid in its disbelief that any woman would blazon her goatishness, her deficit of male flesh before him, before his eyes, before his eunuch eyes.

'The mouths of women beset me,' he called out on the river bank.

9

Oᴺᴇ shoe off, Mrs Daker was found gibbering through the aviary. Her dress was piping red with blood which passed so satisfactorily for her own that, having found brain-sick Ewers by the river, they took him prisoner for it. To double the griefs of the Daker family, *Beryllus*, the kingfisher, was gone from his toppled cage. He was a desert bird, his liking was dry heat, a nest deep in spinous grass, and to peck at the dew of a morning. How many summers would need to pass before he would come back to the futile plenty of the riverbank?

Ewers was brought back down the river. The Judge-Advocate's court sentenced him to hanging.

They had him in an all-but-underground magazine at the Battery. It was empty and had a grille in the roof. In the day-time the grille was opened. Thereby entered the steamy days of early March; and sometimes Ewers reclined thigh-deep in them by stretching flat-out from his wristlet on the wall. Not that the light wasn't hot. But it was as if he were bathing himself in the river of life.

A Marine called Private Terry Byrne guarded Ewers here. He even came to see Halloran one night with a message from Ewers. Byrne was a wide-faced, boyish-looking man. His nose and jaws were made to be beefy and innocent; but beef and innocence were both out of the question in that far station on the earth's rim. In fact, his large face looked pasty, his eyes more stupid than they thought they were, and cleverer than they would ever let on. Twenty-eight gormless years had gone to instilling in him an air of vague and fractious hunger. When with Halloran, he spoke out of this hunger and morbidly of scarcely anything else but Ann and hell (of a night he woke feeling damned, he said). He was hard to suffer after a hot day.

Halloran had been resting on a bench under the eaves of his hut; nostalgic, waiting for a south wind. The night had swaddled him round and over-swaddled him. Sitting still, he sweated. You could smell the spent day particularly stale on Terry Byrne when he came up the street among the company hutments.

'Corporal Halloran darling,' he called from some way off. He always *darling-ed* his friends. He said nothing more till he was conspirationally close.

'You're a friend of that Ewers who tumbled Mrs Daker?'

'I've met him.'

'He sounds to have more than met *you*. He sounds to have great esteem for you.'

'Aren't you just a crafty one, Private Byrne? A person would never think you were trying for the whole story of Ewers and me. A person would never have an inkling. Let me tell you all about it.'

'Good for you, Corporal darling!'

Byrne put one foot on the bench and leant against the daubed wall. He was so crooked and avid waiting there that Halloran felt ashamed.

'No, I'm only gulling you, Byrne. I've met him the once. That's all.'

'Well, he has the sort of message for you that's only sent to friends of long standing.'

'Yes?'

'He says read Genesis, Chapter thirty-nine. And for God's sake come and see him.'

Halloran sat back, watching high-up boughs supine across the face of the big, low moon.

'Thanks, Terry.'

Terry Byrne took his foot from the bench. But he wasn't leaving yet.

'Well?' he said.

'Well?' said Halloran. 'What do you mean, well?'

77

'Aren't you going to read Genesis, Chapter thirty-nine?'

'I haven't a Bible. And he can wait till tomorrow.'

'But they're hanging the poor feller in two days' time.'

Indeed. They were building a high, five-sided gallows on the transport side of the Brook, a cedar frame nearly as high as forty feet, something to look mystic at night, a shape to stick in the mind of the wrong-doer. They would finish it in another day perhaps. Then it would perform its first exemplary hanging.

'He seems to have earned hanging,' Halloran said. 'Almost my last words to him when I met him the once were to be careful of Mrs Daker. And then he goes off with his paint-box and rushes her like a bull.'

'How do you know he did the rushing? That's what occurs to me to ask. As a man of hearty yearnings myself, I ask that question. How do you know he did the rushing?'

'He could have run away if he wanted to.'

'Hadn't you been told, Corporal darling? They don't let felons run away, even from randy women. Why don't you get your hands on a Bible?'

'I don't own one.'

'I know a man who does. Come on, you have to help the poor beast by that much. You know the name of that narrow little Scots sergeant?'

'No.'

'No. But he's got a Bible, anyhow. Let me get it for you, Halloran. Give the feller a chance.'

Even in that hot seam of night, Halloran felt a sturdy distrust of Genesis, 39.

'I'll get it myself,' he said, standing up. 'You can tell Ewers I'll read it carefully. But I can't come to see him. Tell him that.'

Neither of them moved.

'Well, goodnight Terry. And thanks,' said Halloran broadly.

'You said you didn't know the Scot. I'll go down with you as far as his place!'

'I know him. His wife died on the water. He has his own hut over there near Sabian's Barracks.'

'Let me walk that far with you, anyhow.'

Halloran shrugged, and they started off. As they walked, they heard the wind sluicing through the south end of the town, rattling in trees, blowing doors shut. Up their military hill it came in a surge, and men were out to their doors, docile, anticipating it. Washing over Byrne and Halloran, it was one of those luxuries of creature-flesh which make men buoyant. Byrne began to sing.

They found the hut, the spare old sergeant sitting in the door.

'You wait here, Terry Byrne,' said Halloran. 'We don't want the whole regiment reading that particular chapter.'

Halloran went up to the old man and said good night.

'Could my friend and I borrow your Bible for a second?'

'Tell me why?' the sergeant said.

'I want to read to him from the book of Genesis. He's a Wexford man like me and he's got more devils than one of the pigs Christ drove into the lake. He came to me since there's no priest. I want to read to him from Genesis.'

'That's what you tell me.'

'Sergeant, I'm a respectable soldier, a corporal. I'm Captain Allen's orderly. I don't want to sell your book. I don't want to use it for betting. I just want to read it to poor damned Terry Byrne over there.'

The sergeant got up and went into his hut, coming back with the book in pale and covetous little hands.

'When will you have it back with me?' he asked.

'Within an hour.'

'Your friend over there got his coat on him?'

'Yes.'

'Then leave it here with me.'

'All right.' Halloran stepped aside and called to Byrne standing in the street. 'He wants your coat while we have his book. That's fair enough.'

Byrne came forward, but slowly, with distrust.

'You wouldn't sell it on me, would you?'

'No. I'm one of the chosen,' said the sergeant, 'like the two of you.'

He handed the Bible to Halloran, and Byrne took off his coat.

'Better without it on a night like this,' commented Halloran, and thanked the sergeant.

They had not gone far along the road when Halloran decided that he could perhaps make out the print by moonlight. He opened the book. Night made the pages a tranquil blue, but the print was the smallest a printer could manage.

'What's it about?' asked Byrne.

'Shush! Let me read it first.'

It was the story of Potiphar's wife and Joseph, of how Joseph fled from Potiphar's wife leaving his garment in her hands, of how the woman accused Joseph before her husband, of how the woman was believed and Joseph sent to prison.

'Read it to me?' asked Byrne.

Genesis 39 was an accusation by Ewers. It was a hidden accusation, and not meant for Byrne's ears.

Halloran turned the pages back and read Byrne something about Jacob and Laban and Rachel, and some dirty work with a second daughter called Leah.

'That doesn't mean anything,' said Byrne, 'except they would have had a time getting some of them old Hebrews into the Carmelites.'

Halloran agreed.

'Are you going to see him?' Byrne asked.

'No. Why should I?'

'You're probably wise,' said Byrne, pop-eyed and magisterial.

He said goodnight and went off to get his coat back with the book. Before he'd gone three yards, he turned around laughing.

'Hoy, Corporal darling,' he said, 'Ewers probably liked the part where Jacob tumbled the wrong lady.'

'Yes,' said Halloran. 'We'll have to make sure the same never happens to us.'

'I wouldn't say that, two for the price of one is the type of trade that's always appealed to Terry Byrne.'

'Go on, you old bull!' said Halloran.

But the next afternoon, in the dead of the noon rest, Halloran came to that length of rampart and Empire which Byrne, torpidly, kept safe.

'I thought you weren't going to see the man,' Byrne complained.

'I changed my mind.'

'I can't let you see him.'

'Can't you? Well, I've been sent by Captain Allen. Prove I haven't!'

'You're a close beggar, Halloran.'

'A person has to be.'

'It's a shock to a man to find he's not trusted.'

'Come on, Terry. Be of good heart and so on. I changed my mind, I tell you.' He pointed his finger at Byrne. 'Don't you go listening in now!'

He climbed the side of the embankment. All that you could see of the magazine was the bolted double door and the vent poking out at the top. The rest of it had been dug into the hill and covered with soil. The vent stood open. There were three drunken blow-flies on the grating. Halloran knelt down, and the sun scalded the nape of his neck, while the earth was so hot to kneel on that you dreaded burial. He peered through the vent and at last could see Ewers' legs patterned with the shade of the grating. He could not see Ewers' face.

'It's Halloran here!'

The legs twitched.

'You said you wouldn't come.'

'There isn't time to sulk. What did you want to say?'

'Did you read Genesis, Chapter thirty-nine?'

'Of course I did.'

'I am Joseph, Halloran. I swear it to you.'

Halloran squinted down the vent.

'Halloran, don't you believe me?'

'I'd rather believe you than Mrs Daker. But I've heard the story, Ewers. That she had blood all over her.'

Of course, Ewers wept. Poor damned Ewers.

'She is a goat and a harlot,' he said.

'Yes, she is.'

'I ran away from her. I was painting a bird for Daker when she came up at my elbow. She breathed like a cow at my elbow.'

'And you made her bleed for breathing like a cow.'

'No! Halloran, I was unable to look at her, let alone make her bleed. I ran away.'

'Why didn't you tell them at the court?'

'I did, and they asked me where the blood came from. They asked me over and over, until I thought that I was mad and *had* harmed the woman.'

'But you're Joseph. Hurry up. I've got no sort of permission to be here.'

'Halloran, I was brought an envelope yesterday evening. I have it with me now. It contained one green feather. There was no writing on the envelope, but the message was from Mrs Daker, beyond doubt. I had been painting a green kingfisher on that particular day, and when I had run away, Mrs Daker took the kingfisher and mangled it and, no doubt, spread herself with its blood. And being mad, dared to send me this feather.'

'But you can't know this. You can't tell Sabian this.'

'Aunt Norris,' said Ewers. He could barely say the name.

'I'll write to her,' Halloran told him. 'I promise you that.'

'Katherine Norris, near the Newgate, Dumfries, Scotland.'

'Yes. The Newgate.'

'Thank you, Halloran. Thank you, thank you.'

The bay was luxurious blue, and a small, luxurious breeze came up the embankment to refresh the left side of his face.

'Halloran,' Ewers said without warning, 'I am a eunuch.'

'What?'

'I am a eunuch from childhood.'

Phelim shook his head.

'Did you tell them in the court?'

'No.'

'Why?'

Ewers said nothing more for perhaps two minutes. A number of times Halloran asked why as gently as he could. He considered whether he should walk away or, better still, run from Ewers in his pit.

'I was in a dream in court. I thought that they might somehow find out without my telling them. I told myself that there was time, there would be time to tell them even after the trial.'

'My God!' said Halloran.

'I am very noticeable,' Ewers explained softly. 'They would have made a mock of me.'

'You're mad.'

'I've been made a mock of before this.'

'What can I do?'

'Tell Major Sabian.'

Halloran said nothing.

'You believe me, Halloran?'

'What do you think? It's hard. Didn't Partridge know?'

'He never did. You've no idea what extremes I went to, not to be mocked. Don't you believe me?'

'Don't ask me that question yet.'

'Can you see me?'

'Waist down,' said Halloran. He could see quite clearly the sailcloth legs.

'Even from there, you will be able to tell.'

Ewers made inconsolable noises, while his free arm undid the prison trousers and scraped them down over his hips. As he had promised, he was unmistakably deformed, even at a glance through the grating. He sounded to be beyond himself. Halloran looked away.

'Forgive me, Ewers,' he said. 'Don't go crying.'

Ewers became even more audibly upset, while Halloran felt sick from the implications of the affair.

'Now listen to me! Don't go crying! I'll see Sabian. I will. I promise.'

Down below, halved and lepered by light and dark, Ewers was not consoled.

'I have to go. But I'll see Sabian this very day.'

Four afternoons a week he reported to Sabian's office, to

Sabian's orderly sergeant. That much was a start.

'Don't be upset,' he told Ewers.

He ran downhill.

'He didn't do it, Terry.'

'Like all the other fellers who were ever hanged,' said Byrne.

'Maybe.'

What an immense hatred arose in Halloran when, seconds later, drums and a bugle cawed at whoever was sleeping in that two o'clock town.

'Anything for me?' Halloran asked the orderly-sergeant through the door.

'That's not the way to ask.'

Halloran marched in quickly.

'Anything for me, Sergeant?'

'No.'

'Here's the returns from Allen's company.'

Halloran put down a paper on the table. His face had a broiled look.

'You been running?'

'I have. I've got sweat all over the returns. Where's Major Sabian?'

'I don't know. He was here for a second this morning. I think he's at home.'

Home for Major Sabian was on the other side of the bay, across the Brook and past Blythes'.

'Damn it,' said Halloran. He let his arms go limp. He had already run half a mile to make time for an interview. It was beyond him to find the time to go across the town and call on Sabian like a brother officer. 'Don't they do any work, these officers?'

'Sergeants down do all the work,' said the sergeant.

'Will he be here at all this afternoon?'

'Not likely at all.'

Outside, Halloran felt tired and hollow. He sat down in shade, not looking first for spiders and ants. Below him some rusty sapfings lived out their harsh youth without a hint of growth or expectations. They did not yield any piece of the useless hill; they grew in tribal obstinacy down to the very lip of the bay.

'I wish I had an axe,' said Halloran aloud. He ground his teeth in hatred of the place. 'If I had an axe!'

He would have to speak to Captain Allen about Ewers. Whether Ewers would survive handling by Allen was another question. But a corporal is able to move only through given channels; through given straits they were, rather than channels. Conscience can make outright demands on a man. But human affairs were not carried on in an outright manner.

'What can I do?' he had asked Ewers.

'Tell Major Sabian.'

And if you were a Major yourself, you could.

When he was cool again, he moved in numbed peace back towards the hutments. Yet the rancorous afternoon turned on him. Below the road, on the edge of the parade-ground, some Marines were playing cricket. For some reason, Sabian was on the road and had stopped, in his boredom, to watch the game. His adjutant stood by him. Both rumbled and clapped when the batsman flogged the ball far out across the parade-ground.

Halloran was bound to stand and wait in the corner of their vision. Sabian half looked at him. Pride of place fluttered the eyelids. Yet the man was nearly fifty. Didn't he feel the worm of death at all, that he could flutter his eyes as imperially as that? At last, somebody bowled that entertaining batsman. Sabian, turning towards Halloran, growled his aloof amusement at his adjutant. Halloran saluted. Sabian came up to him.

'Corporal Halloran, sir. Captain Allen's orderly.'

Sabian nodded.

'Sir, that Thomas Ewers who was—'

'I know Ewers.'

Halloran coughed. He could hear his tongue sticking to parts of his mouth as he tried for a second to work up some spit.

'That Ewers, sir, there was something he failed to tell you in court.'

'Oh?'

'Yes. He's a eunuch, sir. Very much a eunuch.'

Sabian laughed.

'How do you know?'

'I've seen him, sir.'

'Oh?' said Sabian piquantly to the adjutant. No one could have told how Halloran hated him; screwing up his hands in hatred of this substantial man and figure and officer.

'He was afraid that he would be made a mock of, sir.'

'He has made a mock of you, Corporal. Who injured Mrs Daker, if he didn't?'

'He has explanations for that, sir. I'd be willing to take an oath, sir—'

Sabian lifted his hand above his head and held it there for some seconds, as if the gesture had come to its natural end there, as if he were hailing Caesar. Then he struck Halloran across the jaw. The forests leapt, and over the hill jumped a liquid arc of sun.

'You waste my time, Corporal. Every ravisher from ancient times to this has blamed the ravished woman.'

'They gain authority from Joseph and Potiphar's wife,' the adjutant muttered.

'Exactly,' said Sabian. 'I suppose he says that Mrs Daker injured herself.'

The cricketers below had begun to watch.

'That she got the blood of an animal,' Halloran amended quietly. 'Sir, couldn't you—'

The Major barely managed to hold his anger in shaking ham-fists.

'No I couldn't, Corporal. You had better go.'

Before he had gone far though, feeling damned because he had not said all that might have been said, feeling in a panic of damnation, Sabian called him back.

'Corporal,' he said leniently, 'Ewers, if he is a eunuch, would not be the first eunuch to give his master a nasty shock.'

On the morning of the second day, Ewers was ceremonially hanged; but by then Halloran had begun to see that he himself had done what he could, given the circumstances. Like all men of rigid conscience, he tended to discount any tragedy if he had done all that conscience demanded to prevent it. But he could not, despite this, discount the tragedy and the pity of Ewers. It disaffected him in part, it took all the starch out of his soldierliness.

He was able to stay away from the hanging, but Terry Byrne saw it. As Byrne told it, it was the worst of hangings, a long stifling, when, in the muscular agony, the ravaged animal spills dirt and water down its legs.

10

O NE Sunday, Ann seemed feverish and possessed by a type of haunted gaiety. Her face looked a little sere, somehow, despite her breeziness, making one aware of the odds against fruition. They spent their afternoon on a narrow beach well within the bay. Autumn had begun. They sat on the sand, facing into an amenable sun.

There was no conversation to speak of, until Ann said unrelatedly,

'I think I have a child.'

She did not glance at him, she looked straight ahead, mildly frowning. Halloran watched her straight, brittle neck, and the brittle joy, against all reason, sustaining her mouth and the corner of the eye that he could see.

'How do you know, Ann love? How could you know?'

'Don't you know how, Halloran? Are you really that unschooled?'

'Something to do with bleeding, isn't it?' he asked softly. 'The bleeding stops.'

'Yes.'

'But I don't like to think of you bleeding.'

'It's the way of things.'

'You weren't made for the way of things. You're a queen amongst women.'

'Queens and all bleed. It's you who wasn't made for the way of things, Halloran darling.'

'There are some things I get the way of very quick,' he said as gaily as she could have hoped. He took a rowdy bite of her neck and slapped her on the bottom.

'It would be your child.'

'Of course it would. Whose else? Terry Byrne's?'

She laughed.

'Mr Blythe's?'

She pulled a face.

'You don't seem to mind,' she said.

'Of course I don't mind. He'll be the star of the south end of the world.'

'He wouldn't be up against much,' said Ann.

Halloran put his hand on her stomach and leant down.

'You'll be onto some pretty fine nipples in this household, lad,' he told the maybe-child loudly. 'Take your father's word for it.'

He did not know with what manner of hope the child grew in the womb, but his thin girl would not have the milk for it afterwards. At the back of his throat lay tears for the bud of flesh, bud of man.

Ann hit him on the shoulder and laughed at him and proudly said that he was an evil man.

Yet Halloran's gaiety too was coming unstrung now. He retold the difficulties to himself. They could not marry before Mr Calverley without damning themselves before God. They could not omit to marry before Mr Calverley without damning themselves before the colony. Every society, however rotten, has members whom it considers the arbiters, the standard-makers of its morality. Halloran and his secret bride were unlucky enough to be the moral paragons of their community. If they fell, they became stumbling-blocks, even to the most errant feet, even to such feet as Byrne's. And the question was, how would Mrs Blythe jump, as the saying is? Would she cast Ann out of the house to live with the other women and be pestered by every woman-fancier in the garrison? Or would she lock Ann up and undertake her salvation? And the old agony recurred of how, if he married Ann publicly, the Governor would no doubt pardon her in time and send her home with him, free passage, when the garrison was relieved.

Grinning at Ann, he said privately to Herod's wife, *You're a lucky old crone, suffering many things in a dream only on account of him. In a dream only.*

'We must cherish him very much,' he said, meaning the child.

'Of course we must. Of course, I couldn't swear he was there.'

'When would you be certain?'

'I'd be almost certain in a week. I'd be terribly certain in two weeks.'

'Son and heir,' said Halloran, but mourned the thing already.

'What about the cord?' he felt justified in asking gently.

'I don't know. You have to put your faith in something, but nothing brings what you want all the time.'

'Yes, you're right about that.' He couldn't refrain from saying, 'I thought it put matters beyond doubt.'

'Nothing puts things beyond a doubt,' said Ann. 'Perhaps I didn't wear it in the right frame of mind. If that's so, I'm sorry, Halloran.'

The sun was low and strawberry. Streaks of cloud fumed before its face; the west had gone smoky, the water like mercury. He could no longer pretend to levity.

'Right frame of mind or otherwise, what does it matter?' he told her. 'It must be meant. You'll start to think I'll leave you, nothing surer. You'll have to remember I have no home except you. You'll have to remember I'd be in a desert.'

'I will get fat and splotchy beyond bearing.'

'Beyond whose bearing?'

'Yours, Phelim.'

'Ann, Ann,' he said. 'You wouldn't be fat and splotchy ever, as far as my eyes go. Not even if you were fat and splotchy.'

They laughed together.

'We must just be strong, Ann,' said Halloran, grieving prodigiously for the child.

As much of the situation as they could, they organized. If by Friday Ann still believed herself with child, she was to send him a creamy pebble from Mr Blythe's garden. If she knew she was without child, she would send him two. She would send these signs by the hand of the Blythes' male servant, who would deliver them to him on the garrison side of Collett's Brook, just beyond the bridge.

On Friday, the servant came and tipped one cream pebble into Phelim's cupped hands, who sighed and received the iron into his soul.

'The girl give me two,' said the servant then, 'but I dropped one of them.'

'You're sure?'

'I'm sure. Anyway, pebbles is cheap.'

Valley, bridge, departing servant, all spun, Halloran being a mite in a twirled saucer. And though he had become drunk with release, he felt deprived of the child for whom, all the week, he had been practising his valour.

I I

ASTER rain came down like flint-arrows on the Tuesday of
Holy Week, and people, unaccustomed to its vehemence
because of the dry weather, stood under eaves and grimaced
at it. Suddenly, the clay- and saw-pits gurgled and filled with a
stew. Some alien earth was in the stew, but it was almost possible
to believe, standing above these places with idle tools in your
hands, that each pit was coloured the peculiar colour of the pain of
the men who had filled it summer-full of blisters, heartburn, gut-
cramp, god-hate. Men blinded at the shipyards and brickfields by
tropic gobs of water on their lashes, groped for gear, blinking the
improbable colours of the prism out of their eyeballs, until once
more they could see an adze for an adze, which was the only safe
way of seeing anything.

Rev. Mr Calverley, lucky under hardwood shingles this thatch-
reaving weather, went to his desk and wrote down, 'The rain has
come, and bounty has lit up again the weary land'. It was a suitable Easter theme. But towards dinner, he remembered the heartless way long rain dealt with churchyards and went out with a
lantern to see if his son's grave had sunk in the outline of a coffin,
threatening the resurrection.

In Halloran's hut, the rain spouted through many weaknesses
in the roof. Halloran himself pulled up the flooring of cabbage
tree mats and planking and dug a ditch with his bayonet, in-
corporating many puddles into one, guiding the one out of doors.

He would have liked to repeat his achievement for Ann. It
was close to six o'clock. Soon she would be alone in the equinoc-
tial gloom of her kitchen, hauling her mattress here and there,
seeking a warm place away from the wet, dabbing at her cold
with an apron corner. About nine, she would try to brew miser-

able tea from the Blythes' used leaves.

He was duty-corporal in the cook-house that night; hard work. Every man's plate of meat was weighed, and *he* had to supervise the weighing. He went out of doors barefoot, carrying his shoes in his hand, to attend to this duty. It was blue dark. Sheathed in the rain, he had a rare privacy. Here was good thinking weather, yet he didn't exactly think. First he stood slack-shouldered in the drench, making pledges to Ann and himself. Times when he felt brash enough to spit in the eye of the weather and make pledges to his future were rare, but tonight was such a time. He had confidence, and the confidence came from his having written a verse about the ants. It was such a savoury thing to be a poet. It side-stepped mortality so deftly that you could hug yourself.

The ants of whom his poem was made had known about the rain some days before it had begun. They had come hustling indoors, and Halloran saw them now as having carried in the sunlight on their backs to store it in the wall cavities and under the flooring for the day when it would be, once more, the cosmic fashion. Which seemed at present to be going to be a long time.

He made patterns in the mud by dabbing at the track with one foot or the other. He scarcely cared if he was seen, because a man could be doing any extravagant thing to save himself from whatever of malice there was in the blinding wet. Each time he laid his foot down in the mud, he uttered a foot of the verse. The joy of words and rain, the joy of capering legs. He took the blanket off his head and whirled it once. But it was a bit sodden for abandonment.

'My ant of the red earth,' he said and sang,
'My harvester small,
 Bears sheafs of the sunlight
 To his barn in my wall.

'From his pit beneath tap-roots,
 Once drawn its claws,
 He carries the soft corpse
 Of summer indoors.

'My little, black friar,
A speck of my bread
Will not be begrudged you,
While summer is dead.

'A steak from the lizard
Who died by my door,
Is his by just stipend,
Who scours my floor.'

Halloran, who had none the less crushed with his canvas shoe a flock of ants feeding in blind ellipse round a lizard's tail.

'Very fine, but what about Ewers?' asked someone just behind him.

There, improbably, was Hearn, very close, on the edge of the embankment. He had a blanket on his shoulders, but his big grey face got a drenching. The copious briars of grey hair seemed just as briary despite the rain.

'Ewers? Don't talk to me about Ewers, Mr Hearn. Ewers was unjustly destroyed, I give you that. But not by me.'

He thought how uncivilized it was to allow a man to dance through four quatrains believing himself alone, and then to spring flummoxing questions on him.

'By the system you serve,' said Hearn.

No *How are you, isn't it wet?* about Hearn's conversation. Headfirst into questions of eternity, questions of guilt!

'Not by any system I serve,' said Halloran. 'It was the Dakers again.'

'The system is all the Dakers from here to Ulster.'

Halloran threw one of his shoes five yards. Petulance.

'What are you at? What are you after? *I* know my conscience. Damn you!'

His shoe had capsized in a puddle.

'Christ!' he said flicking it up. 'There you are, Mr Hearn. You have me taking the Holy Name.'

'That stings your conscience,' observed Hearn, mocking in his peculiarly level way of speech.

'Yes it does, if you want to know. How do you come to be here, instead of the Crescent?'

'I've come to help Long, His Excellency's secretary. His Excellency believes that even if the last storeship was taken by enemies of the King—whoever they might be—another one should be with us inside four months. Long and myself are doing estimates for the office-hacks in the Admiralty and at the Home Secretary's.'

'I suppose this is not called serving the system,' Halloran muttered.

'Only on paper. Only by shuffling numbers.'

'If you didn't shuffle the numbers, someone else would have to. They're dirty Hanover numbers, Mr Hearn. You'll catch the pox of damnation from them quick as I will from this old coat. Did you know, by the way, that you're not supposed to be on this hill?'

Hearn tried to shake the water out of his locks.

'I'm sorry,' he said. 'I was never at this place long enough to learn the out-of-bounds for *my* class. Working at Government House, I have a freedom of movement which mightn't always be for the best.'

There was nothing to say to that.

Hearn stroked down his bard's locks.

'What would you have done, Corporal, if you'd had others with you and found me here? Would you have found that your chances of riding the tempest would be bettered if you had me flogged? Then you would have had me flogged, and you'd say to yourself . . .'

Halloran cast up his blanket-shrouded arms.

'I'd say the angel Gabriel could be flogged for being on this hill, unless he's a member of the garrison. Which I've never seen any sign of. I wouldn't go off my singing if he *was* flogged, because he's damned well not supposed to be here at all. I don't have to forswear life and shoot the Governor because you come creeping through the rain like a Redemptorist, booming out omens. I told Ewers when I took him to the Dakers. *You'll get a big hearing and little mercy from Mrs Daker.* I couldn't do any more.'

95

It grated to see Hearn's head remaining upright and uncovered, heedless of the rain.

'Now, go home!' cried Halloran, like a whooping farmer to a cow in the barley. 'Go on! Go home! You're a trouble-maker and seditious as hell. I've got nothing to say to you.'

There were ten seconds. Nothing happened, but the peace-making rain soothed their shoulders.

'I'm disappointed, Corporal.'

'Thank God for that much. The surest way to be disappointed is to live long enough. Besides, I wasn't put here to satisfy you, even if you were Wicklow's Alnegar.'

Though Hearn shook his head, he did not seem any more seriously discomfited by Halloran's blindness than he did by the deluge.

'Let me tell you, Halloran, you're worried by this conundrum about the God of your oath, the God of the Army and Navy that is, and the true God. Isn't that so?'

'It's no conundrum. Go home!'

Hearn's black bulk remained only just visible, but impassive. The night had become deeper, and the downpour more vigorous. One could hear the trees being thrashed.

'Go *home!* Don't you obey anyone?'

'Yes, yes, Halloran. I'll obey you. You think you're safe if I obey you. But I doubt it, since you're honest. But more than honest, you're conscience-bound. You are, here in the dark, in the rain, more afraid of your conscience, what it might ask, than you are of black fever and shipwreck and death from thirst. You're afraid of this system you guard with your strong young arm. You are not afraid of its noose and knout, but of how it stands to your conscience.'

'Damn conscience!' said Halloran. 'And damn this strong young arm you speak of.'

'I'll leave you on your military hill then. I hope the God of the King's Marines looks after you. But look out for the God of the Spanish guards, who's a terror for dropping tree trunks on loyal Irish boys. Not to mention the God of the French dragoons. His weakness is landslides.'

'You're a blasphemer,' Halloran called, beginning to shake with reverence.

'No,' Hearn asserted, 'God is untouched.'

Yet he himself was not untouched. He turned his back on Halloran.

'Blasphemer?' he asked himself. 'No!'

He went away. It was such a night as could dissolve any large man with dramatic swiftness.

1 2

THE rain went on and blew the corner of the Blythes' roof away. Blythe asked Allen for a man to help his male servant shift the furniture in the front parlour, mend the roof with canvas. Some sergeant saw Byrne idle and sent him.

Byrne went in by the kitchen and dried his feet at the hearth. Ann would scarcely speak to him. The kitchen leaked like a cowshed; the fire was out though the bricks were warm. Byrne stood on them in his bare feet, sighing.

'I wish they'd sent me to fix *your* roof, Ann Rush. I wish they'd sent me for that.'

He put his shoes on and followed Ann through the house, staring at her slenderness from behind. In the front parlour, crazy Mrs Blythe sat by her window watching it stream and chatter. She had a rug around her shoulders and a book in her hands, but she took counsel of the gale and never glanced at the book.

At once the male servant pointed his eye-brows at a chest of drawers in an exposed corner, and he and Byrne hefted it down the room, where Ann wiped the rain from it. They next lifted a tea-table, a trunk, a dresser and Mrs Blythe's bureau. They grunted and minced with their loads, but Mrs Blythe did not glance at them. In the end they left her beset by her furniture and put up a canvas partition as Blythe had ordered them to do. They worked behind this. It did not take long to rig a sailcloth roof and tie it to the rafters. But they both got very wet and had to work in silence. The once Byrne tried to speak, the servant hissed at him that the old sow was at her thoughts. When they had finished though, and had begun to tip-toe out through Mrs Blythe's half of the room, Byrne shrugging into his forage coat weathered to pink, the lady seemed to be merely watching the rain and not thinking any more deeply than rain causes a person to think. The servant saluted Mrs Blythe and went out. Byrne nodded and was following.

'That soldier,' said Mrs Blythe behind him.

He turned to her.

'Mrs Blythe,' he said too loudly, since she had startled him. He scratched himself where his sodden coat had made him itchy.

Mrs Blythe asked him his name. When he'd given it, she asked did he know a soldier called Halloran. He became enthusiastic.

'Yes. Yes indeed. If you mean Corporal Phelim Halloran, I know *him* sure enough. We came out of Wexford together.'

They had, in fact, come out of Wexford jail together; but Mrs Blythe was not the style of woman to take account of how easy it is to go to Wexford jail.

'I've heard reports that he's a rather riotous young man,' Mrs Blythe said.

Even Byrne could tell that she hadn't heard any such reports, though with her eyes locked up in serenity, she seemed to be viewing the endless, level plain of her own guilelessness.

'Him, Mrs Blythe? Corporal Phelim Halloran?'

'Yes.'

'Oh no, Madam, you must have heard of some other feller. If all of us was as solid as Phelim, the town would be like a monastery. He's the best type of Irishman they make these days. I wouldn't say the same for myself.'

'I see,' she said. 'Well, you know of course how rumour-ridden the town is, not being at all like a monastery.'

'Oh, it's rumour-ridden,' Byrne assented strongly, wagging his big childish jaws. 'A person can't do a thing, any old thing at all, secretly in this town. It's a town that feeds on rumour, having nothing else to eat, if you'll excuse me saying it, Mrs Blythe.'

His fluency had him beaming.

'Then no doubt you've heard something of my husband. Probably you've heard a story or two?'

Byrne felt grateful for the barrier of mahogany objects, since the lady had all the power of her gibbous eyes open and bearing on him now.

'That'd be Mr Blythe,' he said, for the sake of putting time between himself and the question. 'Yes, well, he's a very quiet sort of man by all reports and keeps to himself, which is the best thing of all to do in such a hole as this. This town I mean, Madam.'

Making very little noise about it, Mrs Blythe began to laugh, but shaking and genuinely diverted. Byrne stared at the floor, grinning shyly. Blythe was being laughed at, but so was he.

'If I were Captain Allen,' Mrs Blythe told him, 'I'd make you a colour-sergeant or something else as grand.'

As if the sun had given up the day at eleven o'clock, the room had become very dark. Byrne wondered how the lady would manage to stay there all day under the chancy roof, amongst the haphazard furniture looking oddly restive, like people taking temporary shelter.

'I'm not made to command,' he said to show her he had some small knowledge of self.

'So you have nothing but good to say of both Corporal Halloran and my husband?'

'Yes, Mrs Blythe. Although I'm closer to Halloran than I am to your husband, as you would know.'

'As I would know. You're no fool, are you, Byrne?'

'Not all day of every day anyhow, Mrs Blythe.'

Once more you've said it well, he told himself. But it was wasted on Mrs Blythe, who had gone forward in her seat, her eyes shut but not contemplating her own candour this time. Byrne felt some pity for her unloveable suet face in its pained corner.

'Are you sick, Mrs Blythe?' he said. He out-flanked a commode to get closer. 'Mrs Blythe, do you want me to get a glass of water? Will I fetch the girl?'

'No,' she said. What a small, back-broken negative it was!

At last she opened her eyes.

'It's gone now,' she said. 'Pain is with me more and more.'

'That's a terrible thing,' said Byrne.

'I have been lamed with ulcers since Rio. It is small enough tribute to pay to our Saviour's cross. Yet I sometimes find it nearly beyond me.'

'Yes, yes,' said Byrne gently. In his day, he had paid a deal of tribute himself. Unwillingly, certainly. But he felt entitled to give quiet assent to the pious. He felt entitled even to ask,

'Do you use a poultice on your troubles, Mrs Blythe?'

He wondered fleetingly if he had presumed. So did Mrs Blythe wonder; fleetingly.

'I have used starch, but it is in short supply. I have even used flour and mustard, in shorter supply still. Kaolin is very soothing, although I gave myself a terrible burn applying kaolin before it was well cooled.'

'You want a drawing poultice, Mrs Blythe. You don't mind me saying so, do you?'

'No. I don't at all. Tell me.'

'I had an aunt and her leg was one dripping sore, Mrs Blythe. She used every cure she could think of, even faith and relics. But it wasn't God's will. Then a land-agent from Waterford was passing, and told her to take the giblets from one of the slightly bigger birds, a shrike or kestrel say. You stew the giblets just for a while, not very long, and then you cake them in soft soap to stop them sticking or going bad, and you wrap them in a hot cloth. She put this poultice on, my aunt did, and praised the God of heaven, because she could feel it working on her trouble. Today she walks this earth as straight as any soldier.'

'Giblets?' said Mrs Blythe.

'Yes, Madam.'

'It sounds likely.'

'It does indeed.'

'Where can I get giblets?'

'I could be certain to get you some out of magpie, or out of a gull. They mightn't be table-birds, but there's virtue in their giblets.'

'You could get me some, yes, you could indeed.'

Mrs Blythe seemed to be growing robust in her chair. The prospect had flushed her.

Three days later, Byrne, beginning to despair, caught a gull by casting a weighted fishing line on the edge of the bay. The hook was baited with a piece of beef, and all the swift young gulls competed for it as it swung in its slow arc through the air. Byrne retrieved the beef out of the gullet and ate the inedible bird; but the giblets were for Mrs Blythe's trouble.

The poultice did so well that Byrne was asked to the Commissary's place a number of times in May and early winter, and was delighted to have such a powerful invalid for a friend.

13

Off would go Captain Allen, at least once a fortnight, hunting down squalour in the corners of his company's huts, investigating excesses of vermin in this or that soldier's bed-roll. His was the only company for which barracks had not been built, and he felt that some obscure point was proved if there were fewer of his men ailing than were ailing in other companies. He was a specialist in proving obscure points, if not in explaining them.

His adjutant always escorted him at such times. So, too, at a distance, did Halloran. On the west of the hutments was a clay-pit, and here one day, waiting at his distance for the officers to finish in one of the huts, he failed at first to see a little bald man called Quinn emerging at the top of the diggings, five yards from him.

'Hoy Corporal,' he heard, 'hoy Corporal sir!'

Halloran saw a little brick-coloured man picking at the earth with his mattock. His brown eyes somehow managed to see from under his bald, servile brows.

'My name's Quinn, sir. I bribed the overseer.'

Halloran laughed. 'Good work. Should be more men like you.'

'So that I could move up here and see you.'

'See *me?* I'm not worth a bribe.'

'I need your advice. I won't go to any officers and gentlemen for it, I've had a bellyful of them. I need to get advice from one of my own. They tell me you're a man worth knowing.'

'I don't think there's any such person, the God above us excepted,' said Halloran.

'I see,' said Quinn negligently. He hadn't bribed the overseer and climbed up the pit to talk theology. 'I can't see you in the

Marine lines, and I can't see you here for more than a minute. But perhaps you could see your mercy's way clear to talk with me one afternoon. If it could be today, I'd know how true were the exalted things they say about you.'

Halloran began to laugh again. But the sinewy shoulders and the sweating scalp bent over the mattock with such fear. He restrained himself.

'Do you know the Government dry store? Near the shipyards?'

The little man looked up, clownish in his delight at the two of them knowing the same place.

'There at half-past two?' Halloran suggested.

'Almighty God of mercy,' said Quinn, and began to call down wild benedictions on Phelim's head, ending in the devout hope that he might become father of a great race.

Halloran laughed.

'Amen to that. You don't come by being father of a great race without a bit of fun.'

Quinn giggled too. It was gratifying to see him, suffused with his undisclosed hopes, work his way back down into the pit.

Quinn told Halloran that it had been nearly seven years since he'd been sentenced in Cavan. He had come to the colony with less than a year of his sentence to serve, and now his time would be up in early May. Whomever he spoke to about it, they all looked blank.

When they had brought him aboard the *Catania* at Cove, he had already served five years in Cavan county jail. There had been some trouble at a market-town called Kilshandra. Two cottages had been set alight, the women of the households screaming for their bridal beds and heirlooms. Five milch cows had been led into the fire-light and their bellies piked open.

Quinn himself, so he told Halloran, had not arrived in the town with his bacon until the next day. He'd been unlucky enough to take a drink with two of the guilty men; a squadron of dragoons came to the town; etc., etc.

'I find it hard to talk to my masters,' he said.

Halloran believed it. For Quinn was the type whose brows are honed to a fine edge by decades of cap-doffing to the agent and the priest.

But despite the long habits of serfdom, on being indentured for transportation, he told his story to every available official, both from the harbour and from the *Catania*: to the harbour-master and officers marine and mercantile, to the commissary officials, the surgeon and Navy agent. So many of them listened. So many of them curled their mouths at the folly of sending a man into the furthest exile for a matter of mere months. So many of them promised to have words about him with so many knights, com-modores, magistrates, members, shipyard secretaries, militia generals, benevolent ladies and bishops.

Despite this hierarchy of concern, *Catania* sailed. The next day, allowed out of the hold, he looked to the quarter-deck, that the gentlemen there might see him and remember what a blunder had been made in him. Yet they seemed to be immune to that or any blunder. Three midshipmen were playing with a sextant and the sky. One of them was probably dipping the great sun into the sea and bouncing it skywards again, as you can with the sextant. The other two laughed.

As final word to the impregnable decisions of the great, there was an armed Marine at the bottom of the companion-way.

It was a story normal enough by the queer standards of Irish justice, nor would Quinn have had the courage to tell it, even to a Corporal, if it had been a lie. Since it would do no harm, Halloran framed a petition for Quinn.

It ran, 'Peter Quinn, felon, of Howden's gang at the claypit, respectfully requests to draw His Excellency's attention to the fact, viz., that on May 5th next, it will be a full seven years since the aforesaid Quinn was condemned to that term of transportation by the Chief Magistrate in Cavan, Sir Ambrose Preston. Quinn begs His Excellency's indulgence for bringing this matter to His Excellency's attention, but assures him that he does so with good intention, and on account of the peculiarity of his case, viz., that he was landed in this country more than six years after sentence was passed on him. With every good wish for His Excellency's continued health and prosperity, this petition is signed by. . . .'

Halloran read out the finished letter, and Quinn hugged himself at its sound.

'That's a mystery of elegance,' he said. 'That's poetry.'

'No,' said Halloran, 'it's not poetry. It's just the sort of letter they get every day at Government House. Just the same, it surely has a good chance of success.'

Yet Quinn, who had never heard such a letter before, was not to be dissuaded from hoping exorbitantly in it. He smiled and his eyebrows went crooked, and for some seconds it was possible to see the Quinn who went to market a quarter of a century back, on the look out for the main chance, whether it wore a bottle or a bombazine shawl.

Yet no answer came from Government House for a month, and Quinn reverted to his thin, subjugated baldness.

On May 4th, about eleven o'clock in the morning, a Marine, well-turned out and patently one of the Government House guard, arrived at the clay-pit to take Quinn to His Excellency. There was no time for any long savouring of hope as Quinn scrabbled out of the pit. The decision was about to fall on him like a mountain.

Two furlongs downhill, two furlongs up, the Marine, whose funeral it was not, strolled behind him. He saw Quinn chafing his hands together, trying to erase the frightened veins on the tops of his hands.

'Chilblains, mate?' he called.

He had the poisonous laugh of a man who will take his terror the day it comes. Which wasn't today.

Throughout, Quinn had a sense of being chained up to the imminence of this clear, orange day; to the florid clouds and the wind shuffling in squat and leek-green forests. The warmth, the clouds, the wind, would all be recorded by an acquiescent officer at the Battery—the passable features of the day in what passed here for autumn. For Quinn, they were so many planks in a casket, narrowing him down to the little plot of time in which His Excellency's word would be given, and himself knocked sprawling one way or another.

Government House was something temporary, a solid pup of a house somehow primitive, like a child's drawing of a merchant-class home. One leaf of a double main door stood open. It was panelled mahogany and had a brass lion's snout with a ring through it. This half-open entrance was eloquent of something, of flustered sovereignty and occult paperwork and hasty final words. Yet however he might have found them, Quinn would always have suspected such paramount doors. For they ushered him into an area where he had never been without suffering for it. Before these doors, Quinn sensed with terror what parodies His Excellency and himself would be to each other.

He was halted in the portico with its poor square, wooden columns, at the head of which some dredged-up village talent had carved Ionic capitals like the noses of Dorset rams. A sergeant came out to take control of Quinn with one of those great man-quartering halberds which are the right of sergeants.

'Eff-rie, eff-rie,' the sergeant had time to sing, and they were in the ante-room.

Full of wind, some berried shrubs pecked the ante-room window. Sunlight had spilt all over the vital documents on one of the desks. The room had two of these low, foreign ones with turreted castles of pigeon-holes rising from them to signify the unwarranted pugnacity of servants of the government. Against the back wall stood a divan for people who didn't work in clay-pits to await His Excellency's pleasure on.

Lieutenant Rowley, the aide, was speaking quietly to Long, the Governor's Secretary. He moved then, back to his own em-battled desk and called to Quinn. On the top-half of a sheet of virgin paper, he wrote down Quinn's answers to certain questions. When finished, he tore the paper in two, sauntered to His Excellency's door, knocked, and heard a permissive rumble.

When Rowley had gone, Quinn was calmer. Because he had

been able to answer some listless questions, he was further able to promise himself that he would not be put upon. He began to stand up like any man's equal. But His Excellency's door swung open too soon, with Rowley in the doorway on his gracious, bent legs.

'Bring in the felon, Sergeant,' Rowley begged.

Ah, the felon was brought in with ceremony indeed, quick-marched in that his malice might be circumscribed, and halted on an unequivocal spot.

The unequivocal spot was on the floor-boards in front of His Excellency's Alexandria carpet. Quinn stared at the mystic, woven splashes and coils, living their own lives which were a shut door to him. He glanced at the window—lace curtains and a striped valance, hateful for their sunny pretensions. His eyes followed the walls around. Behind His Excellency, a number of delf plates hung from a picture rail. All were orange and had, in black, the outline of a ship and its name, and were hung there as a record of His Excellency's years of service in ships of the line.

The potentate himself sat worrying loose thread out of a frogged buttonhole on his coat. He eyed something on the desk, perhaps the half page biography of Quinn.

'Perhaps you could help me with this matter, Mr Rowley,' he muttered.

Behind Quinn the door closed, very crisply and cleanly for a colonial door. Rowley advanced to the Governor's right hand.

'Quinn, is it?' said His Excellency, not looking up.

The sergeant prompted Quinn with his knee.

'Yes, Your Honour.'

'Your Excellency,' said appalled Rowley.

Quinn so amended.

'You claim to have been sentenced seven years ago in Cavan. Seven years ago tomorrow.' There was a certain reasonableness about His Excellency's mottled, staggy cheeks.

'Yes, Your Excellency. A seven years sentence.' This is man-to-man stuff, thought Quinn. 'Up tomorrow,' he added, because he was at his ease.

'So that you actually landed in this place with ten months to serve.'

Choking, 'Your Excellency,' said Quinn in an affirmative tone.

Then came a further good omen. The Governor turned to Rowley and said audibly, 'Damn Dublin Castle!'

He bowed his head again to Quinn's details on the half-sheet of paper. He rolled them round his tongue and found them sour.

'I have no reason to disbelieve you, Quinn,' he said, opening his mouth like a carp and having a last blurred look down the lines of his cheeks to the paper on the desk. 'Unfortunately though, I have no reason to believe you either.'

Quinn nodded and swallowed, too heedlessly. Instantly, he wanted above all to escape from the house. The terror of officials lies in that they can be translucent beings, inhuman windows. With a little wisdom, they can so place themselves that centuries of kingships and Parliaments shine straight through them, flush onto poor creatures such as Quinn. To hell with the friendly cheeks! His Excellency was an official, and officials suffocated anyone they managed to trap down on paper.

'All we have here, in this colony,' the Governor explained, 'is a record of your name, age, ship, date of sailing, skills and subsequent charges laid against you here—of which there are none, of course. You see, the convict indentures for the *Catania* have not yet arrived. There is no way of our knowing how long a term you were sentenced to, or the date of your sentencing. And, of course, I cannot release you after you've been a mere ten months in the colony. You realize that.'

Beyond nodding, Quinn was ranting to himself. He realized that the Register of transports must be kept immaculate, so that no clerk in the Home Secretary's would raise an eyelid at an unwarranted release of a felon.

'My recommendation to you,' said His Excellency, making gestures of amplitude, conjuring with the jagged edges of Quinn's condition, 'is that you continue with your excellent record until your indentures come.'

A sincere man, a deadly sincere man, he frowned.

'How long would that be likely to be, Your Excellency?' Quinn managed to ask.

'On the indications, Dublin Castle is very busy now with the echoes of this and that outbreak. It is impossible to answer your question, Quinn. There is no precedent. I mean, it has never happened before. But I don't expect it will be long, and if you continue in your present docility and silence, you will be freed as soon as we know. I mention silence, because it would be a condition of your release that I should not have countrymen of yours coming to me with *unfounded* stories in emulation, imitation, of yours. You understand that?'

Quinn, damning himself, nodded like a sycophant.

His Excellency ferreted amongst papers. As far as he was concerned, he had reached the peroration of his words with Quinn.

'Be a brave man now! Mr Rowley, perhaps you could write a note of this interview and remind me of Quinn's case when the papers *do* arrive.'

Rowley came to attention.

'Sir,' he said, 'may I say that the felon has received *more* than justice at your hands.'

Hem-licking bastard, thought Quinn, not aware that Rowley had uttered a very courtly denunciation of his master.

But he was right in seeing that, with impeccable righteousness, they were burying him alive. If *be brave*, and *Rowley, take a note* were the final words, he could not live by them. Against the winter, he must have for warmth a few of the murkier tatters of hope.

'Perhaps, Your Excellency,' he began, 'if what I say ends up in being the truth of the matter, you might ask the Provost-Marshal to fix up a passage home for me. Perhaps for a bit off the price. I haven't had time to earn anything, you see.'

His Excellency's red hands with their curly white hair, two genial-looking animals to find at a proconsul's desk, ceased rutting amongst the documents and, as it were, sniffed the air.

'The Provost-Marshal?' he asked. 'Passage home?'

Rowley made an excruciated face.

'I've heard often that the Provost-Marshal fixes up passages home for a just price. I thought it was part of the system.'

'Not of our system,' said His Excellency.

'I hardly know how I'll get home.'

'It's not time to consider that yet.'

Quinn was struck by courage as by nausea. He lifted both his fists to chin level. Though they quivered, they did not altogether give the impression of quivering supplication.

'I ask you, Your Excellency, please don't you confuse a poor fellow close to despair. Because I've spoken to a man who's already paid money to the Provost-Marshal for a quick passage home when the ships come in.'

The Governor leant forward.

'I don't want to hear that man's name, Quinn, and I don't want to hear any more.'

'Sir, you can't . . .'

'Quinn!' roared the viceroy. The big cheeks purpled, with the result that Quinn put down his head and started mumbling with grief.

'Now, be a brave man,' said the Governor, and his voice quavered with successfully expended emotion. 'And a patient one. Lead him off, sergeant. And give him a drop before he goes back to work.'

They sat him by the side wall and poured him a grudging drop of rum. Quinn remembered the man from his parish who claimed to have seen Christ weeping beyond consolation at the bootom of a mug of rum. But God had left no messages in the cup for Quinn.

14

Quinn left a wary silence behind him in the office. The wind seethed, but did not fill the dead sails of the delf ships, or flutter the used years which lay vouched for in black and orange along the picture-rail. His Excellency sucked hard at the petulance in the corners of his mouth, knowing that it was improper that Rowley should so irk him. In the end he had to speak however, petulance and all.

'I can't see any reason why the Provost-Marshal has to be told of Quinn's—well, what was it?—Quinn's *mistake*. It would be gracing it too much to call it an accusation. Not that it would matter a damn if it was.'

Rowley remained in a respectful stance. His eyes took no cognizance of the Governor.

His Excellency hawked without success and picked up the year's returns, as edited by Long and a felon called Hearn. They were capable of being tapped and butted into a state of symmetry. He tapped and butted them severely, these records of the colony's paltry industries, of the productivity of the Briton in an impossible country.

'Good! There's nothing more I wanted you for, Rowley.'

'Sir,' Rowley said, 'the Provost-Marshal is a Marine officer as well. As such, he is not directly subject to your control.'

The Governor exhaled rowdily. He put the returns down at a pace that spun the top two out of line. He groaned against the Chancellery lawyers who left out of the colony's Royal Charter any reference to the Marines in their service to him. So that the officers considered themselves an independent garrison and were, by far, too many independent wills for any professional autocrat to view serenely.

Rowley went on.

'I can understand your not being especially concerned about his honour as a garrison officer.'

'You can?'

'Yes. The officers of the garrison have not always been as pliant as you've wished, Your Excellency.'

'Thou sayest it, who should know,' muttered His Excellency.

'But may I point out that as Provost-Marshal, he is your servant, sir. And he has been slandered to your face by an Irish felon.'

'You don't like Irish felons, Rowley? You speak as if the fact that a slander comes from an Irishman makes it a slander twice over.'

'Perhaps it does, sir.'

'I think it halves it, Rowley. Not that I love them. Do you think I like all that secretive muttering in Gaelic? They are an abomination, whether subservient or rebellious. Any officer quickly learns it. I detest them when they keep to their gods. But when they don't they decay with twice the noise and trouble that an English sinner makes. And you and I eat rations because this colony is top-heavy with them.'

But Rowley continued aloof from His Excellency's anti-Hibernian ardours. Having got to the crest of his argument, the Governor grunted and began to follow it downhill.

'Just the same, I'll lay my soul on it that of all of them, that poor animal Quinn is the most harmless. To look on him as a serious slanderer is laughable. Remember that terrier of yours you shot for meat?'

That told. Apollo Rowley ate dog in his hunger.

'You know how it was always feloniously and treasonably insulting my vice-regal gate-post. Quinn's of that order, his offence is of that order. The simple truth is, he's a harmless animal, below giving offence.'

'A clumsy comparison, if I might say so, Your Excellency.' No *if* about it; he'd said it sure enough.

So that now His Excellency took to the attack, standing up

lightly. His bulk came upright with a very few small, cloth sounds.

'Rowley, you may face me if you like. I'm not a divine presence. Nor am I an exposed stool. I won't dazzle you. That you know. I won't offend your nostrils. I don't think you're quite so sure about that. However, you may face me.'

But at first, Rowley wouldn't. He needn't have, what with his well-connected family, what with the world's width which lay between the two of them and any higher office. Probably because His Excellency was redolent of some form of brisk violence, because it didn't seem unlikely that he himself might be punched by a big man and thrown across the room, Rowley obeyed. Still his eyes, beyond command, kept their aloof integrity.

'Rowley,' said His Excellency heartily, 'it would be impossible for any officer not to be vindicated in court. In that case, vindication scarcely seems necessary. I don't care, Rowley, if the Provost-Marshal is defrauding felons who have brought dirty money with them to this country. That money is forfeit, and he's as welcome to it as anyone. I am willing to consider such a perquisite very much the same as the good cheeses and pork cuts from ship's stores that captains of Royal Naval vessels send ashore to their wives just before sailing.'

Across the valley came a scarcely audible drumming; and then the midday bugle bayed, implying a unity which didn't exist, not even here, in the colony's heart.

So the bugle cut the morning adrift, and when it had finished, Rowley spoke.

'Sir, I believe the contingent of gentlemen in this colony is an embattled group. You forget that when Quinn returns to his comrades and spreads his slander, we will all be weakened accordingly. I would like to be bold enough to remind you, Your Excellency, that nothing was done in the end to dissuade Quinn from peddling the story as truth.'

Slap went the Governor's hand on his twilled leg. There was plenty of firm meat there to resound his honest exasperation.

'I don't know what *you* think *they* think of us in the convict lines, Rowley. I'll tell you. They expect us to figure forth authority. Apart from authority, they expect nothing else. They do not expect benevolence or sanity or probity. They drag our names through ordure. They play merry hell with our more private faculties. Do you know that they have a fable about the reason why all our livestock died off; that I and a few others gave the pox to the poor beasts? If the Provost-Marshal is such a precious gentleman, then he shouldn't care what the sweepings say against him. Let him damn the lower deck, as the rest of us have to.'

There was a pause which stretched itself out to half a minute. Rowley remained immobile. The governor set his chin at the door and then examined his desk. And, as Rowley had hoped, lost his aplomb in the end.

'All right then, get out and thwart me again! Thwart me in every damned matter, big and small! You're able to disobey, and you disobey for its own sake. Go to your brotherhood of officers and arrange for that poor bastard Quinn to bleed! Go on! Go away, you arse-twirling little freemartin!'

Rowley waited for a formal dismissal.

'Go on! *You-may-go*!'

The Aide went away, so pale that Quinn would be sure to bleed for it.

Quinn was detained in a hut without windows. Hailstones had made a hole in its roof, and he could be seen while the moon filled his corner, as it would not do for many more minutes. There was a young fellow further down the hut, out of the light such as it was. He was there for making a ragged hole in a lady's head. He knew he had made the ragged hole—hadn't he done it with a palpable lump of quartz? His crime seemed genuine to him. It did not seem like the crime of another person. He was sure he had wielded the quartz, he was sure of the punishment. He had no imagination, except that he wished he'd made a bigger hole.

Whereas Quinn could not believe in *his* crime; would not believe in the punishment; and his imagination had overflown.

He sat in the ruin of Corporal Halloran's poetic letter, and its phrases came to him in any order, for the sound of words was a great comfort in the dark and in boredom, and even in fear. And the young man without imagination called him a daft old bastard and lofted pebbles at him across the dark, and scratched now and then so heavily that you'd have thought Quinn himself had made him itchy.

Only now and then did Quinn come to himself and was aware.

Me Dinny Quinn man of no malice at all in this downright dark. Why am I here and I mustn't rave about it any more. I am not old. I do not say the crazy things old men come out with. Their daughters move them here and there about the house like a shameful piece of furniture. But they still make themselves heard. That's not me. Not me. Dinny Quinn. By heaven and earth and all things green. I broke a girl on the Learmouth Estate's heart named Mary Hart. Mary Hart I broke her heart. Bound to have it broken from the womb for her with a name like that. But I broke it. Me Dinny Quinn. Not some old man wetting himself where he sits and talking out of the top of an addled head. Girls. Girls in the demoned grey of churches—one of them Mrs Quinn-to-be—nothing wrong with Mrs Quinn-to-be—putting their heads down so the priest won't see who it is. Muttering in the box bless me father I was tempted by Dennis Quinn. My daughter what did he do my daughter. It was the way father he danced at the Barry's ceili and looked at me during it. Or perhaps it was the way he sang at the Redhills market. You must pray daughter and confess often and go to Communion at Easter. The might of religion and sacraments forged by God's hand of steel may yet save you from the shocking sweetness of Dennis Quinn.

But in the end, he always saw that the lavender qualms of girls in confessionals, letting out their lovely guilt in little puffs of winter breath, had not saved him. Was it believable? Could a lover and singer and a man without malice, but with imagination, believe it?

'It's funny till it happens,' he said, yet the moon had left him alone in his urine-smelling corner.

In the morning, the sun was thin gold, and obese thunder-heads nudged it around the sky as if it were a boy king amidst councillors. So that by the time they had brought Quinn and the young man whom Quinn made itchy to court, there was thunder in the north-west. It might have meant only that the town would be watered. Remotely, it could have been a threat to the court. But all the members of the court were Marine officers, habituated to storm; and this was such uninspired thunder.

A woman was there with a bandage round her shaved skull. She had four lady friends to pat her arm when Quinn and the boy were marched in. The women all said that the boy had let out her reason with the lump of quartz, that she was now mad beyond hope. Surgeon Partridge came to court, and said the woman had very nearly died and was very nearly mad beyond hope. The ladies made mouths at Partridge's caution. By a quarter past ten though, the court sent the boy off to four hundred lashes and five years labour in chains. On the way out, he called 'Yah, you old whores!' at the four ladies.

The court was bored by Quinn's case. Most of them would not have bothered to start legal action, but since it *had* been started, Quinn had no hope, and would have been foolish to take any comfort from the languor of the bench. He was foolish, just the same. They gave him a sentence of four hundred lashes, and the burden of what Major Sabian, Judge-Advocate had to say to him was that he was damned lucky.

Later in the morning, at Government House, His Excellency, who had the power to pardon or mitigate, called Rowley into the office.

'Rowley,' he said, holding in his hands a report of the morning's court, 'by how much can I cut down Quinn's sentence? Without having all the members of the court resign on me, that is.'

'Perhaps down to three hundred, Your Excellency.'

'Thank you,' muttered His Excellency, taking up his pen and writing two hundred and fifty.

'Is that all, sir?'

'Rowley, I think you're a stupid young man. I think you're

117

nearly the stupidest young man I've ever met.'

'Possibly, Your Excellency.'

'Get out then,' the Governor told him.

Two nights later, Halloran kept half of his evening meal aside for Quinn. Easily said; but his belly crept at the thought of it. Quinn's back was all blood-bruises, which had broken and begun to heal in a great many places. He hid his head when Halloran gave him the mugful of stew, and Halloran thought at first Quinn was grateful and patted the man's wrist.

'Christ damn you!' Quinn said.

Halloran remained still for some seconds.

'God tread you under!' Quinn said.

'Why?' Halloran asked.

'That lordly letter. It made them wise You sold me to them.'

'Who told you, Quinn?'

'Who sold me if you didn't?'

'Nobody.'

'There you are.'

'Nobody ever sold you. That's what I meant.'

'God tread you under!'

'Don't go mad, Quinn. They want to send you mad. Don't you go mad! Come on now. You'll get better. Your papers will come.'

'You weren't in court to speak for me.'

'They invite to court the people they want in court. They didn't ask me, so I couldn't go. You know that.'

'Did you speak to any of them? Did you tell them what a poor beggar I was?'

Halloran was silent.

'There!' said Quinn. 'God stew you in the pit!'

'They knew you were harmless. It wouldn't have mattered if I'd spoken to every one of them.'

'Your letter mattered, it made them wise.'

'You're talking in circles.'

'Listen. It's evil to curse?'

'Yes.'

'Ever known curses to work?'

'Perhaps.'

'Where have you lived all your life? You know curses work. Haven't you seen them work, under God or the devil, who knows? But they work.'

Quinn sweated. He had already said too much.

'People who are alive die,' said Halloran, 'people who are well sicken, people who are well-off lose what they own. Being alive's a curse no one can better. Especially when you're so weak. Why don't you rest and be quiet now. They're all cur-dogs, but it's no use fretting over it.'

'When I am well and have found the words, I'll curse the balls off you.'

'Perhaps you will. Curse me or not, Quinn, I hope you get back God's own good health soon.'

'God tread you under, you officers' fancy-man.'

Later, Halloran asked Ann why Quinn should have wanted to curse him.

'He was in pain, for one thing,' said Ann very wisely.

But Halloran was not satisfied. Did he deserve to be cursed, like all men who pursued their won safety, like all the worldly-wise? That was what he wanted to know. But he was too uneasy to ask it outright.

'Why me? Why not Dublin Castle or His Excellency?'

Ann had no doubt why. There were some of the profoundest things that women knew instantly, without drawing breath. And when they knew one of these things, it was not simply knowing as a scholar knew; they gave off certainty as a candle gives light.

'It's because you're of his kith. His Excellency's too high to hate the way you can hate someone close. He can see through you, Quinn can. He can't see through Dublin Castle or through His Excellency. Don't let the fellow worry you. It was to be expected he'd turn around and end up cursing you.'

'I didn't expect it,' Halloran said. 'I'm the dimmest judge of men.'

'You're only a boy,' said Ann with authentic sympathy.

15

Aɴɴ had first put on the St Megan's cord five years before, ordered by her mother after a story was spread about a German regiment running wild in a town in Louth. The cord lost some of its dye in the tropics, but kept its virtue until the morning it came apart and fell onto the floor of the Blythes' front parlour. The red cord, as a red cord, was probably more outlandish medicine even than a giblet poultice. Yet it had supplied Ann for some time with faith in her cosmic significance. This faith was staggered to find the cord gone. Seeing it on Mrs Blythe's book-table the next morning brought to Ann a sense of being rarely and especially threatened.

'This old cord, is it yours, Ann?'

Ann blinked, busy with the hot water.

'Ann? Don't dream!'

'No, Mrs Blythe.'

'No? I found it on the floor here.'

'It isn't mine, Mrs Blythe.' Once started, she was lying quite robustly. 'It could have come off anything at all.'

'I suppose so,' said Mrs Blythe. 'Why do you think it has these three little knots on the tassel, like the three knots on a friar's belt?'

'I couldn't say anything about that. Would you like this water cooler, Mrs Blythe?'

Mrs Blythe felt with her right hand, but was very absent about it.

'Do you think that this could have a religious meaning, Ann? Mightn't there be cords just like this one used for this or that purpose in your religion?'

Ann was unravelling a flannel from around a heated brick. She burnt and shook her right hand.

'I don't know, ma'am,' she said, conversational on the brink of the pit. Her stomach quivered with the giddiness of her earth that morning, and she chattered as the chasms opened up and down its length.

She poured the hot kaolin out of the pan into the flannel. Then she dropped a cloth into the hot water. She wondered would this be the last time she would be allowed to minister.

'If you don't mind me saying, Mrs Blythe, we must hurry or it will all go cold.'

When the dressing was at last finished, and Ann was leaving, she dawdled near the table, considering snatching the cord. Considering. In fact, she seemed to herself to have no freedom, as if the matter were being solved outside her own head by two parties who had no love for her. The hair's-breadth supremacy of one of the parties sent her to the door—to all appearances, a sane girl.

Mrs Blythe found Terry Byrne charming to listen to for his store of cures and spells. None of his remedies cured modestly, and most of them worked through various blatant symbols as satisfying to the spirit as are the symbols of a sacrament. His cure for growths on the skin, for instance, was a sacrament far more than a cure. You lashed tight onto the afflicted part a lump of fresh beef. You lashed it so tightly that it became part of the person's flesh, more or less, left it there till it began to smell, then buried it in the earth. As the maggots reduced it to dust, the skin or, at least, the spirit healed.

Mrs Blythe may have welcomed him for the sake of listening to his solemn herbal fantasies, or because what he prescribed often did her legs good, or because, by and by, she had him speaking of Mr Blythe's repute in the town, it being suitably low. Probably, the fantasy and the gossip were all she wanted of him. The time came when he found that in Mrs Blythe's presence, he could safely raise an eyebrow or make a mouth at Mr Blythe's image. That was why he risked a smile when Mrs Blythe showed him the cord one day and said,

'Mr Blythe found it in the town. What is the matter, Byrne?
Is anything funny?'

'No, oh no,' he said.

'Have you seen something of this nature before?'

'Yes,' he said shrugging.

'Ah! I *thought* it may have been a Romish device.'

'How is that, Mrs Blythe?' Byrne asked.

'Something devotional that Papists use.'

His lips twitched. He wanted to laugh again.

'Yes, it's that much all right, Madam.'

'Is it something shameful.'

'No. You couldn't say shameful.'

'Oh, tell me what you know, Byrne! Finish with the mum
show! You're a confirmed sniggerer, young man, and you must
learn to do something about it.'

'Yes, Mrs Blythe.'

'Then please tell me.'

'It's a St Megan's cord. Women wear it around the waist for
this reason and that. It's said to be a help in the keeping of the
holy virtue.'

'What do you mean, the holy virtue?'

'Well, the virtue of the angels, if you see what I mean.'

'Chastity?'

'Yes, Mrs Blythe.'

'Poo!' she said, and threw the cord on the table. 'Hence the
trembling lips when I remarked that Mr Blythe found it in the
town.'

'No. It was just a bit of a joke to myself, Mrs Blythe.'

'You will not have further bits of jokes to yourself in this room
then.'

'If you say so, Mrs Blythe.'

For the purposes of argument, the lady took up the string once
more.

'Now, Byrne, Mr Blythe saw the woman who dropped this, and
he offered it back to her, but she denied most strenuously that it

was hers.'

'She said it wasn't hers at all?'

'Yes. Why would she do that, that is what has me wondering.'
Byrne closed one eye and frowned.

'I can't see anyone in this town being modest about a Megan's
cord,' he said.

'Why do you say *this town*, Byrne?'

'Well, the ladies of the town are a bit brazen, you could put it.'

'Indeed you could put it that way, Byrne. Would ladies elsewhere be modest about it?'

Because Mrs Blythe's owly face seemed oceans away from the
soft decency of Wexford girls, Byrne wriggled his shoulders and
looked up at the roof.

'You're going to keep asking me questions until you know all
about this bit of string, aren't you, Mrs Blythe?'

'Of course I am going to keep asking you questions. Can't you
see how quaint this *bit of string* must seem to me?'

'All right then. Young girls wear it to protect them against
soldiers. If a mother has had too many children and the times are
hard, she wears it to protect herself from getting with child. The
women of Wexford are virtuous women. You've got to go a long
way to find one who's not.'

'Heaven protect us, you have some unfortunate turns of phrase,
Byrne.'

'I've taken unfortunate turns of another kind in my day, God
save me.'

'God save you. Go on.'

'I've even known girls to wear that cord after they've . . .'

'After they've?'

'After they've fallen. To stop themselves getting with child.'

'So that they might be ashamed if anyone found them wearing
it?'

'Yes, the women of Wexford have such decent minds.'

Mrs Blythe sat back gently. Her mouth was tense with satis-
faction, her eyes bunched up shut for the pungency of her cool
anger. How she would scald and flay that girl!

But having hurried Byrne out, she found that her delicious fury would rather wait a day, as the divine fury which Halloran had called on himself had waited many a day, Halloran still walking whole and unblasted. And when her fury had waited a day, and she had been tended for a day by the hesitant girl, she found that it would rather withhold itself for a week. Then Halloran went off for some time on an excursion to the west with Captain Allen. When he had come back to the town, she decided, to her own surprise, that the argument was the Lord's, that she had taken all the safeguards that a Christian mistress could take, that she would warn this Halloran away from the house, but beyond that, the argument was the Lord's. And then, to her further dismay, she did not even warn Halloran away from the house. She waited, prisoner of that precious anger, and knew that she was wrong to wait, that Halloran had involved her in the Fall.

16

Captain Allen and his party went away twelve days in the wilderness, and all they found was that they were weak.

On the first day, for instance, they walked only fourteen miles, though the country was easy. They marched in a plain of grass up to the knees, past sundry councils of those impending trees, raw, double-jointed, feeling boots on their earth and not saying a word, suspending judgement.

In the early afternoon of that first day, they found themselves being watched by a stock-still native family not unlike denuded acacias at a distance of a quarter of a mile. They were very thin, that family, but loped easily away. The crooked grey thickets consumed them like mist.

Allen's party camped at night by a little scrubby river. It was, after its style, a harsh place. The trees raved with small dark birds, who sat like fruit on the branches, singing only a little more sweetly than cicadas. Damp came up through the long tubes of grass, cold at the roots and full of spiderwebs still wet from the night before.

In the trees was flood-wrack, good kindling. Halloran stood watch with the loaded musket. Through the blue twilight, the others gathered in the firewood quickly. He saw Private Terry Byrne aimless and pale in the shadows. Between Byrne and himself that was a startling kinship. For instance, Halloran was able to tell now that Byrne skulked as he did, plucking at dry branches, because he was oppressed by the sense of hell and of what is probably the same thing, of being tethered unto damnation by his own big, starchy boyo's body. This dawdling stupor meant that Byrne would later make an attempt on Halloran's ear and mourn down it about doomsday.

The birds all stopped singing at once, as abruptly as a choir of priests arrived helter-skelter at the last verse of the Office. There was a second of silence, and then, as one creature, they quavered upward in hundreds, reflected an instant and seethed northwards along the river. Byrne came straggling back to the fire-site. He carried a few twigs under his right arm.

'Marvellous night this is, Corporal,' he muttered, shivering. 'No soft mattress and mothering paps tonight.'

'They're waiting for your kindling.'

Halloran nodded at the men, who had made their two piles of wood and were advising the marine with the flint and steel.

'Ballocks to you!' Byrne articulated softly, and joined them.

Halloran feared, from the way Byrne stood apart from their vulgar urgency, that he would indeed become soulful as the dark came on. When the firewood creaked and a tongue of flame jumped, four men hastened to add the choicer bits of faggot, but Byrne turned his back.

The meal was made and eaten, Allen and his lieutenant dining at their own fire twenty yards from the others. At the men's fire, there was a tendency to speak low and stifle laughter, for the inland exacted a mild awe. But Allen, feeling equal to any pagan waste, chuckled whenever he wanted to. In such an open space, beside the little straggles of flame, his laughter sounded like a revelation of weakness.

At last, Byrne brought Phelim his meal and took the flint-lock from him. Halloran moved in towards the fire, but remained standing. He was miserable with the cold and hunger; and some type of feverishness of the flesh, not directed at Ann, numbing all his aspirations, moved in his belly in definite, warm arcs. He felt too blunted even to understand how perilous was its slug-blind persistence. In this state, he didn't wish to debate man's latter end with Byrne, but neither did he want to join the tight little group around the fire.

It was a good fire. He felt its heat on his face and lifted one foot at a time towards it, holding in both hands the very hot plate of beef stew thickened with pease-meal.

Behind him, Byrne let himself shiver audibly, give a small giggle of cold.

'This is a fearful lonely place,' he called to Halloran. 'Here we are, lost in the dark on the scruff of the world. On the very scruff of the world.'

'Yes,' said Halloran. He looked at the darkness between the stars. Since you looked up to the darkness in the northern world, here you were in fact looking down into a pit of stars, and sometimes you saw yourself as poised over their lance-points ready to plummet; yet, behold, you would remain.

He shuddered. He champed his food like a barbarian, to discourage Byrne from becoming reflective.

'How's Ann, God be her light?' asked Byrne, spacious as a bishop.

'Ollump,' said Halloran through clods of meat in his mouth. He had often been involved in strange dialogues with Byrne over Ann. Byrne would be devil's advocate and put forward the reasons why Ann should not be treated with more respect than other women; and Halloran would lop them down with increasing fury, sometimes with main force. The insane thing was that Byrne seemed happy to be quashed, that the argument was undertaken by him in a spirit very much like that of a pilgrim. It made you wonder about the strange, regal place Ann must have held in his mind.

'Is she enjoying life at the Blythes'?'

'Yes.'

'That Blythe is a dirty old boy.'

'And you're a dirty young one, and so am I, I suppose. Name a fellow you know who's put off the old man and put on the new.'

'God forgive us all, I'll say that. But he's a *dirty* old boy.'

'He behaves himself with Mrs Ulcer Blythe to keep her eye on him.'

'Why don't you liberate Ann from the Blythes', Halloran?'

'Why don't you drown yourself?'

'She could have her own hut down on the brook. Mrs Blythe is such a terrible strict woman, Ann could be easily liberated, singing iddiddly-iddididdly-itytyty.'

Halloran glanced at the camp-fires, and with the plate still in his hands, swung his knee sharply up into Byrne's underbelly. When Byrne sunk coughing onto his haunches, propping himself with the musket, Halloran saw him as he must have always seen himself, a large soft Irish boy lost in the wilderness. But, numb tonight, Halloran felt no pity.

'I'll make you unfit to liberate a Slaney sow if you come that talk,' he whispered. 'I might as well tell you, I'm not in the mood for you.'

Byrne cried. His voice was very thin.

'I ought to shoot you here and now, you frowsy-gutted bastard. My God, I will and tell Allen the thing went off by mistake.'

But, of course, he didn't.

Halloran spoke.

'Now you've got your voice back, Brian Boru, stand up. I've got my boot, such as it is, lined up with what's more precious to you than the whole Communion of Saints.'

In fact, Byrne got up as humbly as from prayer.

'I'm a joke of a man, Corporal darling, there's no use clouting you black and blue as I could indeed. I'd still be just as much a joke of a man.'

'If you say so.'

'Yes I say so. How does a man who's such a joke save himself from hell-fire?'

'Dear God in heaven,' said Halloran, 'save him and shut him up.'

'Tell a poor man, Halloran.'

'You tell me, Terry Byrne. I know nothing on the subject.'

'I don't believe that. You're known to be a regular bugger of a good man.'

'*If I have not charity*, says St Paul, *I am like sounding brass*. And I don't think a knee in the ballocks is anyone's idea of charity. You'd better go elsewhere.'

'You're hedging on me, Halloran. Everyone knows you're as clean as a lamb. But me, I've fathered two children in this land.

128

That's a poisonous sin, fathering bastards. Not at all clean, not as clean as murder. Crack, he's dead, you can't do anything but pray for him, confess it and tend his grave. It's clean, you see and finished. But this one? The children are growing in the sun, walking in the street, Halloran. They grow up and the sin grows up. How does a man like that save himself?'

'I've told you before. I don't know.'

'Did I tell you about my dream?'

'About the pit?' said Halloran, warding off the story with his hands. 'You told me.'

'I was deep in a pit of—'

'Of black soil, like at home.'

'Like at home. And did I tell you about the man at the top of the pit hurling clods of earth on me, and the man . . . ?'

'And the man was God, and wore ox-blood gaiters like a wealthy farmer.'

'Yes. Heaven and earth, what a dream!'

'You know the waste-pit beyond the shipyards, how it drips out over the rocks. I had a dream like that after eating oysters there.'

'You're making a mock of me. You're a heartless sod to have the power to help me and you won't.'

'Some people can't even go to hell with dignity,' thought Halloran. He cleaned his plate slowly with flour-cake. He did not think of Ann. His soul was brash and animal, and his feet were cold.

'Listen to me, Terry Sinner!' he said. 'Nobody is saved. That's straight from Rome, my boy, straight from the muzzle of the big gun. Everyone is sitting on hell's brink, one cheek on, one cheek over. Who are you to be let off, with your two bastards?'

'It's wrong to scoff at a poor feller in search of his God.'

'His *God*? Your *god*? Their god is their belly. And in your case, the little bit stuck on.'

'Damn you!'

'Be a *big* boy, Terry. Go and be a *big* boy.'

There was drowsy laughter, not at them, from the fire. Halloran watched the brows, chins, noses of the men all transfused with light, rinsed by flame, all glinting. It was possible to see these fellows as pitiable, riding their raft of light in an illimitable sea.

'Keeping an eye out, Corporal?' came a voice not aware that it was in an ocean. Allen's.

'Sir!'

Silence and the cold. *Eli, eli.*

For his own part, Byrne began to surmise.

'I will have to do something that changes my whole tune.'

Phelim snorted. He cared little for Byrne's basic tune, however played.

'I will have to be a martyr, and pay all my debts in a second, with one gush of blood. Unless I save myself in a second, quick as the temple veil getting ripped, I'm finished. If they give me so much as two seconds, I'll be fornicating in my mind in the second one.'

'Then you study up to be a martyr,' Phelim advised him. 'A lion in an arena won't give you much time to go astray.'

'No, that it wouldn't.'

The boyo gave a well-rounded, sad laugh, and started to go.

'Well, you see, acts of contrition are out for me, and there's no priest. So only a martyr is left.'

'That's right. Here, St Terentius, take my plate back.'

With grunts of comfort bound to be disillusioned once the damp came up from the earth, the camp was settling to sleep. Byrne left Phelim without saying another word.

For the first three days, Byrne spoke of nothing but salvation. Halloran, burdened with his numbness or with nostalgia for Ann, did not seem to be able to insult him away from the question.

There were with the party two transports. Of them it could broadly be said that, though reliable, they were, after their manner, lovers. Byrne became interested in the younger of them and shelved his study of the last things.

By then, they had passed from the plain of grass through downlands into the dusty forests of a miserable tableland. By the fifth day, the plateau became more massive and broken with shadowy clefts down which the tributaries flowed.

One afternoon, they camped well down in one of these fissures, close to water and safe from a furious north wind rioting on the other side of their valley. The two officers had climbed the ridge to take their position. Halloran had the others collecting wood and bearing water.

Byrne got back to the proposed fireplace with what could be called two armfuls of kindling. He sat and began to build a fire. As he waited there, sluggishly breaking twigs, the two transports arrived lumping full waterskins. They drove iron hooks into the trunks of trees and hung the water from them. Then the elder transport marched up to the fire and kicked Byrne in the jaw.

Halloran rushed up and held the man. Byrne got up from the ground with his mouth bleeding. Two more Marines arrived, and Halloran ordered them to hold the boyo.

'He's been messing with my Arthur,' the transport said.

'He's been messing with your Arthur, has he?' asked Halloran. 'Right. You'll carry my gear for the rest of the jaunt. That'll keep your feet on the ground.'

He let go of the man and advanced on Byrne.

'You've been half-way down my ear for days about salvation, haven't you? Nothing like a bit of the old sodomy between martyrdoms. Keeps the old man in trim. Captain Allen had men flogged for sodomy, did you know?'

At that moment, came the noise of the two officers, slipping in the leaf-mould of the steep forests and chuckling to each other.

'Not a word,' said Halloran. And there was not a word.

The gorges became so vertical that Allen turned home after the eighth day. Three days' rations were left. Halloran felt an immense joy. He felt God's blessing smile on him aslant through the trees each morning. He was going back to Ann.

17

THEY slept the last night at the Crescent, Allen meaning to row home in the morning. Halloran and two Marines found a quiet billet on the outskirts of the hutments. Here they cooked their own rations, for Allen had told them they could not draw from the garrison stores, not that night anyhow. 'Perhaps in the morning,' he had promised, pretending for a second that they could depend on him to see to it. With hardly a word, they lay down an hour after sunset and slept.

Byrne found a noisier bed in the hut of a sergeant who was the camp's notorious gamer. The wife, whom Byrne had with some success coveted in the Indian Ocean, had died the previous December. But her spirit did not lay heavily under that roof; the sergeant was gay and had constant visitors, and in his corner, Byrne slept and roused pleasantly throughout the evening and the small hours, always waking to light and warmth.

At least three men, at various hours, told him the news of the village when their laughter woke him and they found his dazed eyes on them. It was vivid news, told to him as a recompense.

What had, in fact, happened in the Crescent while Byrne and Halloran had been pushing theology up and down Allen's bitter gorges, was that His Excellecy had been persuaded to despatch a Court of Enquiry to the Crescent. Somehow it had become known that a rebel committee was operating in the village, and Major Sabian and four other officers were told to winkle it out. His Excellency advised them to be sensible but firm. Firm they were.

They heard first Captain Howard's evidence, fervently given. There had been, said the Captain, an increase in illicit gatherings of Irish, taking place in sight of officers and guards. They had flaunted before the authorities the secrecy of their old, barbaric tongue. A female transport had come to him with a story of pikes prepared and hidden away. Surgeon Daker had attempted to uncover these pikes, but had been unsuccessful. A young Irishman questioned had been unbearably contumaceous, and had had to be flogged for contempt. He himself, Howard, had suffered something he called 'insolence of bearing' from a transport named Robert Hearn, who performed clerical duties at Government House. He had refrained from punishing the man in the hope that, given some latitude, Hearn might betray something of importance about the rebel committee.

He had prepared a list of names for the court's perusal. . . .

Daker's torpid evidence, on the same model as Howard's, was then taken.

After two days, the Court of Enquiry drew up a list of men to be flogged—preventively. Amongst them, *Hearn, five hundred*.

The punishment had been dealt on the Saturday that Allen's party had turned back from the tableland.

The three men who told their version of these facts to Byrne all said with passion, 'I hope they try their tricks now. I hope to God they do. We've got plenty of powder up here, and after that there's the bayonet.' They wanted by these means to make clear what they themselves were not sure of—that they were not the prisoners, and the felons were.

When Byrne woke again, the hut was dark and the door stood open, full of a sea-blue half light. It might have been half past four. By the table in the centre, the sergeant and some intruder were talking as if it were midday.

'What's the matter?' Byrne asked.

'They've gone,' the sergeant said.

'Who's gone?'

'The prisoners, the Pats. The ones from the timber-parties and the government farm.'

'Tell me.'

'Terry,' the sergeant said, 'you'd better get back to your friends.'

'But tell me first.'

They told him, and he dressed and went to find Halloran.

Phelim was woken by the shoulder and saw suspended above him Byrne's yokel head, in shadow.

'Hoy Corporal,' Byrne kept saying, sounding a swamp of catarrh.

Halloran sat up. He was a poor riser, and one side of his face seemed to have subsided from the other.

'They've bolted, they've gone,' Byrne announced. 'I almost wish Dennis Byrne's small boy Terry was with them.' So he repeated the stories which had broken his sleep that pleasant night. 'Last night then,' he kept repeating, having to go through the preamble for the three other Marines awaking one by one in the hut.

'Last night then, some of them broke into the warehouse here. They squashed the guard's head, a Marine from Howard's company. Eternal rest grant.'

Byrne was so feverish with the story that Halloran thought how one man's squashed skull is another man's renewal. But to Phelim too, at this time of morning the murdered soldier did not reek of damnation. Death was a quick pain in the head and a cool sleep. Halloran countenanced it, and breathed easily.

'Straight after, they stole two cutters and a jolly-boat and shipped the goods from the warehouse to their friends along the river. Do you know who their friends would be? More than a hundred from the timber parties and the Government farm!'

'Oh dear God,' said Halloran, for their cause which hadn't a Chinaman's chance.

Byrne frowned. Reverence was a distraction in any good anecdote.

'And you know,' he went on, 'it makes a man far from ashamed that not one life did those fellows take at the pits or the farm. But they chained up guards and overseers and told them to watch out for the next time they'd meet, and to think of what merciless bastards they'd been to their brother-men, and how the Almighty must hold in His hands a few colliers full of coals to heap on their heads. Then they left with some nobility, you could say.'

'No doubt they're sidling up to the hogsheads somewhere across in the woods and thinking the same as you. And they're all dead, between those who'll be shot and those who'll be hanged.'

'You're a long-nosed moping bugger, Halloran,' said Byrne. 'Your darling officers have to find them yet.'

'Poor lost souls,' Halloran was muttering. He remained sitting on his blanket, kneading his ruined feet. He could feel in them the sharp edges of the land they had brought him over. They were wrapped in an old pair of black worsted stockings, formerly Ann's, and evoked nostalgia for the low coast of Wexford, and even for his lost brothers in the woods.

'You wouldn't know a great day if it took you by the horns,' said Byrne.

Inevitably, the Navy reveille blew, singing *Charlie, Charlie, lace up and go* all over the hillside, hacking the morning down to regimental size.

By seven o'clock, the garrison had been fed on wheat-meal cake cooked in ashes and given a half-pint of spirits each. Men had gone shuffling through the open-air bakery, and nudged each other over the murder stains on the doorstep of the warehouse, and scooped cartridges and balls in the armoury. Captain Howard had risen with dysentery, and collapsed in the midst of preparations. Now he passed the command to Allen. Patrols had already been sent out, one into the hills, one down the river by fishing-boat, and had seen nobody. But the patrol by river had found the wreckage of the stolen boats in a place where she-oaks and gums and monoliths crowded right down to the water.

Allen strode downhill from Government House to receive a report on what boats were left for use. On both sides of the street stood a file of Marines in whom the morning sang. This was the hour of level tedium on most days, the hour when the day presented itself as intolerable before the day's work had been more than sniffed at. After long training in boredom and hunger, men turned their faces with an effortless goodwill to watch Allen past. Their faces all affirmed, 'Yes, I am a soldier born to stand up firing lead pellets at my King's enemies, and here I am, arrived at my hour.'

Fallen in by the river were two ranks of men who affirmed nothing; sick men resurrected from the garrison infirmary. A subaltern addressed them. Behind the fulgurating youth's back, some half-dozen fat birds fed, white hoods, black inquisitors' faces. They pecked the earth with an authentic mastery, and suffered the boy.

Halloran came jogging uphill to meet Allen.

'The adjutant says, sir, no cutters and five little fishing boats, but only three of them half-way safe.'

Allen grunted. No doubt he had it in mind to do smart, soldierly things with the boats, feints and sweeps down the river. For want of a few small craft, it would all have to be foregone.

He was still considering, and Halloran stood by him politely, when up from the hospital came Daker and a shambling man with a blanket over head and shoulders. Daker stopped continuously to allow the man to catch up, and was absorbed for seconds on end by the black and white crow-shrikes (*gymnorrhina*) pecking the earth. He conveyed to Allen and Halloran the sense that for him, the morning was salient only in these.

The man, like a ruined friar, came on with his head back in a capuche of blanket. There was no jacket or shirt under the blanket, he wore only canvas pants clutched at the front. The sun was on the man's falcon nose.

'It's Hearn,' said Phelim. He thought, *he used Mealey as a case in point, Ewers as a case in point, Quinn likewise. Now they have given him a case in point in his own flesh.* He noticed the perse under each lid, and the blue, death-struck lips. In this altered face, Halloran was aware of the life flowing in the eyes. He was reminded there and then (not later, or as a result of thinking artfully upon Hearn) of the rivers one gets glints of from fissures in limestone country.

'He insisted on seeing you in person, Captain,' said Daker, arriving. Hearn still grunted on the slope, a very rheumatic prophet Samuel. 'His name is Hearn and he's suffered at the hands of the Court of Enquiry. He heaped such intemperate abuse on the men detailed to carry him that I let him walk himself. He says he has information for you on this Irish affair.'

Hearn's rowdy breathing obtruded itself. From consideration for his back, he held his head arrogantly tilted. Now that he was all death except for his eyes, he had a new defiance, had lost his old satanic air. Seen close, he seemed far too warlike to be compared even to Samuel; but Elisha, who called forth bears to tear the two and forty mocking boys, might have had eyes like Hearn's.

If all my people were like me, said the unquenched eyes, *and all your people like you, we would grow our grain in your rib-cage, we would plough your shinbone into lime.*

'How much credence you give what he says is your matter,' Daker observed, 'a military matter. But I have never found any reason to trust him. Perhaps you'll excuse me.'

Excused or not, he was going, and allowed himself to be delayed purely as a concession.

'Perhaps you could send a litter for this fellow,' Allen suggested. 'I'm sure he won't be able to return to the hospital by his own powers.'

Daker screwed up doubt in a corner of his mouth.

'I'll manage it if possible. If I cannot, perhaps you could detail some of your men to carry him.'

On the narrow back of the last word, the Surgeon escaped. His serenity carried him on downhill as Allen called,

'We have other things to do, Surgeon. You are to bring a litter when I tell you!'

'Jumped-up Surgeon's mate,' muttered Allen as well.

Hearn's laughter at this frightened Halloran, probably frightened the officer more than offended him. It stirred like an animal in the grass and seemed to come, in fact, from the ground. Allen struck Hearn with a clenched fist, but against all reason, the man avoided falling.

'You, Halloran,' Allen called out, turning his back, walking away, 'you talk to him! You're of the same damned race.'

Then Hearn spoke up, loudly, plying the cyanose lips, the sense coming out clotted, two or three words at a time on the brunt of each breath.

'If that Captain of Marines listens to me, he will have His Excellency singing Hosanna to him. He will be a conqueror and have a few honours to take to his pillow of a night. And he may grow up to become a Major-General.'

'Sit him down!' Allen commanded over his shoulder.

'No, thank you Captain. The cat licked me very low.'

'Listen to him, Halloran!'

'*You* listen, Captain of Marines, or lose your chance, now!'

Allen seemed calm, sensibly taking account of the fact that a man punished to his limit is beyond authority.

'Do you know something of this rebel affair then?' he asked quietly.

'Yes, for your face, Captain!'

'My hearing's passable, front or back. But let us humour the dying.'

Indolently, he about-turned.

'Well, Hearn?'

But the man's deathliness shocked him. Beneath the brow and cheeks and nose, the skeleton had asserted itself, had risen like a tide.

'Quickly,' said Allen, aware of the shortage of time.

The adjutant came up. That made the Captain, the adjutant and Halloran who could hear Hearn. To the soldiers further up the street, it must have all looked something like the Ides of March.

'Your people were right,' Hearn said. 'There was a committee, a committee of five, of whom I was one. A man called Benedict Cavanagh was chairman. He's away in the wilds with them now.'

'I know,' said Allen.

'They had hopes of me, poor souls. The committee was a pike-in-the-belly business to them, though.'

'And it wasn't to you?'

'No, it wasn't to me. It was a committee of reform to me.'

'Reform? Who were you going to reform?'

'The administration,' said Hearn. 'Keep it inside just bounds.'

'What do you mean?'

Allen was very ready to take insult.

'Daker, for example,' said Hearn. 'Dear God, let me lie down, will you? On my belly.'

Two men were sent running for a litter.

'Give him some spirits, Halloran,' said Allen.

Hearn was on his hands and knees, the blanket askew, showing the backside out of his trousers, real flogging breeches kept on with thongs round the top of each leg, and kept up in front by hand. The back was healing, one or two places still moist. Hearn had suffered a seizure after only a part of his punishment had been given. The system of which Hearn spoke so often, would, long live its stroke-counting soul, keep the rest in store for him.

Halloran could remember that Hearn had once tried to get liquid into Mealey's downward mouth. Now he was doing the same for Hearn. He hoped he wouldn't catch their condition. An amount of the spirits spilt into the man's hoar-frost stubble. Three yards away stood two men with the litter. One of them was Byrne, knapsacked, with wonderstruck eyes.

'Give him your blanket, Byrne!' cried Allen. 'With your permission, Mr Garside, I'll put him in the adjutant's hut.'

They carried him up through the company lined either side of the street. These men were still exhilarated and anxious to know the what and wherefore of Hearn. They lived in the flush of the morning, the dew not yet dry on the grass. Their weapons were propped in a variety of off-hand positions which hinted at the brave possibilities of the day.

Hearn was let down before the adjutant's hearth, and Phelim took off his coat and made a pillow for him.

'Set the fire, Byrne,' Allen said, bending over Hearn's stertorous rest and scanning the blue features squashed nose-first in Halloran's coat. 'Mr Garside, send a runner, will you, to the outposts. Give him more spirits, Corporal. I promise it'll be made up to you.'

But the warming stuff streamed down the side of Hearn's chin. The man barely smelt it, the thin lips flickered for a second to the taste.

Hearn slept there for more than an hour.

When he woke at last, his eyes explored the hut with the inevitable foxiness of a man who thinks he may have woken up dead. He saw, however, the edge of the hearth and, through dazed chair-legs, a soldier reclining back-on. Halloran leant in the doorway, looking out.

Hearn's mouth and memory were desperately dry though, and he wanted to be assured of the reality of these two man-shapes. However it hurt, he coughed a number of times. Phelim turned.

'Hoy, up off your ribs, Terry Byrne,' he called. 'Run and bring Allen!'

'Do you want a drink?' he asked Hearn, motioning towards his own canteen on the table.

'No. Some water maybe. I never wanted any of this.'

Yet Hearn's eyes flickered towards the hearth, showing that, despite himself, he considered the fire a great blessing.

'Keep yourself covered,' called Halloran, fetching water.

'Indeed. I get the balance of my five hundred when I'm well again. *Surely justice and mercy will follow me, all the days of my life.*'

'Justice and mercy of a kind will follow you if you're able to help Allen. I'll give you that much.'

'That's not your affair. I vomit up their mercy.'

Allen came in with the adjutant and Byrne. He took a chair brusquely and straddled it. Hearn lay vigilant.

'You won't exhaust yourself with insolence this time,' Allen stated. 'If you've anything to tell, tell it straight, and I'll guarantee you the remission of the remainder of your punishment. I will also take you down to the port, to a fit hospital.'

Hearn pushed himself up on his hands but Allen pushed him down gently by the crown of the head.

'Tell it without gesturing,' said Allen.

The man whimpered, for seconds only.

'I came to you standing up in the open to tell you what I know about the committee. For the sake of the committee. Not for your sake or my sake. I wanted to tell you to take your remission of remainders to the devil!'

'Very well,' said Allen, finding a fault of absorbing interest up the sleeve of his coat. 'I'll take your pride for granted. But what have you to tell me?'

One of Daker's fat crow-shrikes had wandered right into the hut. Byrne chased it out with a flick of his foot.

'You're in the business of putting down rebels now, Captain,' said Hearn. 'I know some of them have to die. But if I'm to help you, you'll have to swear of course that you'll destroy the smallest number you need to.'

Here was Hearn making friends to himself of the mammon of iniquity, swearing people in.

'That goes without saying.'

'Oh, no! The things that have gone within saying with you people have broken the backs of my people. You have to swear by God and mean it.'

Who's conscripting God these days? thought Halloran.

The Captain got up and walked into a corner.

'Be sensible, Hearn. How can anyone make an oath like that? What you mean by the smallest number is not what I mean by it. I can tell there's mockery in you, and if you *are* mocking me, I'll hang you, gamy back and all. The Court of Enquiry have my vote of thanks, flogging you.'

'That aside, you'll have to swear.'

'Does he know anything, Garside?' asked Allen over the prone body he would have liked to kick.

'I think so, sir.'

'He knows I do,' said Hearn.

Allen stopped stock-still.

'Very well then. It will disappoint you to see my good faith. Just the same, I swear.'

'Swear what?' Hearn, prostrated, was in a position to ask.

'To take only what lives are necessary,' Allen sang with a venomous sort of patience.

'To save as many lives as you're able,' Hearn insisted slowly.

'Damn it!' the captain roared, but composed himself. 'I swear by God,' he recited, 'to save as many lives as I am able. But just try lies on me, Hearn, and see what! By tonight it'll be martial law and I'll be martial as a pike if you've tried lies. Understand that?'

'Quite a homily for you, Captain Allen,' said Hearn, and fell asleep immediately.

Allen put his fist to his brow and shook his head. But within a short time, Hearn's eyes opened again. The fire, tended by Phelim and Byrne, had warmed away some of the drowned-blue from his eyes and lips.

'Once you have them confused in the dark, they'll be easy as cattle,' he muttered. '*And a little child shall lead them.*'

At this stage, Halloran and Byrne were cleared out of the hut and launched into the pleasant morning out-of-doors. In fifteen minutes, Allen came forth from the adjutant's hut bawling: 'Corporal!'

'Sir!'

'Run and tell the officer at the convict lines that any transport found outside his hut is to be arrested as a rebel.'

'Sir!'

The Marines were being marched back to hutments, their feet stumbled in the red dust. One squad of ten men had fallen out and was listening to an officer. They were to go off on a reconnaissance on this glorious day of sun. They leaned to the officer's words and their faces were tight and intelligent with pent energy.

'It is not expected that we'll find enemy scouts—' Halloran overheard from the officer. And yes, he thought, in an army such as the one in the forest, where you call the general by his first name and act together with your leaders only as an especial favour, scouts are hard to come by.

Byrne remained in the adjutant's hut, where Hearn kept calling, 'Send me back to the hospital!' Desperately allured by the fire and the three blankets, he made a few noises of rebuttal but went back to sleep in the end.

Before nine o'clock, Allen and his officers climbed the brick-brown hill behind Government House. Halloran stood by further down the slope with two Marines and watched the lieutenants nodding as Allen pointed to this or that hard hip of land. The generous morning continued to gild them all with an heroic light. Halloran himself gazed across the river, across mangroves to a tableland as blue and hazed and comfortable as chimney-smoke. He felt himself to be very much the centre of this world. With his hat off, he found that the tawny drench of light through his eye-lashes was made of gold rods all bearing on him. He was the focus, he was the central screw. Take him out and the hills would fall apart. He contained the world and was not contained by it.

Feeling so sanguine, he remembered with an unaccountable pleasure Hearn's prophecy. *And a little child shall lead them.*

The officers nodded for a last time and came down the hill.

18

'Give a man a swallow,' said, as a matter of form, a hoarse guard in the portico.

'Why don't you give this man a swallow of yours?' Halloran asked him, corking up his own near-empty canteen again. For hours, he'd been waiting outside Government House. The sun was still up, but the north wind had come on hard, and had night-damp on its breath. He was beginning to need the part of his spirits that Hearn had drunk, but he knew that in a furore you couldn't ask for such special adjustments as the topping up of a Marine's spirit ration.

He had been forgotten there. He knew nothing of the plan the officers had hurried about cherishing all day. He had no idea of the wherefore of the parties sent out in the afternoon to get in heaps of brushwood. All day people came and went with faces urgent from knowledge; of what, he didn't know.

After the sun went down, he waited there, stock-still, letting the night get at his cheek-bones. He didn't want to be there, but neither did he want to go to the kitchen to boil his beef. At last, his errant legs *took* him there, in the true sense of the word. There he was at the door, aimed nose-first into the rotten bonhomie of his brothers-in-arms. He dipped his raw soul into the place and followed bodily, thinking, *how long can I stand the sorrow of these evenings?* It was warm though; he would have liked to have been there alone.

He took a sliver of beef from his knapsack and a string from his pocket. He tied the string around the beef and lowered it into the cauldron on the hearth. Some men were making bread on the edges of the fire, and Halloran remained watching them, too close in to the fire, the heat thumbing his eyeballs. He got on his haunches and wriggled closer to the blaze and the pain. *Why?* he wondered.

I'm not what you call a man of affairs, he said blinking at the heart of the flames. *I'd shoot myself or drop the business of any mangey empire because of the pain of being homeless.* Occasionally he stood and fished his beef out, but each time it looked more indecent, and he would put it in the pot again. In the end, he knew that it would not improve no matter how strenuously it was boiled. He sat and ate it and finished his canteen. On the basis of being soldiers, the others made a riot of noise, but Halloran thought of how he'd fire so high above the rebels' heads that Goliath would be safe.

It dawned on him that chewing this meat had nothing more to do with his hunger than would brushing his hair. He wrapped it in cloth and packed it away still tethered with string. There was some comfort in tidying up his kit, in hiding away the few scraps on which life and the soul survived. He had some flour in his kit, and with it a pickled cut of bad meat like a lump of drowned man. Out of such scandalously silly things grew all the hanging gardens of the spirit. *They* kept poetry in the poet, vision in the artist, wisdom in the seer. He couldn't feel that this was a quaint truth, but an obscene one.

And then the sense of mortality swamped him fore and aft. Each man laughed in his byre of flesh—he wondered how—and the seconds went on hard, little rat's feet across the roofs, but no one heard except Halloran.

'Allen wants us,' said Byrne above him.

'Oh. Is Hearn well?'

'He's got a fever. He's talking about being guilty.'

'He's a fool,' said Halloran rising.

After the kitchen, it was only a quarter warm in the hallway. Allen bustled past once, saying, 'Wait here!'

'All very well for him,' said Halloran.

A light shone in the back parlour, and where he stood with Byrne, it was not altogether dark enough to excuse Halloran from listening to the boyo, he himself feeling far too exposed to go fingering his own red-raw despairs.

Byrne talked himself in circles. He felt that there was some bond of brotherhood between the two of them, and he couldn't quite lay his tongue on it.

But he tried. My heaven, he tried!

Amongst the rest, he said, 'I think the moment's coming, Halloran. You know what I mean. I mean the moment of my salvation that I've been talking about. It's since those fellers took to the forest that I've felt it. Those fellers in the forest and the men of the regiment, they're all my brothers, see. All sons of God though sinners. I tell you I'd die for any one of them here and now. Here and now in this hallway. In the valley of tears, as the saying goes.'

'Listen!' said Halloran, and Byrne jumped and listened, bug-eyed, for the moment of salvation.

The night had emptied of all human sounds. At the back of the house, a loose door or window yelped. The roof rustled as if the black-butt shingles had put their leaves back on.

'Everyone's gone,' Byrne whispered thunderously.

'Yes,' said Halloran. 'They might all be dead, you know. It happened to the Assyrian army once, so why shouldn't it happen to a few dingy Marines? The angel of death might have touched the lot of them, but missed us in this bit of a hall. And we'll have to stay here in the sting of death for the rest of our lives, because the moment we step out of the door, *he's got us!*'

Byrne dropped his musket.

'You're mad as a saint, Corporal,' he said, searching for it on the floor.

Some time later, Allen and the adjutant came from Howard's bedroom. Allen crooked his finger at Byrne and Halloran, and they both came to attention and marched up to him.

'I have a message for each of you to take down the hill. If you don't get it straight and give it straighter, God help you!'

He schooled both of them in the same message. It was quite unintelligible. He made them recite it five times each, which Halloran resented. When they had delivered it, they would follow

146

the hill behind Government House until they came to a natural terrace they both knew well by sight.

'The pass-word is Pindar,' said Allen, and then, needlessly pedagogic, went on, 'Pindar is an illustrious Greek poet of ancient times.'

Halloran thought of the time Allen had found some of his raw poetry in the back pages of the company orderly book. 'Oh,' he'd said, 'it knows nothing of Greece or Rome.'

Byrne was to take his message to the officer guarding the transport lines, Halloran to take his across the parade-ground, roaring 'Pindar!' when he came level with the adjutant's hut.

They left the house. Halloran, however tired, trotted away downhill to escape Byrne. The fall of the road tricked his legs into big lolloping strides. Had anyone ever made so much noise? he wondered. His breath was loud as a windmill, his cold knee-joints clicked and the knapsack thudded. He was afraid, and his jogging eyes saw confusions of shadows and stars, the way a person sees something hurled and coming fast. Beyond doubt, he thought, some fool will shoot me. His belly flesh felt so soft, and the tender walls of muscle arching up to his ribs so chancy. He reached the parade ground, and walked jaggedly from there on, cringing from the futile bullet.

'Pindar!' he sang.

But no one shot him.

And having given the message with a great show of regimentality, he became the man who had nowhere to go but away. There were two lights burning for the sake of form far to his left, but the shapes of things were hidden beneath the lines of the hill. If rebels were waiting for him in the groins of the dark and would kill him for his weapon, what an unexampled number of pike-thrusts it would take to kill off his despair and his homesickness for Ann.

He came to the terrace without a scratch, to find that he'd forgotten the pass-word. Yet it escaped of its own accord and shot away uphill.

'Come on up!' someone called, soft as a lover.

There were thirty men up there crouching on the terrace. With blankets over their shoulders, they looked like sleeping farm animals. Halloran found Allen, who said nothing but nodded him away to the line of Marines before them.

Here, beneath the big noise of the wind, there was indeed whispering and shivering and furtive nose-blowing. Byrne hissed to him, and he was too lonely not to slump down and be warmed by any human closeness.

'What are we doing?'

'We have to wait up here silent no matter what we see. On the order we creep down to the track there, form up and load. That's the lot of it. What can he do with the few of us he has?'

Halloran shivered.

'You pray for me, Phelim,' said Byrne, 'and I'll pray for you. We'll pray for each other.'

That's a bad bargain for me, thought Halloran nodding.

Five hours smothering in the cold black is a hard experience. He kept thinking that dawn was just over the hump of the next quarter of an hour. He scratched his cold hip, coffined in flesh whose last throes and consummate amazement might come in this very darkness, before he had once learnt not to be lonely. At the end of the five hours, his eyes were well up to seeing a line of men coming down the near side of the glen before him. He saw also that the darkness on the hillside across from the terrace trembled significantly, as if there were a similar line of men there. He heard soon after the pickets yell and fire and flee, as Allen had ordered them to. Then the army of transports went roaring into the town. One column moved across the parade-ground towards the armoury, the other ran towards the barracks from the west. These had a pitch and brushwood fire rise up between themselves and the barrack building and, black against the blaze, heard very close behind them the adjutant ordering his section of Marines to fire. At the same time, those storming the parade-ground saw forty Marines rise out of the ground no more than a spit away. The two volleys sounded almost simultaneously. On the terrace,

Allen was exalted.

Both squads were now onto the rebels with the bayonet. Allen's thirty went down into the glen, corking up the bottle. They stood in one rank and loaded and knelt. Behind them was Allen with his service-sword, and a young subaltern with a sergeant's halberd, which Halloran thought a savage statement of intention. Halloran himself was appalled by the choral thickness of the yelling in the town below him. It was an ambiguous noise, and whether it signified triumph or confusion or fight or dying, no one could have told. He heard one roar, without doubt the death-roar of some man, bull, singer, saint, brother of Christ and of George by the grace. All the rest was Chinese music.

'What about the oath?' asked Halloran softly of the tumult, it sounding such a prodigious slaughter.

But an amazing number of men had got clear of the shambles. They came stumbling up-hill now, and the first half dozen of them saw Allen's men even before the *Present arms!* was called. At this point, the affair, which had been at least speciously a battle, dropped its mask and became an execution. The air seemed full of breathing. Halloran heard the shocking resonance of the breath of the men in line with him; he was sure he could hear the huffing of a tall man who had decided to be killed and stood side-on to the line, hands on hips, getting his last breath back. And then Byrne muttered,

'Fire over their heads,' and *heads* collided with Allen's order.

Halloran shut his eyes and fired very high. More or less in his singing ear, Allen ordered the charge. There were a dozen transports on the ground. One sat up weeping into his hands. The young gentleman with the halberd leapt over him, arrant boyishness on the field of glory. Everyone followed except Byrne and Allen. Allen remained to clout Byrne across the head with his closed fist, and to whack him across the backside with his service-sword when he bent to find his canvas hat.

'You'll get me a felon's tripes!' Allen screamed. 'You'll get me an Irish!'

Phelim hadn't run many yards when he found himself face to

face with a small man in a rotting corduroy jacket. The man jumped back.

'Fall down!' roared Halloran.

'Please,' said the man.

'Fall down, you silly old bugger!'

Not far away, the young halberdier dug the broad, ceremonial point of his weapon into a yelping rebel. With some urgency, Phelim swung the stock of his Brown Bess against the small man's belly. The fellow lay down making extravagant sounds of agony. It was likely that in the dark he thought himself actually wounded; but Halloran bent over him and nudged his hip.

'Don't carry on,' he said, and started weeping. The fellow must have been in his fifties, and had come a long trip with hope to end up hawking here.

The matter was nearly over now, except that a little way uphill and across the narrow valley, low comedy was in progress, as Allen chased Byrne who chased a felon. It *was* like a play, like a bad play, the way Halloran heard it later and over and over from Byrne. Byrne sprinting, the Irishman falling on his knees constantly saying, 'In the name of God!' And like a farce figure was Allen, striking the turf with his sword three times, roaring 'Kill him!'

Byrne gaped because he knew he would bayonet this angular young man yelling, 'In the name of God!' There seemed no good reason to desist. Byrne saw him fully enough to know that he was brother-man and that the bayonet would viper him, craggy as he was, with a small head and curls close down on his forehead. When he rose and broke away again, Allen tried to get him by these curls and hack him with the sword. But he was away, and for some seconds, Allen and Byrne stood still, as if the matter was solved. Allen realized first that it hadn't been solved at all. He changed his sword to his left hand and struck Byrne across the jaw. The yellow blindness all but put an end to the affair for Byrne and for the Irishman, and even for Allen. Because Byrne made off uphill in quite frenzied style and found the boy trying to hide in under the limbs of a native fig fairly spacious and concealing in the dark. Byrne was thinking, *I'm only doing soldier's work*, yet he was bitter against himself, thinking also how if you're no good in the first place, you'll be no good in the melting pot, in the furnace, in the womb of wild events. He ducked under the branches and walked to the young fellow. 'Jesus, Mary, Joseph,' said the young fellow, louder and louder the closer Byrne got. The Holy Family couldn't do the job tonight, Byrne thought. They depended on him, and he had no mercy. The bayonet gestured softly at the boy, who turned his back and took it in the buttocks. He began a whining, too, that cringed on a rising note, back into the mousiest corners of sound. The iron went into his belly, high up because he was rolling; and he was so close to death then that, under the double dark of the fig, his breath sounded more like a felled bird than like true breath. Byrne was enthralled by the barbarous fluidity of his bayonet going in. He actually felt for the man's softer parts with his boot and spiked him a last time.

Down the hill, Halloran was thinking, *What about the oath?*

Hearn had been fed spirits all day, and had gratefully taken them. In the adjutant's hut now, he moaned to the furore but didn't wake.

16

'THANK God for the wind,' Ann said, as it blundered across the kitchen roof and covered their voices.

Halloran muttered, 'I wonder does the wind come from God?'

'Of course,' said Ann, happy and blood-warm, cherished, gratified and securer than the stars.

Halloran felt shivery behind the ears, not wanting to insult God by thinking he was behind the wind if he wasn't; not wanting to insult him by thinking he was as remote as Hearn's God if he was close; not wanting to insult him by thinking that a Corporal of Marines could insult him; not wanting to insult him.

'I'll just do my work from now on,' he said. He was talking about the business at the Crescent again. 'The buggers will be lucky to get that much from me. God is not mocked.'

He felt shivery again.

Ann was the remedy. Some of her hair lay over the corner of his mouth, tasting clean and fresh as if she'd washed it for his home-coming. It had a smell of bounty, like the smell of grain.

'I hope I didn't put you in any sort of danger, sidling in here.'

'Mrs Blythe sleeps like a horse.'

'You brew some marvellous liquor,' he said, speaking figuratively and kissing her. He could tell from the way she wriggled her shoulders that she understood him. 'I've got no compunction. I'm not at all sorry I came.'

'No one's asking you to be.'

The whole kitchen was grating like a ship under sail. It was a miraculous night to be together.

'After all else,' she added pertly, 'we're able to have a talk.'

Halloran chuckled lowly like a satyr. She had restored him so fully that he couldn't help but comment, with some attempt at seeming flippant, 'You seem to believe now that you're my consecrated bride.'

She punched him between the legs.

'You always have to be the scholar, Halloran, the divine. Is it too hard for a sharp mind to lie down man with his wife and enjoy what crowds of dungy farmers can enjoy?'

He slapped her buttocks. He was aware of the correctness of her hips and the virgin flatness of her belly, which lay as a bowl between them.

'It could only happen to a fool like Byrne,' she said.

'What could?'

'That trouble with Allen. It could only happen to Byrne. And then, trying to drown himself.'

'I don't think he did try.'

On the journey back from the Crescent, Byrne had sat in silence, having found, for an hour or two, the flat dignity of despair. In one of the wider stretches of the river, he had thrown a fit and jumped into the water. Yet he had seemed grateful for the oar they offered him, and crawled out of the river with great resignation.

Ann elucidated.

'When you're dealing with a booby, you lose your temper like a booby. Allen ends in being as big a bumpkin as Byrne. It wouldn't have happened if he'd had a nobody's fool like you to deal with.'

'A nobody's fool like me, love, is too full up of worldly wisdom to call out in the first place as Byrne did. A nobody's fool like me goes to hell for doing nothing.'

He was not only grateful to her for seeing the matter so clearly. He was full of wonder.

'Don't talk to me about hell on a night like this,' she said.

The wind swelled until it roared like flood-waters.

'Oh, be ye lifted up, ye eternal gates!' he said.

She turned half side-on to him. Noses and foreheads were a problem to lovers, and your mattress-side arm was always going numb. Her right thigh settled into the warmth of his belly. She asked him not to die. It was jealousy of death, she said, that made her sound grudging sometimes.

'Before the roof falls in,' she said, 'and if we have to go to hell, let us first get in a bit of the gentle art.'

He laughed at her amazing sensuousness.

But within thirty seconds, she was asleep. He uncovered the hair from her ear, and kissed the soft rim.

At the end of May, the meat ration was cut to two pounds. For the first time, Halloran saw starvation as feasible for Ann, who had little fat to withstand a famine.

At this time, Hearn was much talked about throughout the town. He had survived, and had been praised and pardoned, and had resented the survival and the praise, and cursed the pardon. For his safety he was kept in the Marine infirmary, and Halloran was wary of seeing him. But Byrne had spoken to him. Byrne himself had a charge pending against him of attempted suicide, for which he could be adequately chastened but still remain on the company's strength. So that his mutiny in the field was forgotten by all but Byrne himself and Captain Allen. He knew that he was going to be punished, and now that he was damned, had lost the final remedy of being able to identify his punishment with that of the suffering Christ.

The May mornings were like promises, impossible to be kept on five ounces of meat. At seven o'clock the light would be full and level, barred like a tiger with the long shadows of trees. On such a morning, Halloran was called to the Judge-Advocate's, Major Sabian's place, where the roses had begun to bud. Major Sabian sat in the front parlour, side-on to the door, with meaty arms oppressing a very feminine French writing-table.

Halloran saluted.

'Take a seat, Corporal!'

Sabian dipped his pen and wrote across the top of a page.

'Can you spell me your name?'

Halloran spelt it.

'That's a pleasant change for an Irish,' said Sabian, as if all Irishmen had had a chance of going to a grammar school and had wilfully neglected it.

'I believe you're of the Papist persuasion, Corporal?'

Halloran felt somehow that he was safe to play the yokel.

'There was no persuasion about it, sir. I was born that way.'

'No need to explain terms to me, Corporal. You are a Papist. Very well. What do you think of oaths taken in my court upon the Bible? Would you consider yourself free to break an oath taken in a Protestant court?'

Thinking *damn oaths*, Halloran said, devious as a Jesuit, 'I would be bound to tell the truth in your court, sir.'

It sounded like rugged virtue though, and Sabian was gratified. Halloran cringed to see the Major swell with approval for his rustic innocence.

'I ask all this because you are delicately placed as regards this charge of attempted suicide against Private Byrne. The charge is brought by Captain Allen, you see. I could understand your wondering what to say in such a case. You were in the boat. Could you tell from what he did that he meant to drown himself?'

'He was very quiet, and then he took a fit and fell overboard.'

Sabian kept his pen poised stagily over the sheet of paper.

'He fell overboard? He didn't throw himself?'

'I couldn't tell if he fell or threw himself, sir.'

Sabian was pleased.

'Did he stand up before he threw himself?'

'He just toppled sideways, sir.'

Not that Byrne ever did a thing any other way than sideways.

'You see, Halloran, you couldn't very well swear that Byrne threw himself over the side.'

'I wouldn't know whether he did or not, sir,' said Halloran, entering into the game.

'You've answered me with great forthrightness, Corporal,' said the Major. He coughed throatily into a handkerchief, and took the interest in the result which people over forty seem to think themselves entitled to. Then he packed the thing away up his sleeve and looked with a sort of flemmy speculativeness at the rafters and the black tails of the shingles.

Halloran wondered why such demigods as Sabian and Allen bothered to envy each other under such lonely stars and on a handful of daily meat.

'Captain Allen trusts you, Halloran?'

'Not much, sir.'

'Oh!'

Major Sabian was not so pleased.

'He's a man very much to himself, sir,' Halloran explained.

'Yes. He always has been. Dismissed!'

Out in the sunlight, Halloran felt weak as he saw that he'd come out of no small danger indoors.

One night, Hearn, while still weak, walked away from the infirmary to die in the forest. He followed the very track which Marines with assignations in the town often took at night. He had become humbler since his flogging, and he didn't offer his death as anything of importance to God. He kept a large stake in it himself, in this death which was redemptive of nothing. Against the mercy of the system, it was the only protest that was within his making.

The next day, after a cursory search of the fringes of the town, the administration wrote him off. Amongst the larger fish that Government House had that day to fry was that when the sun came up, it showed an American whaler in the bay. This was a prodigy, a manifestation, and made His Excellency nervous. The Captain was allowed ashore, but a heavy Marine guard lined Government Wharf in silence above the whale-boat and its crew —guarding against a word, any incendiary, radical, American word. The men at the battery could be seen at action stations. They had all come a long way, Marines and whalers, to keep silence with each other in a remote haven.

Late in the morning, back came the Captain, sullen in the

company of His Excellency and Rowley. He had been told that his crew were not to be allowed to land, and that no matter how much bad food his victuallers had sold him, he would not be able to buy stores from the colony, not even with cash, let alone promissory notes.

At midday, the American sailed out. He did not dip his flag and, with the peril over, His Excellency did not particularly resent it.

20

Two or three days later, in the afternoon, Halloran was coming back from Major Sabian's orderly office with Allen's orderly book, when he was vigorously waylaid by Byrne. Byrne was a great elbow-clutcher when in full flight, as he seemed to be now for the first time since Captain Allen's triumph. He rose from the ditch by Government Farm, which had been sown with wheat at the beginning of May. He gave two tight little jerks of his left thumb (doing its best to be wary) at his left shoulder.

'I have that Hearn feller over there, in the trees,' he said. There was a wooded slope behind and to one side of the farm. 'He wants to see the both of us together. He has some news. I was with him when I saw you go by with the orderly book earlier. I've been waiting for you all that time, without a peep.'

He marvelled at himself.

Halloran groaned. He'd been sick in the morning and his bowels were still queered. And now portentous Hearn was up there in the timber.

'I'll go with you and help you get him back to the infirmary,' said Halloran neutrally.

'To the infirmary? He has news, Halloran, news foretold in the Bible and all the old books. You wouldn't take him back. I'd kill you with my own hands, much as I love you.'

'You would?'

'I'd have a try, darling Corporal. What do you owe to *them* any more,' said Byrne indicating the valley, 'that you'd want to give him up to them?'

'You're on duty at the shipyards tonight, Private Byrne?'

'That's right.'

'I'll meet you here at seven. I won't tell anyone, but I mean to bring him back to the infirmary. Tell him that much. Tell him I won't listen to his lies and schemes.'

'It's not a lie and it may be a scheme,' said Byrne quietly, 'but if it is, it's God's scheme.'

'Yes,' Halloran said, 'I can imagine the Almighty dodging up and down this part of the world, grinding his axe with a Wicklow Protestant and gallant Terry Byrne.'

In fact, he was terrified that there might be something on the divine agenda to cut straight across the cramped sphere of tenderness where he and Ann lived, lasting the distance. He detested prophets, prophets were a great danger. This prophet had had two raw nights to succumb to, but here he was, voluble with prophecy, muttering omens in the bushes.

They don't feed you enough to take these shocks, Halloran told himself, getting on his way. His hand was very tight and spinsterish around Captain Allen's orderly book.

'Happy shall he be,' Byrne intoned, and the trees waved their arms like ecstatics, and Halloran shivered. There was a phoenix nest of moon in a large tree straight ahead of him, beyond the clutter of boulders. Amidst the wind, he heard a voice wheezing.

'That taketh and dasheth thy little ones against the stones.'

Trust, thought Halloran, a man barely able to breathe to choose a watch-word long as your arm. There was Hearn, wrapped in blankets, without a fire, in a cold crevice.

'I'll take you back to the infirmary,' called Halloran. 'We'll say you wandered off in a fever.'

'Fever nothing!' said Byrne. 'Listen to his news.'

'Damn his news! I have news for him. The two of us are risking our hides moping round the forest with him.'

Hearn coughed tightly in his crevice. He had worked himself to his feet, and waited for them, too oracular for a squabble.

'Talk up then, Hearn. Don't stand there like a phantom with quinsy. Come on, take my poor damned breath away!'

The uncertain shadow that Hearn was, wavered; the man was

only a presence, a rustle of breathing. He had no outline. He made the night seem thick with portents.

'Halloran,' he began by sighing, 'don't be afraid.'

'I'm not afraid.'

'I don't mean afraid of the dark or death. First and foremost, I mean don't be afraid of me.'

'I said I wasn't afraid.'

There came a pause long enough for Hearn to shrug and look as ironic as he might allow himself. Probably he did neither. There was no chance of telling in the dark. But he could be heard handling something paper that crackled as much as the treasure-maps of boyhood or the wicked astrologies of old women. Halloran thought with a sort of hopeful spleen that it might be something just as silly.

'Read this,' said Hearn.

'In this dark? What is it?'

'It's a booklet from Boston in what was the colony of Massachusetts. In North America. It's written by an American. But not any American. One of the signers of the American constitution, no less. It tells of what has come to pass in France.'

Now, a substantial shadow breathing hard, he pressed the pamphlet, crisp and lethal, into Halloran's hands, and though Halloran gave it back after merely feeling it all over, it had somehow added its authority to the scene.

'Well, what has *come to pass* in France?'

In Halloran's mouth the premonitory phrase got short respect.

'You've told me,' Hearn said, 'that you were put into prison for being at a land committee meeting. Did you ever think there'd come a world in which you could meet to talk about land ownership if you wanted? Meet with the men you wished to meet with, speak and act your mind as you've never spoken it or acted it in this town or any town you've ever lived in?'

'No,' said Halloran, sardonic as he could manage on the spot, 'you're talking about this side of paradise, I suppose?'

Hearn coughed, a chain of coughs which stopped on an instant. And in the very *next* instant,

'Yes,' he said, 'did you never foresee a world in which men would speak and act their *minds* and not their *fears*? Because they could freely say and freely do. And because whatever they freely said or did would be judged as good or bad under one law, the same for every man.'

'I never foresaw any such world. Tell me about France, anyhow.'

But it was possible to see Hearn's white hand extended, patting the dark air, as people do who are trying to say, 'Let me get my breath back!'

'Don't rush yourself,' said Halloran, quite kindly.

In fact, Hearn was able to begin almost at once.

'The French nation has forced its king to accept a parliament which is in full charge of affairs,' he said, a little declamatorily. 'To get the story over quickly, they've made a law out of the rights of man, of every man. Notice, a *law!*'

'I see,' said Halloran, casually enough to kill most fervours.

'The courts of Europe are boiling with the news. Or quaking, better still. It's the common people who are boiling. They smell a new world coming. A new order.'

Halloran grunted. He had learnt when young, in Wexford and elsewhere, to be off-handed towards seers, to greet the apocalypse with a shrug. He did feel that the rights of man being made law should mean much to him. But he had had such success convincing himself that Ann and he were mirrors to each other, imposing each other's image on the other, that whatever obtruded itself between them, even a new age, was, like anything caught between mirrors, shown up as suspect and illusory.

'It's likely, Halloran, very likely that God who never spoke for kings and captains has begun to speak for His people and won't cease till He has said His fill. *Come and gather yourselves together unto the supper of the great God. That you may eat the flesh of kings, the flesh of captains, and the flesh of mighty men.'*

'And here's,' said Terry Byrne, after being quiet and temperate for so long, 'one poor beggar who's going to get a good mouthful of that dinner, who s going to eat deep of that supper, who's going to eat up some captains he's got in mind until there's nothing but arse left.'

'How do you know this?' Halloran asked Hearn, who was so full of profound hope. 'Where did you get that book?'

'Mm,' said Hearn.

'You couldn't have met that whaler.'

'What whaler is that?' Hearn asked.

'A whaler that was here Thursday and warned off from here. And a good thing too.'

'Why a good thing?'

Halloran said nothing.

'You see now what I mean by speaking your fears,' said Hearn at last.

Halloran detested him for being so unshakably decretal.

'Why don't you tell me in one gulp?' he suggested. 'Why don't you tell me straight? No texts, not one. Just tell me friend to friend, if you can.'

Yet Hearn wouldn't of course, until there had been another mantic pause. During which, Halloran had to go on shivering. He stamped the ground.

'My God, it's easy for you to stand here all damned night getting cold. You've made up your mind to die. I don't happen to be in that same happy position.'

'That's true,' said Hearn. 'That's very true. My mind *was* made up to die. I was reconciled to death, as they say.'

'And you're not reconciled any longer?'

'No.'

He told them that he had walked all that Wednesday night, reconciled to death, trying to travel far enough from the town to be assured of dying by himself and in peace.

Byrne laughed.

'I was not joking in fact, brother Byrne,' Hearn said gently.

He travelled on the heights behind the beaches. This was the easiest way. He felt very little discomfort, he said, except thirst and some shortness of breath. At first light though, he had a turn. He felt that he was falling out of his own body. A second later, so it seemed, he woke to find himself installed once more between and behind his eyes. He was still on the ridge, trudging, but the sun was high in the corner of his eye. This was the choice he had: had hours passed while he walked on asleep, or was the high sun unreal? He felt so sodden that he voted for the sun being unreal and, therefore, for the daylight and the ocean and his own progress and pain being likewise unreal.

In this state, he came to a small pocket of water in the rock and was happy to come to it. It gave strength to the vote he had taken of himself, in so far as an impossible spider, evilly coloured in black and yellow and blue, had spun a web across it. He did not fear the spider, but scooped the yellow scum from the water and drank. The water was so cool that it gave him doubt. He fell asleep. When he woke and got on his way, he had a ship in the corner of his right eye, and the sun had gone over to his left. The ship put the whole affair past belief. In the end, he went downhill and fell down on a sand-spit, a sheltered place, no waves on the shore. He did not care if the tide covered him.

'*And in those days*,' he said, regardless of Halloran's warning against texts, '*men shall seek death and not find it—*'

'He thinks he's prefigured now,' Halloran muttered.

'Once I would have thought it, the same as you do now.'

'Me?'

'You think you're prefigured. You think you're prefigured to long and easy love.'

'Don't talk rubbish,' said Halloran.

'All I know is that being nothing wrapped up in flesh, still I couldn't die. Even for a place like this, even for men like us, there is a plan.'

Ah. That took Halloran's breath. There *is* a plan, he thought in terror, Hearn having said it with such mortal certainty. There is a plan. Outside of us, not having regard for us, never to be distracted. It hovered over the cold forests. Its claws were aimed at him, at his soft sides.

'While I was asleep there,' Hearn went on, unaware of having scored, 'the ship, the whaler, came into that bay, the very ship that I thought was part of my sickness. Anyhow, it came sailing up out of my sickness and saw me without delay. They were very Christian to me, as it turned out. I ate and slept well there two nights and a day. And I spoke with the captain.'

'Now that you're back, come down to the town with me,' said Halloran. 'Please.' He was polite. Awareness of the plan had taken all the starch out of him.

'Not the town, Halloran. I'm going to France.'

'By whaler?'

'Yes.'

'You'll have more chance walking. He'll sell you to the Fiji natives. He'll give you to them without cost. Some little black heathen will play peek-a-boo with your hip-bone.'

Hearn considered this.

'I can't imagine it,' he said. 'Of course, I have to find my own way from America.'

'He'll push you overboard before New Zealand.'

'He's lost too many crew.'

'Fine crew you'd make! Whales wouldn't wait for you to get your breath, you know. And you don't know whether this miracle of a parliament is still in charge of things.'

'That is one of the small doubts that are met with in all human affairs,' said Hearn.

'Oh,' Halloran said, 'just one of the small ones.'

'The men on the whaler think that all of Europe will become a republic. The parliament will still be there. It's the old that's under threat, not the new.'

Halloran struck his pockets to show they didn't jingle.

'No money. I'm sorry. You'll have to pay your own passage.'

Laughter came as a stranger into their debate. Byrne and Halloran looked up and saw that, yes, it was Hearn's unexpected laughter.

'You wish it was a money matter, don't you? In fact, the captain needs stores. I promised him stores.'

Halloran merely shook his head. Disbelief took such an effort of expression and gesture, most of it wasted in the dark. He knew, besides, that people had been voicing for centuries their rank disbelief in this and that mad, prophetic scheme, without being saved from one of them.

'Why not promise him Dublin Castle?' he asked.

'Luckily he didn't want Dublin Castle.'

'You get hanged just as dead for stores.'

'Just as dead either way. I want you to help me, Halloran.'

Now it's time to go, Halloran thought. He could actually feel his flanks itching as if to turn away.

'Even if it wasn't mad,' he said, 'I still couldn't help you.'

'Your oath?'

'Yes.'

'But remember how they gave us that oath?' Byrne asked suddenly, sounding rational enough to terrify anyone who knew him of old. 'The oath rushed through by a sergeant and then they lock you in the gunner's mess, just before they go ashore to get drunk on the bounty of the free recruits. What sort of oath is that?'

'I can tell who's been talking to you,' Halloran told him.

'I have a vision,' said Hearn, his irony so tight-reined that you hardly recognized it for irony at all, 'of God hanging on every gasp of that groggy sergeant's breath, the unknown God standing by to be bound by what a sergeant says in between drinks on the deck of a little ship in Wexford Bay.'

'Take no notice, Terry Byrne,' advised Halloran. 'He's after your soul.'

But some distance away, a bough creaked and fell down the tall night, affirming by its purposelessness the large purpose that lies over all things.

'I'm within a spit of thirty,' Byrne said, 'and I have to get started on my atoning.'

'You silly bugger!'

'There's something to atone for, surely,' Hearn claimed. 'In the three of us. You, for example, stood in line at the Crescent.'

'I have an oath to stand in line.'

Hearn waited, to let the words set in the cold air.

'You have an oath,' he said at last. 'Be honest now. You didn't stand in line because of your oath.'

Halloran wanted to lie of course, but how useless it was in the face of the large purpose.

'I'm thinking of my oath now.'

'Then let's pretend your oath might be one God takes an interest in.'

Hearn *did* pretend it. Someone had schooled him in the infamy of kings and parliaments. He spoke of Henry Tudor, who took an oath to King Richard and broke it to return and put a sword into Richard's bowels and pick the crown up out of a bramble bush. How good were the oaths men then made to Henry?

Collecting his breath, he went on to create a riotous picture of oath-taking and -breaking out of the odd-ends of history—King James and his perfidious in-law, the coming of the Germans, the arrogance of the Crown towards the oaths men made to join honourable societies and strive for honourable ends.

'A stew of bad faith,' he said finally, 'and in the middle of it, Corporal Phelim Halloran still believes himself bound.'

While Hearn was being thus fluent with oaths as a species, Halloran reproached himself for being badly prepared to stand by his. Since the day he had met Hearn for the first time, he had known that he would one day need to have ideas on the matter, something more than an emotion of perverse loyalty. He had tried so strenuously to be safely and rationally bound by his oath's reality as a man is bound by the reality of the earth on which he stands.

As things were, he could no nothing but argue meanly.

'Terry Byrne, do you really want to be strangled up high bogging yourself in front of multitudes? I don't believe it.'

Byrne said nothing. Hearn kept a long damning silence.

'Come on, Terry, you get his legs and I'll get his arms and we'll cart him back to the town with us.'

'Not me,' Byrne said. 'I know he's right.'

'You're oak right through, aren't you, Terry? Head, heart, belly of oak. A hero of your race.'

'I know he's right. That's all.'

Now the prophet was beginning to be in need of his rest. His wheezy breath could be heard, biding their argument.

'Halloran,' he said when he was ready, 'say you sell your pig to a man for five bags of barley, which he'll pay you at harvest. Harvest comes and he doesn't pay. Can you take back your pig?'

It would be an indignity to answer. Halloran didn't.

'Well, can you?' eager Terry Byrne asked for the winded seer.

'My mind keeps choking on this stores business,' said Halloran.

Byrne called, 'Back to the pig!'

'Damn the pig!'

'You give your oath to a king, but the king is unjust to you,' Hearn said. 'Can you take your oath back?'

'No.'

'Even though the king swore at his crowning to rule with justice?'

'That's his affair.'

'You know that the king, *your* king, swore to keep faith even with us?'

'I had a notion.'

'This is all the French and Americans have said. If you can take your pig back from an unjust man, you can take your oath back from an unjust king. Now, do you think the French and Americans are all damned for this opinion?'

There was no doubt that they were not all damned. On the other hand, Halloran felt safe in that getting stores was the final impossibility.

'And you're going to work through Byrne,' he said. 'He can't be trusted. You're a fool.'

Byrne coughed. His better side was that he couldn't bear grudges and that deep-dyed insults embarrassed him. When seen against Halloran as Halloran was at that moment, he seemed a man of considerable dignity.

'We're all leaky boats,' Hearn said. 'In any case, Terry doesn't worry you. Because you're what is known as a man of faith. That means that you know peace with your Ann isn't had by luck. It's earned. It's earned by Halloran joining himself to some divine purpose. A divine purpose uses yourself, Byrne and me with equal ease. Now there *is* a purpose working in us. Against all odds, it has brought the three of us together here in the dark.'

Halloran raised his arms and stiffened them to show his freedom.

'No damned purpose has its hands on me. If it has, it can get them off again.'

For a second time, Hearn laughed.

'I don't think it hears you,' he said.

And they held, the three of them, a listening silence to see if Hearn were right. Halloran wanted to go. The ring of cold around his heart and the nag of events had him squirming.

'I can't promise I won't give you up,' he told Hearn. 'Not for a price either, I'd like to do it for nothing.'

'Very well,' Hearn said. 'You could tell them I intend taking perhaps three hundred pounds of beef and two hundred and eighty of flour . . .'

'I don't want to hear any of that.'

'Eighty-four gallons of rice, eighty-four of pease. Four firkins of cheese.'

Halloran insisted, 'I'll tell them, don't you worry. I'll tell them.'

'He will,' Byrne said, having become sober and responsible to the point of provocation.

'I have means to get inside the warehouse,' Hearn admitted, 'and I know the place on the inside, having worked there.'

'Not wise, Mr Hearn,' Terry kept counselling. 'Not wise.'

But the man had not finished burdening Halloran yet.

'Taking the food by night, I'll load it into a cutter and take it to a place within the bay where a boat from the whaler can take it and myself on.'

'You'd sink your cutter for one thing,' Halloran said like a true Marine. Which he wasn't.

'It *would* be well-laden.'

'It would be twenty fathoms well-laden, that's how well-laden.'

'It can be done.'

'I'm sure. You've got a key, you said.'

Somebody's joints cracked knowingly. Hearn's or Terry's.

'You could say we had,' said Hearn.

'I don't want to know what I can say. Have you got a key?'

'We can get one. We know a man who has one,' said Byrne.

'There was a time when Byrne and myself considered taking a cutter and stores and sailing to the East Indies. Only a week ago we were thinking of it.'

'Why not?' Halloran said. He sounded feverish with sarcasm.

'On the other hand,' Hearn told him, 'it can easily be done, this whole thing. I promise you that much.'

'Whether it's easy has nothing to do with it.'

'I see.'

'I'll be back in the morning. Perhaps with an armed guard.'

'You'll find me in this same place.'

'You're sure of yourself, aren't you?'

'I'm sure of the purpose working in us.'

'Damn you.'

They said goodnight. Halloran walked away, and lost his patience with the wind palpable in his eye-sockets and in the back of his jaws as a pain. He heard Hearn speak but pretended not to, having heard enough already.

'Hoy, Phelim,' called Byrne like a friend, and shamed him into turning.

'Yes?'

He even walked back part of the way.

'Everything has worked together in a way that will shock you,' Hearn said. 'People who tell you that God is with them are an abomination. But it's very likely that the true God is with us.'

'If that's so, why isn't there a sign?'

'It would only fit in with the pattern if there were. I wouldn't be the man to say an adulterous generation required a sign.'

'You wouldn't want to be the man,' Halloran said, hated his own bluster and turned back into the wind. He felt very like a man who has signed an august contract, and the keeping of it is utterly beyond him.

2 1

Some optimism of the blood had kept Ann awake half the night. In the small hours, she felt strong and became feverish with expectations of the future. She woke before dawn in a very still morning of tonic cold. No sound came from indoors where Mr and Mrs Blythe would not rise, each from his own unbridal bed, till seven or later. The roof creaked with soft and sudden sleeping noises this morning, noises quite unbidden, quite unintended. She lay and enjoyed the sting of her morning strength untouched in her belly and shoulders and legs. To live on, she thought, it is needed only for a person to keep within her daily strength. It was one of those simple pre-dawn truths which by eight o'clock become not so much untrue as wholly beside the point.

Once she had decided to be canny with strength, she rose to squander some. She took her chamber-pot with its baize cover and walked slowly out of doors. The wet trees had just stopped shivering and looked a little like exiles themselves. The earth was wet and grey and was, surprisingly, tamed. Down her throat went the smooth pink of cock-crow air in mouthfuls. The sleek cold rushed up her nose, nettled her brain until it threatened to crack into chilblains along the bottom. Of course, she found herself capable of believing that she would walk out one morning mistress of her own home. She would see sleeping cattle and listen to the sound of stirring house and husband.

Fifty yards into the morning, however, and already she wished she had slept more. The presentiments of a sweet destiny had turned tight and indigestive at the back of the throat and belly. She went on some way, emptied the pot, seeing herself for what she was, a skinny girl tipping out her slops. Coming back to the kitchen, she stopped at a cassia tree. It had hard winter pods that had taken her interest. She put down the pot and picked a pod and began to strip its shell. There was a man in a military coat lying in the grass only four yards or so away. Nearly flat out, he had his sideways eyes on her and breathed heavily.

'Don't call out!' he said to her. 'It's Terry Byrne, but please don't call out!' And then, as if it went to prove his good faith, 'I rushed down here fast as I could soon as they changed the guard.'

Terry Byrne it was, even though all the saggy skin on the earthward side of his face made him look uneven and dangerous.

'What is it, Terry?'

'It's about Halloran. It's about Halloran's safety.'

'Is it?'

'If you just step into the woods about a hundred yards to the other side of that hut up there, there's a feller wants to talk to you about it.'

'I'm sure.'

'Ann, it's a man in his forties.'

'I see. Tell him to come down here.'

'He can't.'

'Why?'

Byrne sighed, lifting his head straight to do it.

'Have you ever heard of Robert Hearn?'

She squinted or even winced.

'He was here once—six weeks ago. Doing paper-work for Mr Blythe.'

'Halloran's been helping him.'

'I don't believe that.'

'Just this week. Before God . . .'

The urgency of the matter had him on his knees.

'Lie down, Terry!' she told him.

He flattened himself back into the grass.

'I'll go straight on home from here, you won't see me again today,' he said, 'but you've got to talk to this feller.'

'Is it like the Crescent?' she asked him savagely. 'Are you

lining me up for some sort of steel in the belly?'

She couldn't see his eyes amongst the yellow spikes of grass. He must have been very cold there, hiding his face against the lean earth.

'No,' he said.

'Go home now,' she told him as tenderly as she could afford.

But they couldn't move off together, and she had to leave him behind her in the grass, his plan being that he'd battle upright after perhaps five minutes, as if he'd been felled hours before and in that very spot by drink or sickness.

So she felt vulnerable at the back and approached the woods sideways, with pauses, having no workable idea of how much was a hundred yards.

'You'll have to find me,' she muttered, and stepped into the forest, all of whose tongues were furred with frost soon to melt to a dribbling olive.

'Hallo,' she said conversationally. She walked circumspectly, not wanting to find him with a start. Once or twice she looked over her shoulder. What she expected to see was that she had come maze-deep into the trees. Yet both times the open spaces showed luminously only a short dash behind her.

'Hallo!' she said again.

'Here,' the man said.

She had not seen him stepping out of any shadow. He was revealed whole to her in a long cowled smock made of seal-skin. He tried to produce a smile of buoyant leniency, of the type that priests use who pretend they know of the special agonies of being a woman. It was from the plentiful grey coils of his hair, bard's, scholar's hair, avuncular, that she took most of her hope.

'Do you remember me?' he asked. 'I did some work once at Mr Blythe's.'

'Everybody expects you to be dead.'

'I hope I haven't disappointed you.'

He grinned. He couldn't deal easily with women. Mrs Hearn, whoever she was, must have felt she was living with a monument.

'I think you have,' she told him. 'What's this about Halloran?'

'You know that strong box the Blythes have? It's usually in the front parlour. It's iron, it has brass bands across its top and leather-work on the front.'

'I can't remember it.'

'Well,' he said. 'Anyhow, its twin is in the warehouse. The same key opens both of them, the one you must have seen and the one in the store.'

'I wouldn't know.'

'It's the truth. I wouldn't mislead you. I need an imprint of the key.'

'Not from me,' she said. 'How much do you need it?'

'Halloran and myself want something out of that box. We have reasons.'

Though, across the valley in the hutments, Halloran had not been told of them yet. For Halloran needed to believe that the plan had dropped whole and mandatory from heaven, that it was woven all of a piece. He could not be permitted to see the thing customarily put together out of oddments.

'Halloran didn't tell me.'

'You don't see him often. In any case, he wants to save you anguish.'

A sudden wind alighted in the tree-tops and shook beads of frost all over Hearn's unaware shoulders.

'You have to understand this,' he said, leniency going. 'We have an enterprise on hand. There's no danger. We are able to get inside the store and out without leaving a trace. With the key to the strong-box, all will be by stealth. Again, not a sign left behind us. The other course, not having a key and breaking the lock, that *is* dangerous. I told Terry Byrne to say that I wanted to speak of Halloran's safety. It is just that. Halloran's safety.'

He coughed.

'Let me show you how to take an imprint in soap.'

'Is Terry Byrne in the *enterprise* too?'

'He's my messenger.'

'Sweet heaven!' she laughed.

'Terry doesn't know about the strong-box. No one does, except the two of us. Certainly not Byrne. Certainly not Halloran. Though for different reasons.'

Again she laughed. 'Byrne,' she said.

'Why laugh?' he asked her. 'We are all leaky boats. But this is a matter of conscience with Halloran and Byrne and myself alone. A matter of conscience and atonement. You must have the imprint this evening if a key is to be made in time.'

She stood in silence and at her ease for some seconds. Rods of light shone in the wet tree-tops, saying, 'Nearly half-past six.'

'You made a mistake telling me, Mr Hearn. You don't have me. After I see Halloran, you won't have him either.'

He began to smile at her, not with an assumed smile as before. It was so evenly triumphant and so long that Ann became afraid, worse than when she had first entered the forest.

'If you wanted to put him on the rack,' he explained, 'or pull him into three pieces, if that's your purpose, then of course you'll tell him all about what I've asked. But before you *do* tell him everything, say that you've seen me. Pretend you got a glimpse of me by accident, but that you're sure it was the notorious Hearn. Ask him what you should do. Judge by his answer whether you should give me what I'm after. But, as I say, don't tell him that I asked you for it. He'd rather break the lid off the thing than have you as a part to the plan. That is, he'd rather be caught.'

He spoke to her quickly, dominantly, presuming that she had nothing cogent to put into the dialogue.

'Suppose that you tell him how I've asked you for the imprint. What does he do then? If he takes no more part with us, he has already conspired. He's already guilty, he's in as much danger as we are. What does he do then? Does he go to those in power and kill Byrne and myself? Of course not. Does he merely keep his silence, having stood out of an enterprise of conscience and atonement? And does he let the others be caught for lack of him? Does that sound like him?'

She said, 'I don't know. We seem to be talking about a different man.'

But he cleared this idea away with the heel of his hand.

'He'll stay with the enterprise, you know he will. How much of the lover's talk between the two of you has been made up of Ewers and Quinn and the slaughter at the Crescent?'

She wouldn't say.

'Begin by telling him you've had a glimpse of me,' he said again, 'that you were sure it was me. And then judge.'

And he went through his whole argument again, more gradually, schooling her in the alternatives and saying in the end that there was no choice for her.

She said, 'There's always a choice.'

'If there is, how did you end in this town?' he asked her, off-handedly spiteful, like the very sunlight which put a false youth on his briary hair. 'Let me tell you how an imprint is taken.'

22

THE north wind set in later in the morning. Halloran woke with a light fever and a cough, but had no time to indulge them. He came to Byrne's hut just in time to see the boyo, dressed for church-parade, vanishing downhill through the Marine hutments. Halloran stumbled after him. There was a terrible lack of harmony between the wide blue of the bay and the fig-trees exercising in the wind on one side, and on the other, his own undigested fear and shallow breathing and spongey ankles.

Byrne heard the scrabbling of feet on the shaley hillside, recognized Halloran and waited for him in peace. And peace was rare in Byrne.

'You have to take me to Hearn.'

'Yes.' Byrne frowned in an uncharacteristic way, like a man of affairs. 'Yes. I've been looking for you. There's so much to get done.'

'Never mind that. Take me to him.'

'You're in a rush. Anger and all.'

'Anger? I'll say anger!'

'Why?'

'Brother Hearn's lying, that's why. I'll give him *brother!*'

'You might give him away too.'

'Never mind. Take me just the same.'

Closing his eyes gently, Byrne stood for a while with his mouth open in thought, intelligently poised on a sentence. But he grunted down whatever it was he had intended to say and led Halloran away. From the back, he did look depressingly like a new man. He walked as if he were illustrating what Hearn had said, 'There is a purpose working in us.'

It was a mild day to the eyes although the wind was up. Winter had somehow softened the lines of the forest which still seemed a place of self-contained and ancient ease. Halloran felt free since it made no claims on him, not soliciting his admiration as forests elsewhere did, and weakened his sense of moving on a path plotted by somebody else.

Today, not being in fact as angry as he would have wished, he was able to follow in his mind the way they went. They veered to the west slightly and after half a mile, came to marshy land and beyond it, the boulders where Hearn was hidden. Once more the ornate, Biblical password was traded.

Hearn rose out of the stones. Phelim was astounded at his vigour, for he seemed to have succeeded in rebuilding himself—on a lean scale, perhaps; yet very nearly completely a new man. And he'd been warm last night. He was wearing a dark, hooded coat made from the pelt of some Antarctic creature. The whaler had been Christian indeed to Hearn.

'You've been a pharisee with me,' Halloran said.

Hearn lifted an ear but not his eyes.

'I beg your pardon.'

'Don't bother begging my pardon. You haven't told me the whole story. Three hundred pounds of meat, you say. See how I trust you, you say. I tell you every thing to the nearest ounce. Like hell you do!'

'What do you mean?'

'Three hundred pounds of beef won't feed *you* halfway to America, let alone any of the others. So it seems your whaler is getting no profit out of you at all. A rare man he must be!'

'There *are* rare men.'

'Yes. Most of them aren't whalers,' Halloran contended, although he'd never met any whalers and was prejudging them.

Hearn stood waiting. He could afford to play with his breath and, amazingly, he had breath to play with today. His grey face seemed made to dominate in pulpits; it had been harrowed but now owned an irrefutable repose, as if it had survived immensities, as if the worst had been.

'But you hardly understand the captain's problem,' he said. 'His need is stores.' Hearn coughed then, not from his illness, but like any mere temporizing windbag. 'Stores, you see.' Then over his eyes which had been momentarily vulnerable, a thick skin of infallibility took only a second to grow. 'Stores, not profit. Now he'll be able to take in stores at Valparaiso, which is straight over there.' He pointed eastwards at the unintelligible warp of forest. 'Seven thousand miles certainly. But between here and Valparaiso, what we have taken from the store will keep three or four men alive.'

'I still don't believe it. I still don't believe he'll come. It isn't worth his trouble. There's no profit in it and it's not like him not to want profit.'

After all, Halloran thought, cats want milk and whalers, like all men of business, want profit. It is a law of nature.

'Profit isn't all things to all men, you know,' Hearn told him.

'I'm not going to risk my life on that proposition.'

And certainly within Halloran, life ran pale and prone to argument but not to tranquil faith.

'Has he told you everything, Terry?' he asked. 'Has honest brother Hearn who wants your soul told you all the story?'

'Terry knows more of it than you. That's to be expected.'

It may have been Halloran's mistake then to stare at Byrne. Yet he believed that if Byrne could be dislodged, Hearn's purpose would be beaten. Behind Phelim's back, the seer frowned and made a sealed-lips gesture at Terry. So that only the traditional Byrne was visible, a creature of dish-eyed unenlightenment.

'*Does* he know more?' said Halloran, as Byrne's face became even more bluntly and conscientiously ignorant. 'You don't look much to me like a man who knows things.'

'He'll tell us everything in the end,' Byrne said. 'Your nose is starting to run.'

It made Halloran furious to have his nose so thoroughly betray his mortality. He became noticeably taut. Hearn could tell that he might stamp away at any second.

Hearn said levelly, 'The captain is a man with his eye to profit, yes.' All things were level to Hearn. All valleys had already been exalted, every hill already laid low. 'If it's any comfort to you, he spent a great part of the time ranting against his brother-in-law. He'd got some water-casks from his brother-in-law, you see, bought them on trust. He didn't know they'd been used to hold vinegar and were full of mould. The first one broached killed four of his crew. Now he's out to ruin his brother-in-law, take him to court, destroy his name. So, there you are! He's what you'd call a normal man.'

'Thank God for that much,' said Halloran.

And he *was* grateful to find that most men were dishonest in the traditional way, conventionally vengeful, and could be trusted to be corrupt for the sane and long-established reason of personal greed.

'Well?' he said.

'You remember Rio?'

'Damn good place to live,' Terry Byrne claimed. 'Live like a king on Marine's pay.'

'When our fleet got to Rio, you might remember Mr Blythe was busy meeting merchants of the city. He was meant to buy seed and oil, and before bargaining with the merchants concerned, he asked His Excellency to sign three of the printed promissory notes. Blythe himself was to sign them and put the amount on them when the sale was closed. As it turned out, there was no sale. For one reason and another. Blythe was meant to give the notes back to His Excellency. He didn't.'

'Feathering his nest,' Byrne assumed.

'I don't think so, I think he forgot them. Anyhow, there they are in a strong-box at the warehouse, and Blythe has even gone so far as to sign two of them. Just in an idle moment perhaps, just for something to do. I found the notes last month when I was helping Blythe. I said nothing, I put them back in their place and locked the box. I've promised the captain one of these.'

'Break the box open?' asked Halloran. He made a face at Hearn's ample guile.

'I've made it my business to have a key,' Hearn said, with his eyebrows warning Terry Byrne to be wise.

'Once he has that note, he'll kill you and fill it out for thousands.'

'I'm keeping the note.'

'That's what you say.'

Hearn played with his breath for a while.

'He'll get it from my hand in Valparaiso or he won't ever get it.'

'Brave words,' said Halloran, even though Hearn hadn't sounded self-glorious. 'Then he'll kill you in Valparaiso and fill it in for thousands.'

'Do you think so?' asked Hearn without any genuine interest. 'In any case it will be filled out already by myself for £100. He should get sixty for it from the merchants. Of course, they'll take it to the British consul, who'll say yes, it's on the proper form which viceroys alone have. And you must remember, this little town of ours was meant to be a Corinth of the south, as they say. The consul in Valparaiso wouldn't be surprised to see a note signed by His Excellency for an amount within the bounds of reason.'

'And the beggar wants stores as well? A promissory note, all right. But there's so much danger in the other.'

'He's in a bad way for stores, he's in a position to insist.'

'Unlike me,' said Halloran. He tried to look ironic, but a sneeze scattered his efforts. 'Didn't he doubt you? How could he know just what you were at?'

Hearn nodded. He looked utterly humble.

'Like one greater, I had wounds to show.'

'So you did.'

'Well?' Hearn asked after thought.

'Don't think you've talked me round. I'll be surprised if he comes for you.'

'Of course he'll come. He's a whaler, a man used to danger, the only danger he can't face being loss, the loss of his ship, failure to make his fortune.'

Halloran had his mouth open again when Hearn raised his right fist and pounded it down on his own thigh.

'Damn reasons and arguments,' he said. 'He'll do what he's meant to. So will I and so will you.'

But raw and vigorous faith had run aground before today, thought Halloran. He damned raw and vigorous faith and the ache behind his eyes, his belling ears, his tight breath. He felt as ill as Hearn should have felt but perversely refused to feel.

'Why?' he asked. 'Why will everyone do what they're meant to when no one has up to now?'

'There's a pattern. I'll tell you.'

Apart from the whaler and the new age in Europe, Hearn explained, Terry knew where a warehouse key could be got. The peculiar thing was that not only was Byrne crazed for redemption, but he had even been partner to some earlier thefts of supplies.

Halloran rolled his eyes.

'Is this true, Brian Boru?'

'It is,' said Terry, proud of it. 'Of course, I was forced. And it was before taking stores was made a hanging matter. But just the same, yes.'

In fact, there was that about Byrne that reminded a person of the Easter Mass at which the deacon sings, 'O happy guilt, to have deserved so great a Saviour.'

'God of Mercy!' Halloran said.

'A lot of it used to go on. It was just a bit of sport.'

'I know a girl who's splotchy with hunger. That's not sport.'

'You always take a serious view.'

'Do I? That's because I have to look at shit like you from the outside. An agony you've never had to face, my boy.'

Hearn said in a soothing way, 'Corporal'. But mainly he was allured by the pains his destiny had taken with the entire affair. 'There's no moon on Wednesday night, and slack tide will be a quarter to midnight. About half past midnight there'll be a strong run-out tide. We won't rush it, muffles on the oars, just an occasional pull to get us into the middle. I've been down to the bay in the middle of the night to look at the tides. I know that even there we'll be helped.'

The image came to Halloran of a humourless seal-skin coat dropping like a bad dream through the white, young town; not deviating, as the chain-cranked angels rising and descending in religious festivals in Rio did not deviate; bending at the end of its descent to watch the swirl and suck of the bay.

The key belonged to a man called Miles, Private Albert Miles. Did Halloran know him?

'He's that tall, mean-looking bastard,' Byrne supplied, 'who's always got someone else's watch to sell.'

'You mix with the best, don't you, Terry?' said Halloran.

Hearn explained, 'You and Byrne would see him together. You'd have to threaten him. You'd have to say that you wanted the key . . .'

'If he's still got it,' Halloran said.

'He's still got it,' sang Terry out of the fullness of either faith or knowledge.

'. . . and you wanted him to row. And if he won't, you'd go to the officers and report all you know of him. And you'd have to tell him it's no use murdering either of you, that there's a third person who'd report him as soon as you come to any harm.'

'A spirit of hearty brotherhood,' said Halloran.

Terry Byrne became equitable all the way down the length of his strange mouth.

'We'll have to let him take a bit of beef. That's only fair.'

'Yes,' Halloran said, 'so is the backside of the whore he'll buy with it. No. No beef.'

'It's only fair.'

'No beef.'

'He'd knife us.'

'I'll talk to him.'

'I'm not willing to die to no use,' Byrne said.

As, the sun being on his face, and his soul robust with plots, he was quite willing to die to some use.

All their dealings would be with Miles, Hearn told them. But at the same time, a guard would be needed at the warehouse and another at Government Wharf. Now Miles had a friend called

Barrett and a friend called McHugh.

'McHugh's wife to Miles,' Byrne laughed. 'And Barrett's sort of fancy-lady to both of them.'

'They're not to be told anything, you understand. They're servile to Miles. They'll do what you want them to if Miles beats them enough. Or so I'm told. You'll have to see the two of them are the guards for the warehouse and wharf on Wednesday night. After all, you're the orderly.'

So Hearn's eyes and intentions probed Halloran, while on the slope behind those boulders, some pigeons mourned sanely, bringing to Halloran's notice once more that he was not bound. Amongst the rocks, a tribe of grudging starlings went scrabbling, as mean, as unaspiring, as assured of the sunlight as one could wish to be.

The plot ground on in Hearn's mouth.

The officer of the guard that week was a Subaltern from Major Sabian's company and could be relied upon to be slapdash. He would be at the wharf at ten o'clock, one o'clock, and possibly not again. If the cutter, having stranded Hearn, were back at Government Wharf by two o'clock in the morning, they had, so Halloran gathered, God's and Hearn's permission to go on breathing easily for an unlimited toll of years.

Halloran looked at the earth, at the strewn complexities of dead leaves, patterns of dying which must somehow have a designer.

'If he doesn't come for you,' he said, 'and the sun rises and there you are, sitting on the sand with three hundred pounds of beef. . . . We'll look the silliest dead ever.'

'He'll come. You pretend he's as hard to believe in as Michael Archangel.'

'He is. Very nearly.'

The three of them looked at each other until Byrne went red.

'It's no use,' Halloran said at last. 'I'll need that sign.'

'I'm not dismayed.'

'You never are. I'll wait on the sign. There are risks, you know. Present company not excepted, as they say.'

So Halloran went away to wait for the sign not to happen, and Hearn watched the tired young image stepping on the charred shadows of the forest; the unaggressive colour, the unguarded back suddenly dwindled in the chaos of grey and olive.

Byrne whispered in the prophet's ear.

'I know him. He's for you.'

The sign came to Halloran as he stood easy in the ranks at the start of a Church-parade. Waiting there, he was attuned to expect it. For a grey island of flesh, large as anything that ever foundered a ship, had risen in the bay, and two boatloads, Marines and transports, had been sent chasing it through the mulberry, deep water.

Unlike the transport ranks below them on the slope, Halloran's company, lined up on the edge of the parade-ground, could see all, the entire whale chase, for surely a whale was what, with fantastic appositeness, the hump awaiting the boats was.

The transports and guards were lined facing inland, yet had their mind's-eye at least on the chase. The Rev. Calverley stood isolated by his interest in the deity at the door of the white-washed long church of St Jeremy. Halloran felt sorry for the man, and for the church like a humble beast. With nothing to thrust heavenward, it nuzzled the windy side of the hill, and kept the black, unglazed, Gothic sockets of its windows very much to the ground. Both the priest and his temple seemed to sense, as did everyone else, that whatever of truth and sacrifice there was in the town that morning was to be revealed on the blue of the bay.

A sergeant, tatty waist-sash and all, went on with the convict roll-call. Half a mile away, one of the cutters had come within throw of a cow-whale, big as a town-house, and her twenty-foot calf. Neither beast moved. The cow hissed without malice. Perhaps exhaustion had visited the walls of those barns of meat fleeing from sharks into a mere thirty fathoms.

No one in the cutter knew much about whales. It was thought wise that the harpoon be thrown into the mother; and so it was thrown. Her pain made the bay seethe in front of her. This clear day, the men on the parade-ground could see for some seconds the classic fountain of red water she snorted into the mid-air. At half a mile, it was a bounty of colour, not the agony-flower it was to the whale, not the unspeakable banner it was to the men in the cutter. She vanished for a moment, but then was solid again athwart the boat which splintered with the leisurely sound of a felled tree.

Her shape and the shape of her calf were gone. Twelve men agonized with no urgency in the grey turmoil of her wake. Across a bay of silence, the slower cutter bore towards them. It was far too slow. The whales came back in white froth, and went again; back and went again. Whenever they went, they thwacked the water with what looked like wrath in such big creatures. Yet perhaps it was horror. Whichever way, men disappeared amongst the curds of angry water, and the second boat stood clear.

The creatures did not come back the third time. Halloran saw them in the fore of his mind nosing down into those foreign shallows. Behind their pigs' eyes, the brains and foundry hearts groaned busy with dismay, busy with deprivation, busy with pain. The bay healed back to uniform blue as if they had never come.

In the world of men, the remaining cutter hauled up an improbable number of survivors. 'I can't even swim,' said one of them laughing, settling back intact between an oarsman's legs. 'Hold on!' they told the only three left in the water. Another cutter had put out from shore. One of the three clutching the gunnels sneezed. 'Us?' the sneeze said to those who heard it. 'We were meant to last.' For in the cutter were nine drenched men, and the three in the water made twelve. Not one had been lost.

Byrne made a prodigy out of all this, a clumsy parable. To Halloran though, it was merely a sign, a sign in the strict sense, an indication. The indication was that no man could plot his course away from moments so extreme, so drunken with terror and uproar that, emerging breathing by accident from them, he might as well have died in them. It was meant that man should weather a number of these occasions with a whole skin, and so go home to dinner.

If a man was meant, and if he knew he was meant to chance himself three hours on a given Thursday night, under a whale of a different complexion—he might as well. That was all that could be said. He might as well. He thought on the other hand, and immediately, that there was nothing mystical about whales, that they were as seasonal as turnips.

So, agonizing, he saw the town, the woods and the bay. The wind splashed their thick insensitive colours across his eyes. Ann and he could pretend to be a universe to each other, and all the rest of it. He could pretend that he was able to hold her safe from the extremes of her destiny. But the ironstone world was always there, it said that one day it would penetrate the avid heart and make it meat.

He shut his eyes and remained there, hating the enemy world.

23

Mrs Blythe's silver-ware had seen too much salt air these last three years. There was a salver which rode the muslin table-cover in the back parlour and two cruets on the sideboard, all of them badly tarnished. Ann took them to the kitchen that Sunday afternoon to remedy them before Halloran came. She sat in the door, in the sun, her lap vulgarly wide just for comfort.

She had the salver covered with paste when Mr Blythe came in. His entry took time. With a grimace of pleasure, he let himself down the two steps from the house as cumbersomely as a man walking on his hands. He was in shirt-sleeves, bearing a glass and, perilously, a decanter of brandy. Once he had the steps behind him, he saw Ann.

'The last,' he said, holding up the decanter. 'The very last.'

'It must be, sir.'

She frowned and turned back to the salver.

He came across the room carrying his shoulders shrugged, as if actually pulling the nimbus of the liquor about him.

'It's no better out here,' he said, however. 'It's just as cold. Or nearly.'

'Wouldn't your own room be warmer at this time of year, sir? It's got a window facing north.'

He had put the decanter down on the table.

'No!' he said. 'I'm sick of the view. I'm sick of that clay road and I'm sick of the same bits of bay you see through the same trees. I'm so sick of it that I can see it all by closing my eyes. Look, I'll just show you.'

His eyes snapped shut and the muscles of his cheeks strained to keep them shut. Ann felt forced to ask herself, is this Mr Blythe, this friendly man who does not prefer clay roads? Sober, he looked to be blank of preferences, and when his sober lids closed they never gave any hint of not closing on darkness.

'There,' he said, blind. 'Myrtles of a kind. They seem to be dying, but I think they've seemed to be dying for two thousand damned years. And one of them has a wasp's nest wrapped around its fork like a poultice.' The eyes opened. 'You see, Ann, there's very little profit in looking out that window.'

Watching him with the broad furtiveness which cannot be used on the completely sober, Ann wiped a thumbful of paste off the flange of the salver and had a glimpse in the exposed silver of the day gone molten, ruled by her own face jowly and pompous there. She had no time to hunt for a glimmer of Mr Blythe in the fragment of shadow, though he would have been there, even in that thumb-nail world.

'It's not very comfortable for you out here though, Mr Blythe,' Ann said, more capable with him when he was humanized by drink.

'I know better,' he told her genially while hitching himself onto the table, 'than to expect to be comfortable in my own house.'

So perched, his right arm, glass and all, was prodigal with gestures of reassurance.

'No, you mustn't worry about Mrs Blythe. At the moment she's asleep in the front parlour. The condition isn't permanent or eternal, although a man could do worse than drink to that merry possibility.'

He held his glass up.

'To that merry possibility!' he said, drinking too long a toast and recovering as an athlete recovers from his excesses, huffing.

'To the passer-by,' he went on, 'she presents a picture of deep maidenly repose. Her nose is blocked and her mouth is open.'

He showed Ann how, even making noises with his nose.

'There's a blow-fly on her forehead too. But that's his business. No, Mrs Blythe's well asleep. Don't you worry!'

So Ann didn't worry, and there was silence.

After some seconds, Blythe said, 'Ann, you are so lovely. You're an agony of loveliness. No cancer ever scalded a man as —'

'No, Mr Blythe,' Ann told him, no longer unsure now the situation had broken, 'don't get carried away with words. It's not wise and it gives you short breath.'

'My God,' said Blythe, 'short breath. Did Thisbe speak to Pyramus about short breath?'

'I wouldn't know, Mr Blythe. All I know is that you worked yourself into a state with words last time you started along this line of talk. We had to get a Marine in to put you to bed, if you remember.'

He giggled like a school-boy.

'That *was* a dry argument,' he said. Then he raised his voice. 'No cancer ever scalded,' he began.

'Thank God,' said Ann, because Halloran was coming down through the garden.

'I beg your pardon,' Mr Blythe told her.

'It's Corporal Halloran.'

'Oh.'

Halloran came on doubtfully when he heard Blythe, and his eyes peered and his eyebrows were arched and interrogative.

'It's only Blythe,' Anne hissed at him. 'He's been drinking.'

'Come in, come in, you lucky boy!' sang Blythe.

The lucky boy stood stooped in the doorway, sniffling and wary.

'Aren't you well?' said Ann.

'Just a fit of the shivers,' Halloran admitted.

'Come in, come in, you lucky boy!' Blythe intoned once more. 'Ann, get him a cup!'

Eyeing him for signs of illness and, more still, signs of Hearn's enterprise, she got up from her chair and found a cup in the old dresser by her bed.

'It's a marvellous thing to be young,' Blythe told Halloran, who had come in but looked haggard and still disquieted.

'If your nose isn't dripping, sir. If you don't mind me putting it that way.'

'You put it any way you like, boy. Come and get a nip, just the thing for dripping noses.'

He went to Blythe with the cup Ann had put in his hands.

Blythe poured him a large dosage.

'Your best health, sir,' he said, and took a mouthful. He felt less feverish then.

'What did you think of the whales?' he said, grinning into the cup.

'Yes,' said Ann, helping him make talk.

'I didn't want to smoke whale-meat all next week,' Blythe told them. 'I'm glad they got away.'

'I suppose so,' said Halloran. He had some more brandy.

'But not a man lost,' he said after drinking.

'That'll teach that Government House crowd to go playing with whales.'

Blythe nodded his head and was not able to stop nodding then. The glass in his hand began to tilt and Halloran tried to take it from him. He woke for a small time saying, 'No cancer ever scalded a man as you . . .' Halloran helped him into a chair and he went to sleep, his head on the table, his pink mouth crushed open.

'You're flushed,' Ann said.

'Only a small bit.' He pointed at Blythe and laughed. 'Just imagine, the old fellow.'

But even if the man was asleep, they were still constrained. They kissed well but quickly. Halloran turned his head away sneezing.

'I'm sorry,' he said. 'I'd tell you how homesick I've been to see you all the week, yesterday and today worse than anything. You don't believe me though.'

'I've seen that fellow Hearn in the forest,' she told him.

'Oh no. He's run away. He's dead.'

By way of obsequies, he closed his eyes.

'I know Hearn,' she said. 'It was Hearn.'

'What did he say?'

'It was only a glimpse. I went out to find cassia pods for a tonic for Mrs Blythe. There he was.'

'A meeting by accident?'

'Yes. He had on a grey coat, very big, with a hood. What am I going to do?'

He coughed and took her hand.

'How do you mean?'

'Who ought I tell?'

The corners of his eyes craved pity from someone or other. Then he looked at the floor.

'He didn't say anything?'

'No.'

'Say it *was* Hearn. Probably, he'd be helped by some poor beggar. Say he is. If you tell anyone, that's the end of them, Hearn and the poor beggar. You couldn't do that.'

'But isn't he dangerous?'

Halloran scratched his neck.

'In a better world he'd probably be something in the nature of a leader.'

'Let him run wild then?'

'*Wild* isn't the way he runs.'

'You wouldn't help him would you?' she asked without any warning.

'Ann,' he said, looking at the floor still, 'if I asked you or begged you to drop the subject, would you drop it? I feel so sick.'

She stiffened herself.

'I see,' she said.

He led her back to her silver-ware and her seat in the sun.

Having to poke her, more or less, into her seat, he said, 'What is it?'

'What if I asked you, just to be certain, not to have a thing to do with Hearn?'

'Please,' he said and wagged his head, 'please drop the subject. Sweet peace, sweet repose, just a bit of that, eh?'

His voice was small, dry, close to rage. He found himself a chair, sneezed and sat beside her. Ann treated the salver brutally with a cloth.

'I'm sorry,' he said. He blew his nose. He did, as he said, feel so sick. 'Sweet repose,' he murmured.

While they sat still, the afternoon lay in their laps like a tawny cat, and sparrows came to roll themselves in the dust of Mr Blythe's garden, and twitched with delight as the wind nudged the corners of the house with sleepy regularity. If anyone had, from a distance, seen these two people side by side, so young yet like penates in the doorway, he would have thought, 'My bet is those two have found peace.'

Leaving Ann, he kept halting on the way back to the hutments. He would lean against tree-trunks and nurse with both hands the ache behind his jaws, groaning theatrically, as he would never have done had people been present. The edges of his mind began to melt under the warm suggestion of sleep. At one time, for half a minute or more, he slept on his feet.

Back in the hut, he wrapped himself in two blankets, taking great, mean care over it. Sleep came instantly, and his fever produced a dream laborious though clear.

It opened upon a courtroom. Hearn was judge behind a high brown bench, Allen prosecuted. The defendant was largely, but not entirely, the man whom Halloran had butted in the stomach at the Crescent shambles. He himself was the fourth party in the chamber. There was a strange flavour about the situation, in that Hearn said nothing, Allen seemed awkward and apologetic, the defendant privileged and above the argument. Halloran too was privileged—he knew that he was present as a privilege and had liberty to move about the open part of the court and comment on anything Allen might say. Yet this freedom had not given him any happiness. The roof pressed low on the courtroom, a fug of death grasped the mind. Halloran knew both that he was the most afraid of the four, and that the others did not know it.

Not so much by words as by attitudes, the dream proceeded; Hearn becoming increasingly aloof, though his existence increasingly weighed the mind; Allen becoming more tentative; the man growing hides of dignity; Halloran tasting more and more the prisoner's coming death. The legal arguments in favour of condemnation were regretfully advanced by Allen, who stood at the foot of the bench and frowned. Since everybody seemed anxious for his opinions, Halloran strode to and from the back of the room, concentrating on Allen. The defendant sat on a table in the corner.

Allen had been speaking for a long time. Begging approval, his eyes constantly referred to Halloran. Halloran remained grave, interrupting at last to snatch a word Allen had uttered—'reasonable'.

'Reasonable? But you'll never be reasonable at your own last choke, Captain,' Phelim said. 'Remembering that for the sake of a House that to God is only a house, you made this man's last choke. When your own breath whizzes out, you'll see you're hanging with him. Hanging him, you hang yourself. How does that strike you for reason?'

Professional and human hurt spread over Allen's face and transfixed him.

'Aye, mate?' Halloran asked the man in the corner. The man said yes, while Allen turned his back and limped towards Hearn. At liberty, with Allen distracted, Halloran began to wink and grimace at the defendant. Unskilfully grinning and cajoling, he knew that he must look insane. Yet if Allen wanted Halloran's favour, Halloran wanted the defendant's.

'What you don't understand,' Allen called to him, 'is that hanging is not a subject for argument. Why do you think the judge has been so silent?'

'Judge?' Knowing it to be perilous, Halloran said with some irony, 'What judge?'

Allen winced. '*What judge?* Don't you see that this is a court of conscience?'

'Conscience?'

'You should know,' said Allen.

Then Hearn spoke, patience short, in a voice one didn't raise one's eyes to.

'You have the freedom of the court, yes, but only because so much is expected of you.'

Halloran could not prevent himself from saying, 'You mean

concerning the whales?'

'I mean,' Hearn began, but grunted and abandoned explanations to Allen.

'As I said, the judge has been silent because he knows what hanging is. It is a ceremony which begins in the cradle and grows from the cradle. Its ministers are the mother and petting father, the priest, the boys a boy fights, the girls he desires. Cooks advance the ceremony by cooking his meat, tap-boys by pouring his ale. Horses advance it by flying him over stiles, ships by buoying him across the seas. Must you be so cruel to us only because we are its last ministers?'

Hearn nodded at this. His chin descended like sledge-blows. Then Allen nodded and the room shook. Halloran realized that the building would shatter if the defendant's iron chin assented. He saw it begin to fall and ran outside into the dusk.

Here Ewers waited for him. The two of them fell into step beside each other. They strode away through the stuff of which the dusk was made, an overcast of charred orange out of which the forest grew downwards, as if leaf preceded root.

'Do you think he should hang?' Halloran asked.

'There are reasons why no man should hang. Within the noose you have the worst madness. Within the noose a man commits the sin against the Holy Spirit, uttering without a voice the screaming lust to poison God at his eternal well-springs.'

Halloran walked on but was stiff with fear.

'Why then . . . ?' he asked.

'Because there are other reasons.'

And Ewers began to repeat all that Allen had said on hanging as a ceremony. Halloran was aghast, fear becoming absolute, as Ewers said, 'Were you so cruel to me only because I am the final minister?'

At this, the hanged Scot took from his waistcoat a tiny egg. Halloran, careful from childhood with eggs, extended both hands, yet Ewers didn't place it there intact. He cracked it open and tipped it across Phelim's palms. The thick white contained a yolk of scalding brilliance. Halloran, blinded, groaned with joy.

194

'I can't look at it,' he said, trying to look just the same.

'Wait a small while. It dies out in the hands within minutes.'

Already its light did not so needle the eye. It was, in fact, seen to be bean-shaped now. Its radiance had become a gloss, intense yet growing less so all the time. Halloran panicked at this responsibility.

'What . . . ?' he begged Ewers.

'This,' Ewers told him, 'is the seed of your gibbet-tree. As Christ planted his, I planted mine. Now it is your planting time.'

Staring into Ewers' eyes, Halloran became furious.

'Do you think I *would* plant it?'

'It will certainly not live long in your hands,' Ewers observed.

And every glimpse of the dying seed compelled Halloran.

He said, 'In any case, if I did plant it, Hearn would want it for his tree of judgment. Terry Byrne, who is a child, would dig it up for its shine.'

'You can expect a ready ear and no mercy from me,' Ewers told him. 'By all means, make it safe from Hearn and Terry. But by the time you have, it will be dead.'

Coerced to gaze at the bean and, gazing, to plant it, Halloran was free enough to seek Ewers' face only once more. The artist was strolling off, muttering.

'Please yourself. It is quite clearly not my seed but yours. No one can do worse for it than you can, holding it in your palm.'

The gusts of dying light worried Phelim's under-chin. He lowered his eyes the fatal time. The bean of his gibbet-tree spoke to him now with a pitiable glint, to plant it being the only mercy at hand. Still nursing it in both palms, he yet dug with both hands in the black soil. Leaf-mould he turned up, red roots and white worms, and put the seed in the heart of a conical black pit and pulled blankets of earth across it and himself. Just in time.

Happiness seemed to wake him; but if it had not been sufficient, decision formed like a fist at his back and jolted him in the nape. He rose without delay to keep an appointment that same night with Miles.

Miles sat on the ground fingering the split in his ear. Halloran kicked him on the hip. It was dark. Above them, on the hill, the wind and curlews were inconsolable.

'Now,' Byrne said, beginning to hold Halloran with both arms. 'Now, now. You gentle people. You're the cruellest bastards of all.'

In a voice croaky from excess and not fully returned to itself, Halloran told Miles,' Do what you're told.'

'He will now,' Byrne assured him, 'he will. Stop kicking him.'

They stood above Miles, who was white and extremely interested in the blood from his ear. Byrne was gratified.

'You went mad with him.'

'I'll teach him,' said Halloran.

'I wouldn't have known you,' Byrne told him.

'I'll teach the bastard.'

He began to cry.

'No tears, Phelim,' Terry begged of him. 'It's all settled now. No tears.'

During the night Hearn moved his home to a forest slope two miles to the east of the boulders he'd hidden amongst. Above him rose the forest in silver bark, luminous at night, mourning the dying of the tribes. Halloran had come near this place in February; now as then it smelt like a jaded cemetery. Each day Hearn buried himself in blanket, earth and bark. By night he made a wind-break of a fallen tree. He ate serenely at dusk, pork, cheese, rice uncooked and swallowed one or two grains at a time. His small store of food was the whaler's gift, a warranty from an acquisitive, hard-put man that he meant to have profit out of his meeting with Hearn.

Each night he returned to his first sleeping place for a parley. It meant for him a two mile walk over gormless earth that shifted and broke as he walked; no chance of settling in stride and forgetting himself.

Whenever there was argument, he'd say, 'You are not your own man nor am I mine. We hold each other. The earth holds the trees as we hold each other. We cannot offend each other any more than the earth offends the trees.'

A concept that frightened and induced silence.

After each parley, he returned to the wind-break. With his talent for living in the open, he seemed as always to detect a yellow warren of sleep and to be down in it in seconds.

24

Now Private McHugh turned the key on them. Hearn, Terry, Phelim, Miles shuffled forward into the store-room itself, holding back in the dark from bruising themselves on its hard-edged plenty. This was the room which Halloran had dreamt of for four nights without fail. It had been blue, Arab, sumptuous in the dream, but tonight black and smelling of mould.

Byrne lit the lanthorn.

'Beef is in two sizes of cask,' Hearn told them. He showed them where the eighty pound casks were.

Miles and Byrne began to carry one, but dropped it when Hearn and Phelim were out of sight, and packed meat into the canvas loops they had slung from their shoulders and wore under their tunics. A minute or two later, the others were back, carrying the strong-box to the light. It was opened then, and the note taken out.

The forty-two gallon casks were heavy as elephants. Within five minutes though, they had everything they wanted standing, like barrels out of a tall tale, by the door in the hint of light from the lamp.

McHugh opened the door to them and they carried the casks across the road and dropped them where they could find room in the malicious undergrowth. Hearn, once back from locking the store-house door, threw the key into the bay. There was trouble with Miles over this and bullying from Byrne and Halloran, and at last they were humping the casks away, welded to them by the dark; graceless animals and frightened along the scraggy bay-side.

The cutter, guarded tonight by Miles' friend Barrett, being a cutter made in the town and leaky, rode so low under the load of stores that they boarded it slowly and one at a time. There was such quiet all around them that they worked in the darkness simply as men at work in the dark. Forgetting the gravity of what they did, they were absorbed by its discomforts: cold and the loads they had to carry, push, kick against without seeing.

It made them jovial to find the tide working for them as Hearn had said it would, to find also the town as dark to their sight as they were to its.

They landed Hearn where he told them, perhaps two miles up the bay. Not wanting to be whaler's crew themselves, they had to leave him straight away.

'Don't you feel free?' Hearn asked Halloran, shaking his hand before they left.

They rowed home and dispersed through the woods. Phelim did not yet feel free. He supposed it was a talent, and would come to him.

25

THE winter nights that July were amazingly cold. Friday night was so cold that Halloran slept camp-style, put his legs into his waistcoat sleeves, wrapped his breeches around his shoulders and himself in his coat under two blankets. It rained in the night, and he exulted, thinking, *We're safe, however hard to believe. We're safe!*

When he woke up it was still very cold, his forehead cold as a tombstone. There was no rain, but the rush roof let out its nightful of water little by little and groaned like an animal. The door had come open. The night was visible, smoke-blue, very still and sharp in the doorway, still as a farm-dog, as if it had never gone away.

A tall man in a big Holland hat and a caped overcoat was stooping just inside the door, whispering, 'Corporal Halloran.' One at least of the Privates was stirring.

Halloran struggled with his waistcoated legs and trousered arms, to shed his blankets.

'Here!' he said.

'It's Blythe, the Commissary. Come with me please, Halloran!'

He was still so much asleep that the man in the large hat brought him that broad sense of dread that is peculiar to dreams.

'I beg your pardon, sir.'

'I said, come with me!'

So he got ready. He thought, *And that's that. I am a dead man,* he thought, getting his legs free of the waistcoat.

'Hurry up!' Blythe said.

'Anything the matter, sir?'

'Ann.'

'Ann is sick?'

'Hurry up!'

Halloran found himself with his breeches on. He wondered who had done it, and decided it could have been himself alone. He found too that he was taking care to do up his gaiters, and snorted and got up in a rush, following Blythe outside. How blood-warm the waistcoat was as he put it on, and even the coat was warm.

'Ann, sir?' he said.

As soon as his hands were free the cold pounced on them and hung on the fingers like weights.

The Commissary wouldn't answer.

'Sir, you mentioned Ann.'

Blythe had his right hand tucked into his double-breasted coat and resting on the second button. He took it out. In it was a horse-pistol, just too large for Blythe's hand as it would have been for Halloran's. Halloran, in his boyhood, had noticed these slung in front of the saddle on the mounts of officers of militia, and had always felt that he was predestined not to have a hand large enough to handle such manly things adequately. Neither had most of the officers of militia, but they seemed never worried by this and wore them nonetheless, because they looked gallant. This one in Blythe's hand didn't look gallant to Halloran.

'It's that our work now is to save her, Halloran.'

The pistol was all that threatened. The Commissary himself spoke confidentially as they went off. He stopped when they were at the edge of the claypits. A half-uprooted peppermint leant over them and was in the secret. 'Captain Allen has a warrant on its way to the Provost-Marshal's. Ann and yourself are on it. Perhaps we can combine to save her.'

'Ann? How could Ann be on a warrant?'

Blythe's jaws shuddered. The man was, in fact, gargling anger in his throat.

'Get on!' he said. He could barely say it.

On downhill, Halloran saw Venus unambiguous as alabaster, seas away, above the bay, above China; and reeled in confusion.

'Ann,' he said. 'It isn't possible.'

'Get on,' said Blythe.

On Collett's Brook, the little bridge rang clear as a mallet when they crossed. Blythe pushed him along the back road by His Excellency's fruitless farms. Behind a sapling fence, the furrows were silver with frost or spider webs this still night. Harvest for the wheat would be October, the far side of the perils of the equinox. It was unbelievable that he, like the soft grain, was not likely to see October.

'Sir . . .' he said, stopping.

The Commissary steadied the pistol-stock with his left hand and pointed the weighty thing at Halloran's side. Behind the stillness of their bodies, a frog bleated himself to a late sleep. There was some light and a few black birds wheeling, giving off rusty calls. Then Blythe and Halloran heard a cat-call and the tops of male voices and the clumping of the bridge.

'It's your brothers-in-arms,' said Blythe, 'under some corporal who can't control them. They're taking the warrant back to the hutments. When they find the others and don't find you, they'll be at my house for Ann.'

'But Ann? Ann's safe.'

'Is she?'

'Yes!'

'Get on!'

'How did they find out?'

'Byrne told them.'

'God help him.'

'Get on!'

They got on through the edge of the woods, woods known to Halloran, woods of love, poor as they were. They came to Blythe's place from the side. Even in this area where his colleagues lived, Blythe held up the pistol high, peculiarly unabashed. He opened the front door and the weapon tilted in his hand. It was far too heavy to carry for a mile with the necessary deft belligerence. Nevertheless, the Commissary was very much master as he pointed the way into the front parlour. From Ann's stories, one would not have expected him to be master, to seem independent. Perhaps he had grown tired now of waiting for the potteries' fortune, and dreamt of blatantly controlling his own house, to his own taste.

He turned the key on Halloran, and Halloran was locked in with lumpy mahogany shapes, bureaus and chests of drawers. Across the room, a stub of candle burned in a candle-stick on a walnut table with friable greyhounds' legs and shells on the knees. The single poor light kindled the bosses on a copper shield, product of Rio, hung from the top of the wall.

Before Halloran moved, the door opened again. Blythe brought Ann in by the elbow. This morning her skin was grey, nothing Spanish about it at all.

'He tells me you're safe, Ann,' said Blythe, nodding at Halloran. 'Terry Byrne tells us all differently. Who's right, eh?'

Halloran put his arms around her as Mr Blythe went to the curtains to let in the dawn. While he worked there, he held the pistol tucked under his left arm.

'Let in some light,' he muttered. 'That's my function. Let in some light.'

When he turned back from the window, there was adequate grey light in the room. He stared at Halloran holding the girl, at the two pale, profitless hands straining on her back. His eyes were full of a bleak, level rapacity; they were cannibal's eyes, an embarrassment to ardour.

Halloran let down his hands and faced the Commissary.

'Let me tell you something,' said Blythe. While he spoke, he laid that vainglorious pistol on the sideboard by the candle and kneaded his small hand. He told them that Byrne had turned King's evidence. The Provost-Marshal had got at all the truth there was in Terry, even what concerned Ann.

'So you are a dead man, Halloran,' he said at the end, reaching out to kill the candle-flame with his fingers. 'And the only question is how to save my servant.'

Not aware of trespassing, Ann sat herself in Mrs Blythe's chair.

'Is it true?' Halloran asked her.

She lowered her head.

'That Judas bastard Byrne,' he said.

In that same subdued manner he had used to be angry with Halloran earlier in the day, Blythe began to shiver.

'There's no use in calling him *that Judas bastard*,' he observed. 'For one thing, it isn't true.'

'Oh no, Mr Blythe? I know Terry Byrne, thank you.'

Blythe attempted to hitch up the long Garrick coat he still wore. It seemed that he was looking for the strong-box key, which he would wave above their heads as a hell of a sign of contradiction. Not able to locate it, he shrugged and allowed the folds of his coat to subside around his knees.

'Could you find it in you to believe,' he asked Halloran, 'that Byrne visited a lady in a hut along the Brook last night? Seeking a hero's diversion. You understand?'

'I could guess if I didn't understand.'

'He gave the lady two ounces of meat. So she denounced him. Could you blame her? Two ounces are an insult, while four are a meal. In this town anyhow. So there you are, Corporal. That is where he killed you. By two ounces of pickled meat, you're dead. Imagine.'

Halloran shook his head to clear it. He looked up especially appalled, as all sufferers are, by the dispassionateness of things, Blythe's unconcern, the sobriety and detachment of furniture. He turned to the chair but found that Ann had walked away into the corner.

'I won't have you gloating,' he told Blythe.

'Don't tell me what you won't have.' Blythe stood side-on to Halloran, back to the window gone gently saffron. 'You've had your revenge already on the three of us. On Byrne and that clerk. *And* on me. Did you know that they beat Terry Byrne with green wands according to a method used by the Spaniards? They didn't rush. They had all night. Even so, Byrne endured for three hours. He brought out your names only with the greatest anguish. It's cost him something indeed to give evidence for the King. As for Hearn, they'd have him over the side by now.'

'Perhaps,' said Halloran. But he knew that Hearn would live

to nag them in France. Because who could imagine Hearn drowning, or Hearn's bard's head broken in?

'And then me,' Blythe began.

'I don't want any revenge on you,' Halloran told him.

'Thank you indeed.'

'We'll lie. You lie!'

'I beg your pardon.'

'About Ann.'

Blythe considered this with one eye shut, the pistol tilted at the ground like a cannon abandoned in battle.

'There's no chance for lies,' he said. 'The court has a belly fed on short navy rations like every other belly in the town. You have threatened it. Even Ann has in her way. Lies will be treated without mercy. Believe me.'

Between Mrs Blythe's brown drapes, the odious sunlight began to be profuse. Halloran eyed it and raked the hair on his forehead.

'You've got something in mind,' he was suddenly certain. 'What is it?'

But Blythe coughed judicially. He chose not to rush the matter.

'There's a pleading that girl can make,' he said slowly. He grimaced, just like a specious lawyer. 'It would save her life. Almost certainly.'

'Yes?' asked Halloran, Ann remaining dazed and leisurely in the corner.

'She could plead she was with child.'

Ann turned round.

'No,' she said softly, appalled to softness.

But Blythe drew his head in between his shoulders, gave it a small shake with all the eagerness of a mouse. How could the court prove she was not with child? In such a case, they must wait and see, and while they waited to see, the matter would solve itself. Three thousand tons of shipping, mainly store-ships, were expected any day. When they came in, there would be what is called by decree 'general jubilation', and as a mark of it the girl would be pardoned.

'You'll see,' he said.

'I can't imagine it happening that way,' said Halloran. But they were simply words to say and showed that he was devoid of purpose.

'Am I a milch cow?' a voice asked. It had such a quiet, stinging edge that although it could only be Ann's, they looked around to make sure a fourth person hadn't dropped into the room.

'No one says so, Ann,' Blythe said.

'It's my fate. I have the say on it.'

Halloran suggested, 'Ann, if it's your one chance . . .'

'There aren't any chances,' she decided, and then, without believing in what she said, 'and it's too early of a morning to be afraid of dying.'

She took Halloran's slack forearm in both hands and shook it and moved it back and forth.

'Don't leave me in this town,' she said.

'Do you know what it is to hang, Ann?' Blythe called to her.

'It's not something that takes beforehand knowledge, is it?' she said. 'There have been dozens of men hanged with complete success the first time they tried it.'

'I mean, the indecency of a crowd at a hanging,' amended Blythe. 'How they sweat to see a woman strangle pop-eyed. You know that.'

They knew. Ann hid her face against Halloran's shoulder, while he composed himself to give her all his futile tenderness. She had pulled away by the time he was ready, and gone to the window. He could see her outlined by the winter's morning and thought that no one could consider making Ann so alien to it as to hang her. On the surface, practically speaking, he was frantic.

'I can only say the bastard's right,' he said.

'Don't leave me in this town,' Ann told him.

'There's no decent town of death,' announced Blythe.

'They're really coming to get us,' Halloran called out. Awareness kept recurring in his throat. On the other hand, there were the moments when his mind took hold of what was certain, that they were neither evil nor tragic, that the gallows dealt only in the evil and the tragic.

'They really are.' Blythe nodded.

'What am I going to do, Ann? Tell me, for God's sake. He's got all the truth with him.'

'Don't leave me in this town,' said Ann.

'You won't say that when the day comes,' Blythe advised genially. He had, in the past half-hour, achieved a brand of cricket-in-a-tomb gaiety. It had become by now a chronic condition of his eyes and cheeks, this slow, indecent levity which sapped Halloran's reason, such as it was.

'I can't kill you with silence,' Halloran was deciding in Ann's direction. 'How do you know you're not in fact with child?'

'How indeed?' said Blythe.

Ann said, 'If I scream and pull back, still don't leave me in this town.'

'Curse that Judas—' said Halloran.

'Yes,' said Blythe. 'But the question is of saving Ann.'

There came a liverish rat-tat-tatting on the door.

'Hello!' came Mrs Blythe's voice.

Blythe waited for some time, staring flippantly at the mid-distance. His rakish pistol still pointed at the floor and looked, far from something militant, like a personal deformity. When he wanted to, he sang,

'Hello, hello!'

This was too, too succulent by his standards, to have the young locked in and the lady locked out. Now he became frankly buoyant, now he was spry.

'You, Mr Blythe?' the lady asked.

'Yes, Mrs Blythe.' As if at the end of an interview, he said, 'Good morning!'

'Why is this door locked?'

'Christ have mercy!' said Halloran.

'Hello,' persisted Mrs Blythe. 'Why is this door locked?'

'Don't leave me in this town,' Ann kept saying.

'You'll never believe me,' said the Commissary, 'but to keep you out, Mrs B.'

'Let me in!'

'No chance of that.'

'I can't think,' said Halloran, hitting his temples.

'I'll wait till my legs crack,' Mrs Blythe announced.

'Legs like yours don't crack, Mrs B., they fall away into lard, that's all.'

Mr Blythe gave himself up to a long, gargling laugh.

Halloran was affronted by this poor farce that had degraded their disaster, his and Ann's disaster, as death is degraded by bott-flies.

'Oh my God, I can't think,' he said.

'Who is it in there, Mr Blythe?'

'I am interviewing two felons, Mrs B. concerning Government Stores. Now, Madam, however great a resemblance your complexion might bear to pressed beef, Government stores are beyond the boundaries of your bailiwick.'

'Is Ann Rush one of the felons?'

'Yes. And a young man called Halloran. He *was* a Corporal of Marines, but I believe his discharge papers are already being made out. So I call him a felon.'

'Ann?' called Mrs Blythe.

But Ann had gone to Halloran, who had not been well lately and stood shivering with his fingers pressed hard into hair at the back of his neck.

'Sit down,' she said, helping him by the elbows.

When he had sat and still shivered, she told him,

'You can see, there's no one to leave me to.'

'Aren't you afraid?' he said bitterly, as if she had betrayed him. 'You will be.'

'I know,' she said.

Mrs Blythe walloped the door. Her voice was rich with out-rage.

'Ann, why don't you answer me?'

'They want you to run along, Mrs Blythe. They can't think for the noise.'

'Oh, my dear Lord!' said Mrs Blythe hushedly. And she began

to recite at top voice one of the psalms, whose symbols fitted the three, the hollow master, the false servant, the perjuror in the locked front parlour.

'She can be saved,' Mr Blythe said simply and beyond the door Mrs Blythe's husky contralto loosened a pack of measured curses against unjust men. 'In any case, she can hardly be said to have benefited. I suppose they take account of these things.'

'Keep quiet,' Ann said.

'You think they might treat her with mercy?' Halloran asked the Commissary.

'Well, she scarcely benefited. Not in any large sense.'

'You know everything,' Ann told the man.

'Well, of course you didn't benefit,' Blythe said.

'Suppose I told you Terry Byrne came along here solemn as Patrick Sarsfield, made a small speech and gave me a whole pound of meat.'

'I wouldn't believe that.'

'Is it true?' Halloran asked her.

His eyes cringed from the possibility. She saw this and said nothing. Halloran jumped up.

'Where is it?' he said.

She caressed his arm, a girl of infinite ease.

'Darling Halloran,' she said.

He swore.

'Tell me!' he said.

Beyond the door, Mrs Blythe proclaimed that somebody or other's mouth was full of cursing and deceit and fraud, and under his tongue was mischief and vanity; and that he sat in the lurking places of the villages.

Ann was not malleable.

'I might have eaten it,' she said.

Halloran lunged for the parlour door and turned the key in it. There was Mrs Blythe cringing back from his rush, her owl's eyes craterish, Davidic righteousness frozen in her mouth. He ran down the hall-way, through the back parlour. In the kitchen, so often locked against loving Corporal Halloran and not-so-loving

Mr Blythe, both doors stood open. The sunlight had angled itself through the outer door and lay utterly quiescent on the earth. Yet there was nothing anymore that was not a threat.

'Where, where?' he roared.

Inside the far door was a water-butt, and inches from it a small ridge of clay looking dug up from somewhere. He laboured the water-butt away; it slopped and gurgled, and the hoops ticked after their three years of easeful standing in the kitchen. Where the butt had been was a cool little hole and a parcel wrapped in cloth. He had his fingers on it when Allen clumped indoors and was yards past Halloran before turning and seeing him. Two Marines, looking orphaned, muskets in hand, had edged in after Allen and were staring at Halloran, now become subvertor, rebel, all things sinister.

'Oh' said Allen over his shoulder, more amenable than he had been for weeks, apologetic as a man who has overlooked doing something mannerly. 'Halloran! Good God, just inside the door.'

He laughed as he had in the wilderness one night, when Halloran had been still alive.

26

I N court it is sentencing time.

There are the bench, Major Sabian and his brothers, all busy
garrison officers with plans for their afternoons. Their work
here is summary justice, judgment before midday, punishment
after. Now it is a quarter to midday. The bench were drummed to
court at half past nine and have not had a disturbed morning.
They have kept a blunt face towards the guilty, a face like a
hammer, but have laughed once; at Terry Byrne, since gone from
the court. For Terry Byrne came in dressed like a classic sea-
soldier. Someone had gone to the trouble of putting him in the
town's best Marine coat toned up with red ink or blood or ochre,
the green facings brightened up with crayon. Poor traducing
Terry whom they'd beaten half the night, over two hours anyhow, on and off, with green wands, appeared in pain within a
lean grey waistcoat, with a ruffled shirt-front poked out between
his second and third buttons. And he had good kersey breeches on
and a plausible pair of shoes and gaiters.

The court, the guards, the prisoners, Blythe and a locksmith
near the door all held their laughter when Byrne stepped into
court, sensing that someone on the bench would say what was
needed to cement them all in massed and licit guffaw.

In view of Byrne's clinching breeches, 'Which side does he
hang?' asked a subaltern-judge.

They all roared together, Halloran beyond himself; his dead
guts jumped at the sharp justice that had found Byrne out, his
bumpkin guts went on a spree.

Byrne had decided overnight that Hearn was Satan. He had
now come to bring it to the court's notice, that Hearn's presence
drove out reason.

'We had no chance of seeing things as they are. He had us dazed. A girl like Ann Rush wouldn't have a ghost's chance with him.'

(Ann is in court now. She is grey, whereas once she was willowy, actually evoked the image of a willow.)

Sabian said, 'This court takes no cognizance of devils. What you all planned, what you all did, that is what you turned King's evidence to say. So say it, please.'

It has all been said. There has been no delay, no baulking legal fiction. Marines have rights of appeal, but Halloran and the others are no longer Marines, Sabian having brought their discharges to court with him. Judgment swift, workmanlike, heavy will be on them by noon.

The court declares Halloran and Ann dead twice over, the other three dead once only, although Miles is declared more gravely dead than McHugh and Barrett. The afternoon lies intact before the court's various purposes. But then that strange fellow Blythe stands.

'Your Honour,' he said, 'in view of the court's decision, I must . . . '

He was interrupted by a bugle from the barracks. Midday and the affair settled. Except that Blythe's *in view of* sounded like a lawyer's tag, a disrupting phrase. For fifteen seconds the bugle prevailed. Blythe didn't question it, held his mouth firmly. Behind him the court's two glazed windows throbbed with the far and lovely ambience of the day.

The bugle stopped.

Blythe said, 'I feel bound to make known to you that Ann Rush is with child.'

There were two Hallorans in court. One was chained to a rail on the left on the bench, the other was as distant as an historian. What chance had the historian, being so neutral, of soothing the other one, the one in shirt-sleeves and blood-warm wristlets, who began roaring what a lie it was, and straining so hard in the chains that the historian thought, 'He'll cut his thumbs off if he pulls any harder.'

Ann stared in front of her, saying, 'No!' too low to be heard. The historian admired her pained brow and the deep sockets of her eyes from which arose, as from two centres, the lines and planes and subtle formulas of which her face was made.

Halloran was restrained by two Marines, one of them grunting quite amiable common sense in his ear. If there is anything calculated to send a madman madder, it is quite amiable common sense.

'Strike him, Sergeant!' the Judge-Advocate bawled down the room; which was done. Halloran stood quiet and blinking in the arms of a guard.

'Are you serious, sir?' Sabian asked Blythe. 'It's after midday and the thing's settled.'

'I am serious, sir.'

'You could have told me earlier. It's after midday.'

'There's nothing in the letters-patent to say justice stops at midday.'

'Keep your humour, sir.'

'I will,' said cheerless Blythe.

'Why wasn't I told earlier in the day?'

'It's such painful news. Now it must out. Whatever happens.'

It was already so clear that nothing would happen except mad Blythe would be disbelieved, that one of the bench began to laugh.

'Painful? Who would it be painful to? Painful to you?'

'Yes.'

'You're the father?'

'Yes.'

'I don't believe you.'

Halloran too and Ann began again to disbelieve him, Halloran making a great noise out of his dissent.

'Strike him, Sergeant, strike him, strike him!'

The Sergeant, too literal a man, hit Phelim three times. How the impact ran before his eyes in acid colours. The Sergeant was a large man, if half-starved.

'You can't afford not to take my word,' Blythe said.

'Can't I?' Sabian sounded fraternal in a deadly, spurious way. He turned to Ann.

'What does the prisoner say?'

Ann shook her head.

'The prisoner says no.'

'The prisoner would say no. Her young man is in court.'

'Who? The rowdy one?'

'Yes.'

'He looks a fitter sire,' Sabian said, just because it was a joke that came easily, and to show that he distrusted Blythe.

'That might be so,' said Blythe. His impartial jaws chewed the words. He was the most judicial figure in the room. 'But I was the one she told, you see. Women have some acumen in these matters.'

Ann was in a death of shame, in accordance with her great talent for it. But there was no quiet in Blythe or the bench. They did not see her; and Halloran still was dizzy from the literal-minded Sergeant.

Sabian kept asking her was it the truth; above all, to undermine Blythe. In the end, he was able to restate the sentence with a good conscience. Before that though, he laughed when he could at Blythe, who, with Mrs Blythe to face, still seemed possessed of his normal deadweight of composure. Halloran saw obliquely Sabian's red chin trembling, the largesse of safety, the largesse of power rolling in that fifty-year-old mouth.

'Ann,' Phelim started to call beneath the court's brotherly laughter. They were heaping a cairn on her, short slabs of laughter. He succeeded in being surprised that he had always expected the forces above him, the kite-eyed forces who laid plans for the waste of men, to be as sharp as surgeons. Whereas they were no more artful than the savage who clubs your back to a jelly. So that you were numb for many of the worst things. He was numb, and Ann so numb that to see her emptied him in that poisonous way you are emptied by striding into a house you have

214

always known, the house of your childhood say, to find stony strangers sitting at the fire.

The judges had gone, but Blythe stood on at the back of the court to see the iron collars put on Miles, McHugh, Barrett, Halloran. Each collar connected to another one with chains and was a weight on the collar-bones. Within these chains, it was hard to walk as a team so that the others mightn't be choked or chafed, and no one felt like learning the narrow art of it today.

There were no chains for Ann Rush. It was difficult enough to get her to move.

27

Tнıs was, according to the Court, their second-last dusk.
They lived it out in the utter box of the detention hut, and
would not have been aware of it as dusk except for the tear
in the roof. Halloran had a porcelain fragment of sky in view.
Cut off raw from heaven's haunch like this, it was at first deep
blue, and bled itself away until cloud came between. In the
clouds there were bronze throes and then a pinkish sort of sub-
mission. Halloran couldn't keep his eyes from all this, though it
hurt him; and he was grateful he saw clearly for a change, so
that he *could* see it, and know what a kingly thing it was to live.

He was of course frightened, and aware of two things, though
not in so many words. The first was, what a lie it is to compare
the life of man to a day, and the death of man, stinking, apo-
plectic, pop-eyed, to a sunset. Human death had no dignity,
Ewers had none; he and Ann would look monstrous, and even
those who died gently were hardly less for very long. Hence, the
poetic lie of the sunset of life, of 'Here rests . . .', 'Here lies at
peace . . .' and all the rest of it. To save man from going mad
at being mortal.

The second thing was of what coiled violence there would need
to be in the noose, if the constellations of the mind, the far
countries of emotion, the warrings of powers, the roarings of
loins, the hordes of twitches and gasps, purrings, shudders, itches,
aches, funny-spots were all to be killed out in a second. Could
you depend on hemp for such violence? If Ann had the sense
that he had, of time passing, of time washing a person adrift from
his agony, if he could have known that she had this sense
strongly, he could have been braver. More than hell, he feared to
have her jerking in the full, uninformed terror of strangling.

216

It was very dark in the hut. The other three started to sing a foul and funny song called 'The Colonel's Lady'. It was practically the story of Daker, except much funnier, and the Colonel was a far better kind of man than Daker, so that the song ended very benignly. Just the same, they sang it hysterically loud, emphasizing the rhythm. The words came like hammer-blows, like curses. When they could not see each other for the dark, they gave the song up.

Then they were on their own, as Halloran had been all the time. What they each wondered was what Halloran wondered. How will there be colours, how will wind bluff and crackle in ears, how will hot meat call to the nose, without *me* there to give the circle of sense its centre?

McHugh and Barrett were dependent on Miles, calling out, 'There, Bert? Hey, Bert. There?'

The wind rose, put a knife in the ribs of the detention-hut, scathed Halloran's neck. He knew he had no right to avoid it. He took it flush, in case it got at Ann.

The Reverend Mr Calverley came early in the night. He held up a lanthorn, not for vision, because it gave him little, but as a gesture, a symbol, little more practical than a crozier. He had refused to be escorted by the Constable, and pushing the door to behind him, began his message far too quickly, betraying his ill-ease.

'He rained flesh also upon them as dust,' he said, and straightway the three began to pelt him with the best blasphemies they had. 'And feathered fowls like as the sand of the sea.'

He lifted up the lanthorn to throw light on the hatred of the Word coming from all sides. He raised his voice against the mystery of wanton hatred.

'So they did eat, and were well filled.'

Halloran shook his head at the little fellow's awkwardness.

'For he gave them their own desire; they were not estranged from their lust. But while their meat was yet in their mouths, the wrath of God came upon them and slew of the fattest of them.'

They rang their chains. They had heard the vinegar of his message, though. They were listening better than he thought they were. Now he raised his voice to get the honey to them.

'And they returned and inquired early after God. And they remembered that God was their rock, and the high God their redeemer.'

He didn't quake backward one step from their impiety, though it stank like the hut itself.

'Oh my people,' he called, his ankles cringing from the heads of serpents, 'what have I done to you, that you should repay me thus?'

The door bounced open. Moonlight drenched Halloran's feet. 'Sweet,' he muttered. He felt himself to be knee deep in the bounty of fish from a burst net. 'Sweet God,' he said.

Following the moonlight came the Constable with a chain in his hand. He beat at the four man-soft corners. The chain clattered and plopped across wood and flesh, hissed along Halloran's scalp one way, then another. It was hard and noisy. Halloran kept his hands up to his ears, and it fell like hoofs on his shoulder, then roared away after the obscenities still running wild at the far end of the hut.

Mr Calverley's belly leapt with the chain, bit the blasphemers, head and shoulders. Both his hands were tight as paws, folded chin-high, his lanthorn in them. When he saw that he was standing so, like an eager little animal, he filled with shame, or rather was drained of anything else.

'Stop it, stop it, stop it, Constable!' he roared.

He brought down his foot, such a small foot that he seemed to be merely taking the first step in a polka. 'Stop it!' The chords of his little neck were hard as bark. He was horrified, in part at himself. 'In God's name, stop it!' he shrieked, while silence took him unawares.

'Go away, please!' he said.

But still he thought that stripes these four deserved, and stripes they would get in their pit in hell.

The Constable left, dragging his chain to show that he thought officers of the Government should not slight each other in public.

'There is no other name but the name of Jesus given in heaven or on earth by which it behoveth a man to be saved,' proclaimed the chaplain quietly.

'And *he* works for Government House,' John HcHugh called, feeling out his chain wounds and crying over them.

Four big steps for such small legs, and the chaplain stood over him, holding the light up, looking for the impious features. McHugh snuffled through a moustache of blood, sounding and looking like a frightened horse. The chaplain struck him on the jaw, and gave up the four of them.

'You consecrated bastard!' Miles called out behind him.

'Who when their children ask them for bread they give them a stone,' said Halloran, feeling weirdly hilarious from his beating.

'What?' asked the little chaplain, who was nearly at the door. 'What?'

But he showed no sign of waiting, so that Halloran indulged his tipsiness and called tragically, 'In God's name, help me!'

'Ah!' said the spirit of Mr Calverley. It was full of interest in this brand of anguish. Interest, not pity. As far as he knew he was bereft of pity. He knew that he was no more to blame for this than a store-keeper whose store was empty. He was not ashamed of being arid. He wished he would die. But this, in one dark corner out of four, was the anguish he was called to cure, this was bruised reed and smouldering flax. He turned the light of his lamp upon it.

'Yes,' he said. 'My poor son. My poor brother.'

'I am, I am,' said Halloran starting to cry.

'Hush,' said Mr Calverley, and shook Halloran by the shoulder. 'Redemption is at hand. We shall pray together.'

'If you say.'

But he continued to cry, it was so easeful. His scalp was stinging and his ears roared like hives.

'The girl's on her own,' he said when he could speak. 'The hut's as bad as this one. I know. Then there's the Constable.'

'I've spoken to the Constable,' Calverley told him, thinking that here was at best, brute loyalty and at worst, brute jealousy; knowing that he lacked the vital energies to exalt whichever one it was to the level of redemption. 'I shall be seeing the girl when I leave here.'

He was so disappointed. He could not avoid saying, 'You need not be afraid that she might trade flesh with the Constable.'

Halloran roared, turning away, and bit into his chained left hand.

'I grieve for you,' Calverley said. By heaven he did, but this fellow wouldn't believe him. He did not go away, and he felt sure that here, in the eight o'clock pit of the death-hut, was the final collapse of his mission to men.

'My wife will sit with her the whole night,' said Calverley, and added, not without mild wonder, 'my wife is a Christian.'

'Don't pester her with texts,' Halloran said without facing him. 'Please don't.'

Calverley hissed.

'How dare you!' he said. 'The girl is not even a decent wife.'

Halloran kept his back to the chaplain.

'The girl is *my* wife.'

He said it with so potent a calm, that Calverley thought, how he must hate me, how he hates the London Mission Society's prize vigneron of souls. But how could he fairly detest the prestigious editor of *Tibullus's Elegies*, who has hauled his erudition across the windy night to throw light on the faces of the damned?

'You never came before me,' he said.

'You aren't one of our priests.'

Calverley laughed a short time, or the laughter in him laughed, while he remained mourning beside Halloran.

'That's an excuse for concubinage,' he said, 'if ever I heard one.'

The boy looked at him.

'You give your blessing to hangings, you call God down on the gallows.'

'The gallows are better for my being there.'

But if he had really believed it, he would have left then.

'If they hang my girl before a crowd . . .' said Halloran incompletely, the light of the lanthorn washing over his face, and one of his eyes within the light but stark, seeming to be all pupil, not drawn by the light. 'And if you're there blessing it . . .' He remembered a phrase of Blythe's. 'If you're there blessing the long sweat of indecency of the crowd,' he said. 'Rape by hempen rope.'

For some reason, he was almost asleep.

'May the Lord High God of Glory spit you up,' he managed to say in the end.

The pastor stood up straight. He had a habit of surface rage from the times when he had felt sure of his calling. Without this certainty to temper it now, it ran wild and inordinate.

'Do you think the All-Highest will listen to *you*? Do you think God will avenge *your* harlot on me, his minister?' He cast his eyes up. 'I am wasted on you. I am wasted on this town,' he lamented.

'Yah!' Miles called at him.

He turned to the hut in general.

'I carry the Cross to you, the Saviour's Cross to the four of you. And the single man who will speak to me does not speak of justification but of a—of a randy girl.'

'Yah!' Miles told him again.

'I leave you to the worm of death. I leave you all to the worm of death. He will bite deep on you while I still laugh.'

He gave three hacks of laughter to show them. He opened the door. In the flouncing skirts of the light from his lanthorn, he rushed out, roaring to the Constable, 'Flog them if they move!'

The Constable saw the light of salvation jogging away into the darkness. Towards the small, black fury who carried it, he made a pronounced motion of the hand. Then he locked the death-hut door.

28

I n the death-hut, they were half-mad from the cold. Halloran could not tell from the hole in the roof that the day was made of low cloud, pearl-grey, pearl-radiant. Everything on which the morning lay, especially the water, was touched with the lambency of the pearl. Beyond the bay, the sea ran like a beast with slick, numerous muscles.

Above the sea and amongst the wet undergrowth on the headland, a Marine had the work of watching for a convoy. He sat on a pole, on two blades nailed either side of the top. His coat had edged up round his ears. He had ceased to feel the blades cutting into his buttocks. The frostiness made his legs and feet itch. He was certain that this was not the acceptable hour. By the time he sighted the pin-new East Indiaman, it had already ripped through the oyster-shell horizon far out to the south-east, and daylight poured in behind it. The Marine did not believe in what he saw. It was too sparkling and spanking and lissom a ship, seven and eight hundred tons.

But half the main topmast had gone—something never missing on dream ships. He climbed down the pole screaming. There was a hut below him, and a Sergeant and a servant jerking wide-eyed out of the door. The Sergeant had his stare, and they got their muskets and fired three shots twenty seconds apart—the Sergeant, the Marine, the Sergeant. Their *feu de joie* split the china-ware morning.

'Rowley, Rowley,' screamed His Excellency, trundling down the hall of Government House. He had been gaseous with hunger, and now his bowels jumped at the deliverance. 'I'll cut their tripes out if they're larking.'

Across to the headland, where the dew had melted and the

morning become more solid, far too solid when you had to climb its spiky sides. Having surmounted it and come halloing through the snapping undergrowth, His Excellency snatched a glass from the Sergeant. He screwed it into his eye-lid with such savage hope that the Sergeant backed away and hoped that the superb vision would show up on those hard, sovereign eye-balls.

'Where is it? It's all right, I see it. It's a beautiful ship, Rowley. Looks as if it came from the shipyard yesterday. Well, not quite. It's had trouble with its main-topsail. East India company pennant. About seven hundred tons.'

He laughed, still ogling the streamlined salvation of his town.

'It's not exactly what I expected.'

Of his bounty he let the others look. While they searched for it, he laughed in their ears. He was very taken with that limber ship.

'Rowley, take the boat, bring the pilot. Oh, and warn the battery. Eleven gun—no, thirteen gun salute! Then straight across and collect me. You understand?'

Rowley did, and minced away across the headland. The brush snapped at his button-up gaiters, private Marine's issue.

At the look-out, His Excellency was sobering, thinking, *What if it's only one of a convoy, what if it's a matter of hundreds more felons on their way to me, a half dozen ungovernable cargoes due to be with me by dusk?* He felt sick and climbed down to the bay to wait for Rowley.

A brush bonfire had been built on the headland to guide the ship in. But the white smoke did not show well against a west of pewter. All morning the sergeant looked for a bark that would make black smoke, but gave up at noon to cheer the sleek shape through into haven.

Chatham, said its stern.

Aboard it, His Excellency heard the details of his rescue. The *Chatham* was one of a fleet; it was under charter as a store-ship. This was its maiden voyage to India. The Navy agent happened to be on board, having crossed to it in the Indian Ocean to look into some routine matter. Since then they hadn't seen any more of the fleet, for they soon entered a five-day gale. The *Chatham* was the first of the convoy to reach Batavia, and left messages there for the rest, if there were any.

Callow in his joy, His Excellency nodded. 'I hope they've all drowned,' he said.

Allen was at Government House that afternoon to ask for barracks for his company. He was a blunt enough man to think that since His Excellency would that day be extraordinarily happy, he would be more willing to stretch his resources. His Excellency was not happy in as unmixed a way as that. For one thing, which of the condemned could now be pardoned? He asked Allen, whom he thought the most thorough-going officer amongst the Marines.

'You could safely pardon the two guards,' Allen said. 'The gravity of taking food depends upon whom the food is taken from, how great was their actual need of what was taken. That is, such thefts are of varying gravity. Our need was not as great as we thought at the time of sentencing, because the *Chatham* was just beyond the horizon. But once treason enters . . . There you have something whose seriousness never varies.'

His Excellency had already reached the same conclusions, although he was far more disturbed by them than Allen could ever be by what was manifest justice.

At last His Excellency got up and crossed in front of the fire to the door. His mouth was genuinely crooked, and his big, arched eyebrows channelled doubt down to the wrinkles above his nose. He called for his secretary.

'If that's all, Allen . . .' he said, and he lumbered back to his desk, having a decree concerning 'general jubilation' on his mind, as Blythe had predicted.

'That's all,' said Allen. 'Though I've got something here for you.'

He took three folded pages out of his shallow waistcoat pocket.

'It's some verse of that fellow Halloran. I thought you might like to keep it. When you've retired from public life, it may remind you of what a varied herd you ruled in this place.'

His Excellency took the pages, still frowning. He couldn't understand how he would ever need souvenirs.

'Thank you, Allen.'

Allen bowed and went.

On the desk, the folded pages began to creak open. The secretary came in.

'Sit down, Long,' the Governor muttered, and screwed up his eyes at Halloran's idle art. The pages looked threatened in his big hands. What he saw was the debris of minor inspirations, much crossing and blotting. Two verses seemed to be written whole, although a great number of rhyming words had been written down beside them and scratched out.

'Let the sun cope golden,' he read,
'With the shoulders of my eaves.
May the hale throats of Beauty's sons
Shake old eardrums and the summer's leaves.

'And when Beauty nods silver—
Kine cropping the lushness of my edge—
May the smiles of our shy grand-daughters
Bring larks and heroes to our hedge.'

'Larks and heroes,' he said, 'smiles of our shy grand-daughters. Not my kind of souvenir.'

He rolled the papers in his palms and put them in the fire.

About noon, the massive sounds of cannon penetrated the death-hut, thirteen roars sown like oak-trees amongst the other, ankle-high sounds of this day, their last of all. Albert Miles travestied hope by jumping up but rebounding in the limits of his chains. To Halloran he looked painfully elastic, but capered and laughed.

'What price the French, eh? What price the rotten old French?'

McHugh and Barrett hauled themselves up as if there were windows. The mad hope had kicked them in the belly.

225

'The French?' said McHugh.

'Why not the French? If Halloran and his bit of snuff could think of it, why couldn't King Lou think of it off his own bat?'

Miles looked for Halloran down the long dimness of the place. 'If you and your whore could think of it, Halloran, why not King Lou?'

Halloran said nothing. For one thing, he fretted for Ann as a sceptical philosopher frets for a God. That is, he was not engrossed in whether she was ashamed, fearful, cold, fevered, nagged or soothed by big-breasted Mrs Calverley. These fringed a larger agony. Did she exist? Did she exist in the way he thought she did, was she in the women's hut waiting on the rope? Was she; when he remembered her only as a tallness and a presence, the way a god is remembered.

He blamed neither his fever nor last night's beating for his sense of disbelief. He blamed Hearn partly, for Hearn so powerfully sowed misgivings. Hearn's whaler, for example. Who could believe in Hearn's whaler? There had been a whaler certainly, who had visited and been expelled from the bay. Perhaps he had already been days across the Pacific before Hearn and Terry and Halloran himself had begun their grinding debate. Hearn had been left at night on a small beach and was gone in the morning. Yet it was easier to believe he had descended into the pit, stores and all, than that he'd really been taken away by a fleshly, profit-making whaler.

Now, as if through Hearn, doubt had begun to corrode the sureties he had had through Ann: of having possessed and having been possessed. Which no mere disaster could bear away; apart, of course, from the disaster of ceasing to believe in the tissue of your world.

At the same time, he had begun to vacate his house, his house of life. Or so he believed. He sat and let his senses numb and his lights burn out. He had the illusion of closing the door on so many rooms, the comely, the lurid, the useful. He felt that he lived in a porch in the front of his forehead, and was a stranger to the walls behind him.

The others had not yet begun to prepare for the journey.

'Tell us what she's like when the decks are cleared,' McHugh said, speaking of Ann.

'Yes,' Miles said, 'how's it done?'

And they kept at him until he found that there were rooms where the fires still burnt amidst shrouded furniture, because he began to resent Miles and the other two.

He was angry, but he waited; and when they were quiet, he began to speak out of his serene hatred.

'Wait till tomorrow,' he said.

'Go to hell!' Miles told him.

'Tomorrow,' he said.

'You silly bastard.'

'Tomorrow.'

Tomorrow a third time made them listen. They listened in utter quiet, not able to afford neglecting anyone with words to say on that unthinkable occasion. Not even, ultimately, would they neglect to listen to Calverley.

'What will it be like, do you think?'

They thought but couldn't achieve anything.

He told them.

'Tomorrow when we drop,' he jerked his right fist, 'every bit of song and prayer and curse will come roaring up our throats. And every insult a man ever spoke to a man. They'll scream and push to get past the rope. But it might be minutes before our heads blow off. And all the time, as I've said, every insult ever spoken will be roaring through us. So save yourselves till then is my advice, friend Miles and friend McHugh.' He thought of Barrett who had merely laughed with them, would laugh with anyone, a poor bugger without two words to rub together. 'Friend Barrett,' he said.

At the thought of their familiar skulls exploding, they started to roar. Their rank terror made him ashamed. McHugh took a fistful of rubble floor. He threw it like a free man, jarred his arm, saw his hatred fall as a spatter of pebbles in the middle of the hut.

'Look here,' said Miles, 'I believe in the French.' But now he was aware of the odds against belief.

'Listen!' Halloran told them.

From the town they heard a thin croak of cheering, hardly more vocal than the wind.

Halloran could then have been ironic, but irony was a waste on your very last day.

29

THE sky above their broken roof, expressive yesterday, was today devious and fish-coloured. It was so dark by three that they thought it was twilight. They were very sober now, in the corners.

The fraudulent three o'clock dusk broke when the door clapped open and showed the grey day to be still in business, showed steely, straight, robust, absolutely non-golden light. Shapes of men, two Marines, clattered in the doorway, curiously flustered with the onus of living, no way assured of death's amplitude. They showed some interest in Halloran's head of hair clotted from the chain.

If you only knew how my ears are ringing with the daylight, he thought. The daylight stung the back of his brain, and rushed belling like a festival down his spine.

These two men made noses because of the waste-bucket. They became aware too of Halloran taking a vehement interest in themselves. They did not understand how remote they were from him, how remote as angels in their sinewy, off-the-cuff living. He listened for oddities in their breathing, the distinctive pulse, the lope and gallop of their insides. 'No, I'm not mad,' he wanted to tell them. 'It's just that I've lost the habit of life.' So he observed them and hopelessly admired their prerogatives, as the pious hopelessly admire the prerogatives of angels.

They stood back from the door to let somebody through. But there was a delay. Outside, the white eucalypts grew, five trees from the one bole, gusting outwards from each other, very much a conclave, more habituated to life than any coterie of aldermen, colonels, judges, who ever stood, heads back, gargling a clannish joke. Life arrogant there, outside the death-hut; life astringent in white trees.

Then, with his notorious grandeur, Lieutenant Rowley came in.

Rowley took in the hut wincing. Halloran giggled in his corner at the dead young man, at the series of vacant stances so plausible that they would one day festoon it with the braids and gold threads of, at least, a Major-General.

The Lieutenant had a paper in his right hand when Halloran came out of his soft mirth. Perched in his fingers, it trembled, and he tamed it with two shakes of his wrist.

'Whereas,' the document began hatefully, and went on to tell them how they had been condemned to death the Saturday before because of Act 28 Geo III, C.2 and various letters patent. It said that in view of the general jubilation surrounding the timely arrival of the East India Company's ship *Chatham*, the death sentence attaching to James Barrett and John McHugh should be transmuted to life imprisonment in this colony, that the two of them would work with the timber gangs for the rest of their lives, or do anything else they were told to.

Rowley nodded the Constable in to unlock the chains on Barrett and McHugh for their short journey to other fetters. The two of them felt their way up the wall, fish-gaped and chewed their breath. Their faces were curdled white. Then they began to smile, and Barrett winked and McHugh whooped and whacked his thigh.

'Take them outside!' Rowley told the Marines. He crinkled his nose at their indecent joy. The Marines nudged and nodded the way to the two of them.

Halloran saw Albert Miles's big nose jerk in panic. He came forward lop-sidedly on his knees.

'You'll rot in chains,' he roared at them.

Both his flat eyes, moored close in to the bridge of his nose and swamped with his own futile cunning, wept slowly. McHugh, being shuffled to the door looked back. He grinned. He had been saved so instantaneously that he equated himself with life itself, and you could see in him raw hostility for a man so immutably doomed as to be a death symbol.

'We'll *know* we're rotting,' he said.

They were pushed out into the silver universe. Miles would be alone with the mad Irish all night. He cried rustily.

'Sir,' Halloran said, 'anything for the woman?'

Rowley looked into Halloran's corner. Halloran shivered and pulled the blanket straighter on his shoulders. Rowley shook his head, nearly like a real person, and went out.

They shut the door. It was so dark. The clumsy eaves cried in the wind, and Miles cried.

'They've escaped nothing,' Halloran said, but Miles went on despairing maladroitly at the far end of the hut.

'I have killed you, my lovely bride,' said Halloran very softly.

But no slow fire of time for them. Time would not eat Ann at the roots of her body so piecemeal, so daily, daily, that she would find with surprise that she was old, brown glue for her eyes, no traffic on the poor beaches of her lips. They would be eaten at one gulp, and when again she rose, she would be all olive skin, all brown gloss of the body.

'They've escaped nothing,' he called out, certain of it.

Someone jiggled his sleeping elbow. He stared, and it was true dusk. While, where his neck joined his shoulders, a shivery heat ran.

'Hello,' said Calverley.

'I was asleep,' said Halloran, simply as an explanation.

'Tell me!' The parson licked his lips, the better to swallow pride. 'I take it you don't wish that Ann Rush to die before a crowd?'

'Is she there?' asked Halloran. To himself, his voice sounded cavernous, he spoke out of a grotto like an oracle.

'Where?'

'In that hut.'

Calverley cleared his throat.

'Yes. There's no hope now except heaven. You must know that?'

231

'What does she look like?' Halloran asked, squinting.

'She's quite well. She even—' (The chaplain inhaled) 'sends her love. My wife is tending her.'

'What does she look like though? Is she there? You wouldn't lie?'

'My poor boy, you have a fever. Luckily I've brought you a blanket each.'

Indeed, he had them over his right arm.

'Here,' he said, 'I think you should sit on one of them. The damp comes up through the earth. Although, I suppose that I don't have to tell a soldier that.'

'Here!' he said to Miles, simply throwing Miles the other blanket he'd brought, as if he and Miles were old, knock-about kinsmen.

It made Miles gape, of course, to have a clergyman give such laconic charity.

'Don't let the crowd see her,' Halloran said.

'I see,' Calverley nodded.

'What does she look like?'

'My poor boy.'

'I know she's tall.'

Calverley shook him by the shoulder.

'Listen. I'll see His Excellency who is, after all, decent.'

'Long sweat of indecency,' said Halloran.

'I know. That's my very point.'

Halloran shrugged. Calverley would see His Excellency. But it would be like Hearn seeing the whaler, and Mrs Calverley being with Ann. Symbols.

'Our Father,' said Calverley unopposed.

30

IN the morning, Mr Calverley came early to the death-hut with his hat off, and holding his head sideways, trying to make out Halloran's face. He didn't speak until he had it clear in view.

'Halloran,' he said. 'It's been done.'

'Oh God!' said Halloran.

He fell back into his corner in a clatter. He was all dead wood; his head hung loose from his neck, and his jaw from his head.

Now he believed. Almost.

'Are you sure?' he said. 'Did you ask His Excellency? Did you ask in words?'

The chaplain would have liked to tell Halloran how hard it had been to invade a Government House dinner of celebration, especially as he was one of the few officials not bidden. The viceroy, full of the wine of brotherhood, had been appalled to see the little priest purple and roaring threats in the ante-room. 'I will not preach for you or pray for you or chain God as a watch-dog to your gate-post.' But His Excellency had been dull and lenient. Of course he thought the public death of a young girl an indecency. Of course she could be quietly executed. Ninety minutes early, say. No drums, no trumpets. No excess.

'I persuaded His Excellenecy, and I tried to let you know of it last night. Did the Constable tell you?'

Halloran started to wave his head sinuously, making a low wail. After some time, Calverley half-knelt and took the head on his knee. He held it very firmly. His fingers were quite tense. If ever he wanted to infuse something of the Master through his priestly fingers, he did now. As if he had imparted something of worth, the head revived in his hands. Halloran sat up.

'Was it hard for her?'

'It was the right thing, whether hard or not. But no. She did not find it hard.'

'Is that the truth? Tell me.'

'Yes, it is the truth, Halloran.'

'I'd be calm now if I knew it was the truth.'

'Halloran, I stood not ten feet from her. You know how these things are unmistakable. I heard the noise. Her neck broke immediately.

Halloran turned his head away and vomited. He finished, but stared at the floor of clay and rubble, at the insensate little downs of clay. He felt divested for good of his belly, of his stupid, loud, first-hurt and inconsolable belly. He wiped the bitterness of his lips—there was something in him that was discomforted by the bile taste and didn't know that the romp was finished. To it, the cataclysm would come as a thunderclap.

When Halloran looked up shivering and the tongue still flicking round the acrid mouth, Calverley suffered a thunderclap too. For he saw that here was what was called *the moment of grace*; that now he might be able to sell God as a cow is sold, and that if he tried to, God would spit him out. He felt liberated suddenly from his vested interest in brotherly love. He could be kindly, just kindly, without motives, good or bad.

'Chaplain!' Miles was calling.

'You will have to wait a little longer,' said Reverend Calverley, staying by Halloran.

But Halloran told him to go to Miles, and before long, he did go. When he returned some minutes later, he was used to the dark and could see Halloran's face from yards away, very white in its corner.

'Was it the right thing to do?' Halloran said, before Calverley had even reached him. He was wondering who had the right to say that Ann should enter the furnace even two hours before her time. Yet *he* had said it.

'She couldn't have been more grateful,' said Calverley. 'She was very quiet—upset, as you can imagine. But she was indeed grateful to die modestly.'

'She should have cursed me.'

'She indicated the gallows and said to tell you she was sure they would be a type of wedding for you. There. I carried the message quite faithfully, without qualification.'

'Thank you, sir. Thank you. Why didn't I thank you earlier?'

'You are not to worry about that,' said Calverley.

He did a hard thing then, for any man of the cloth to do. He did not commentate on the tragedy, he did not try an exegisis of the girl's agony, of Halloran's bereavement. He remained silent by the boy, and at last said that he must go but would be back.

'Have some breakfast, it will settle your stomach,' he said in parting.

From politeness, Halloran agreed, although, mindful of Ewers, he would not eat anything.

Calverley went out. Halloran, who could not consistently remember that Ann was hanged, thought what a strange delight it must be to walk out of doors of a morning.

Likewise early, Mrs Blythe limped to her window to have one look at the gallows through the trees on the west of the house, intending then to go back to her chair and pray for Ann. She saw a woman already swinging dead on the gallows. A man on a ladder was mounting towards the woman slowly, carrying a sail-cloth to cover her.

Mrs Blythe clutched her mouth and began to sweat. Her chair stood five yards away. Now she wondered if she could reach it. Without being aware of her efforts she managed to find it and sat shivering.

Some time later, disgraced Mr Blythe knocked.

'Go away,' Mrs Blythe called.

'I would,' said Mr Blythe. 'But you have the only westward-facing window in the house.'

'The door is locked.'

'I have a key.'

She heard the key scraping in the socket.

'I forbid you,' she shrieked.

But hopefully, she had her black-thorn by her. She would raise lumps on that blatant ear of his.

This hanging day, Mr Blythe, who came straight in, wore a suit of blue serge. He wore it as neatly as a man who had someone to impress.

'Are you at peace?' he said dismally. 'Or were you taken by surprise too? It should be twenty-two minutes to noose-time. Still, there she is.'

He peered out the window quickly, rid himself of a small yelp whose meaning he gave no hint of, and faced back indoors.

'You hot old fool,' she said.

'You flatter me, Mrs B. My blood's full of polar bears.'

'You're laughable.'

'I might well be.' He seemed to have no interest in the question. 'What a letter to father you can write now! So much to tell.'

Prodigal of pain, Mrs Blythe slammed her shoulders against the back of her chair.

'I'll tell you straight, sir. My father never rose before a court and claimed and argued that he'd got a servant broody with child.'

He sat himself down. There was a remarkable pallor around his mouth. It seemed to have been painted on, as on a clown or actor.

'You are the total of all the riots of his blood?' he asked her, sighing and closing his eyes.

After a silence, Mrs Blythe laboured upright on her left leg, which she considered a quarter or even a half good. She had her stick and hopped towards him and struck him on the shoulder. It hurt him, she could see that much. It shocked him out of his chair. He grabbed the stick and kicked at her shins, tripping her. She seemed to herself to be a long time in falling, to be striving back from the brunt of the floor for a very long time. Her teeth bit when she fell.

She lay neither greatly hurt nor in great pain, and could have risen of her own accord; but her mode of life forced her to pretend to be as helpless as an upturned beetle. For form's sake, she groaned, playing at pain, and didn't rush to speak her mind, didn't risk to any chance words the new stature which, being flat on the floor, she had achieved. While she waited, someone knocked on the outside door.

'Beware the ravisher, Madam,' said Mr Blythe, stepping over her to answer the knock. 'I can see at least four inches of your delightful leg.'

He let somebody in with warmth and was soon back, ambassa-dorial in the door, his right heel tucked into his left instep and one shoulder inclined.

'It's just like Christmas day, Mrs B.,' he told her, 'and all our old friends come to visit us.'

'Somewhat more like Good Friday, Mr Blythe,' she said.

'Good Friday indeed. Betrayer and all.'

Mrs Blythe frowned, but not for long. She was no fool.

'Terry Byrne?'

'Yes.'

She made a face.

'Help me up, thank you!'

'Not yet,' he said. 'Come in, Private Byrne.'

'How dare you! When I'm in this state.'

'State my eye, Mrs B.,' Blythe said, and was ready then to go back to the window, though not yet to look out again.

Terry came in dressed as he had been in court.

'Look at the silver braid, Mrs B.,' the Commissary called lightly. 'Look at the greenness of the green and the redness of the red.'

Terry cowered within his hard, regimental clothing, and could be heard hissing from the pain of his interrogation according to the Spanish.

'Yes, Terry?'

'Could I help you, Mrs Blythe?' Terry offered.

But his eyes were not willing. One could understand it, given his new state of life. He had traded his kith for the discontinuance of pain. Even the pain of politeness to a felled lady proved that the bargain was a bad one; even the pain of politeness was insufferable.

'It is Mr Blythe's place to help me,' said Mrs Blythe. 'What do you want?'

Byrne began to shrug, but decided against it, for the same reason that he had decided against manners.

'It's nearly time for them to start beating the drum,' he said. 'Do you mind if I stay, since you've been so kind before. I'm so sorry, and there's nowhere else to go.'

At least he *sounded* very urbane, as if the beating had done him the world of good.

'You could shoot yourself and go into the pit,' Mr Blythe suggested.

His wife cautioned him from the floor.

'The smouldering flax, Mr Blythe. The smouldering flax and the bruised reed.'

'He certainly is the bruised reed. They tell me you've been beaten with green wands, Terry.'

Byrne stammered from the pain.

'Yes,' the Commissary nodded, 'it must sting you. You poor Judas-faced bastard!'

'No,' said Byrne, not hard enough to smart though, 'it was that Hearn had us bewitched to the back-teeth.'

'Don't blame Hearn,' said Mrs Blythe. 'Blame yourself, like a good man.'

'That Hearn was Satan,' Terry insisted. He shuddered like a demoniac.

Blythe laughed and pointed to his wife, saying, 'And meet Queen Mab. Or perhaps the Lady of the Lake.' He peered. 'After fifty years drowned in the river of life, the features coarsen.'

'Mr Blythe,' said the lady. 'I am waiting. In considerable pain, I might tell you.'

Mr Blythe turned his back. Whether he intended to stare at the gallows, they were his only alternative to the other two, both of them so insistent to be put on their feet, both in the same degree incapable of profiting from that particularly mercy.

'You had better go, Terry,' Mrs Blythe decided, withdrawing

her eyes to show there was no court of appeal from her decision.

'Like this? You can see how the Sergeants have been dressing me.'

'You must face the world, Terry,' Mrs Blythe said grandly. 'Let it be a friendless world. God is your friend. Out of these despised ruins, Terry, the new Zion!'

At the window, Mr Blythe had a laugh to see that her canons thundered forth just as irresponsibly now that she was on the flat of her spine.

'Remember to grunt now and then, Mrs B.,' he called. 'Remember to be pained.'

Terry began sobbing.

'They won't let me take my meals in peace, Mrs Blythe. They won't let me go for a walk or lie on my belly in my hut. They'll have me carrying the corpses if they can find me. I know the beggars.'

'Face them if necessary, Terry, and do it.'

'With a tow-row-row-row-row-row-row,' said Mr Blythe, 'to the British grenadiers.'

'If I could stay here till this afternoon . . .' Terry hoped. 'There's a lot I still haven't told you about the quaint habits of home.'

The lady shook her head and crawled a foot closer to her blackthorn. Achingly, Byrne sank to his knees to retrieve the stick for her. What occupied him when he had got that far was how to move ever again.

In any case, 'Don't touch it, Terry!' said Mrs Blythe. 'You have to go.'

'Go on, you Judas bastard,' the Commissary at the window said. 'Get on your way. I'll give you a few good English pains to go with your Spanish ones.'

'Where, Mrs Blythe?' Terry whispered, swaying on his knees.

'Outside,' she told him. 'There's nowhere else. You have to learn to face the world.'

'Just an hour or two.'

'Oh, get out when you're told!'

'Ah,' Mr Blythe said over his shoulder, 'they have her all tricked out in canvas.'

'Get up, Terry, you stupid boy,' said Mrs Blythe. 'Sir, I am waiting to be helped up.'

She stared when her husband snorted, turned away from the window, away from Mrs Blythe, hiding his face.

'Tears?' she asked. 'You old fool. There's no fool on earth like a hot old fool.'

He could be heard sobbing now, but not because she had called him a hot old fool.

'Get out, you Judas bastard!' he said to Byrne, who found his feet quickly and by accident.

'I am not one of those people who think that tears mean grief, Blythe,' the lady explained. 'People can *cry* in theatres, where tears no more mean grief than do belly-rumbles.'

But he clearly didn't care what they meant, and he clearly wept for the pity of things. It shocked her to see *him* weeping for the pity of things.

'Oh, stop it and help me up!'

'Mrs Blythe,' Terry said gently.

'Go away, Terry!'

'Where?'

'That's not the point. Go on now, go on! Don't you have an excellent piece of gossip? Didn't you see Mr Blythe strike me down? Most days you couldn't have got outside quickly enough with news like that.'

'That's not being fair to me, Mrs Blythe,' Terry said.

'Get out!' she said.

Productively; because he went, though it may have been that he had suddenly despaired on his own initiative of the poor comforts of her parlour.

'Now,' said the lady when he had gone, 'assist me please, Mr Blythe.'

Yet Mr Blythe was still much embarrassed by grief.

'Sad it all may be,' she admitted. 'But they merited it for themselves. That good soldier Halloran merited it for them. God is *not* mocked.'

The pattern of it all, of Halloran's oath and laxity, and the devilish cord, and of God redeeming his pledge, was quite awesome, quite a parable. She should write it down, for, as a cautionary tale, it would be unmatched.

'But it does make one go pale, nonetheless,' she continued. 'The death of the young is always a harsh mystery. If it be so in the green wood, Mr Blythe . . .'

Blythe left the wall and came across the room, rubbing his forehead. Halfway to her, he stopped and frowned a private frown, as if he'd discovered himself in a small, domestic forgetfulness. Then he continued. He looked as if he might walk over her, and even try to go through the wall. She squealed and crawled away from him, but he reached her in the end, and bent to draw her upright by the shoulders. She simpered, not knowing what to expect.

He simply drew her across the room, back to her chair. As with girls in romances, her feet barely touched the ground, so firm and strong was his hold. He sat her down and kicked her hassock into place and lifted her legs to it by the ankles.

'Madam,' he said before leaving her.

And after a time, when, from having been handled so oddly, the dizziness and shudders had passed, she felt so brisk that she promised herself she would hobble out into the rational winter sunlight, perhaps even that very day. As well, she felt entitled to take out Ann's heathenish red cord and shake her head and nod over it. Through her window, she could see the glossy sides of wet leaves spangled with sunlight; she could hear them tinkling with chandelier music, and she wanted to dance to it. Perhaps her leg could stand it, because perhaps her leg was dry. There had been dry westerly winds since Sunday. She threw her shawl off, and pulled her robe and petticoat and loose-legged trousers practically up to her hip. She unwound the poultice from the worst of her ulcers.

'Of course, I would be very tottery,' she confessed aloud, but the music of the leaves went slowly on, promising to keep time with her weakness.

Yes, it was dry. She had never seen it better. She inspected the others. They were well.

'Thank God,' she said, and shards of music dropped from the leaves. It was a jig that she heard, about a man who was more blessed than lovers since he has a whiskey flask for his love, and it never flounced or answered him back. She laughed at it for being so scandalous. The tempo was gentle with her, and did not push her off balance once. She was slow and club-footed at first, but before long, danced with increasing movement and joy.

31

When it was time, the Provost-Marshal came for them. He entered the hut with guards and a constable. He was perhaps two years older than Halloran, and wore a cut-away coat to show his young man's loins. Previously he had been a subaltern in Captain Allen's company. He knew Halloran, his eyes flickered towards him, on his haunches by the wall.

Did your ears drown with the crack, love? was what was occupying Halloran. *How far north and south in your flesh's fair country did the torment run?*

The Provost-Marshal lost nothing therefore, by turning full-face to the prisoner.

'Halloran,' he said. 'What possessed you?'

Halloran stared. He could make out the young man's face in the far left corner of his anguish.

'Sir,' he said.

'You were well trusted. You would have been Sergeant by Christmas.'

'Sir,' said Halloran.

Ten seconds later, he began to laugh whole-hoggingly. *Sergeant by Christmas.* Belly sash of red and gold. Touring the countryside for recruits. Administering the oath. Administering the *oath*!

They let him out of his chains and shackled his hands before him. Outside, he found himself drinking the honeyed light. At least, his skin went on gorging it vainly in. There was so much of him that would not bend the knee to death, so much of him still living with pointless care. With similar pointlessness, the peppermints along the flat part of the town frothed in his sight. Hard colours pelted his brow; his head ached. Sheaths of sound fell on him.

He limped across the doomsday earth between two files of Marines. Ahead were the drummers, silent drums bouncing on their crooked hips. In this column, only Miles spoke. He had woken up in the night reciting a grace, and he had hardly stopped reciting it since. Now again, he nagged the God of the table of childhood.

'Here a little child I stand heaving up my either hand,' Miles said, at a furious rate. 'Cold as paddocks though they be here I lift them up to thee for a benison to fall on our meat and on us all. Amen.'

Calverley had opened his mouth to begin Psalm 143, but decided the prisoners were beyond it, and would not say it for the sake of custom, just to edify the Provost-Marshal.

The question was, would Miles be saved for saying grace in terror? If God was of the same mind as theologians, he would have no chance either way. For the grace was by Herrick who had written those scandalous lines about night making no difference between priest and clerk, Jane being as good as my Lady in the dark. And terror was not supposed to be admissible in the heavenly court. Yet, since his son had died, the Rev. Calverley had thought with increasing conviction that God could not have views in common with the bulk of theologians, for then he would not be God but a machine of vengeance, a salvation mill.

They came within the crackle of voices. There was a woman's voice wailing a sound that had pontifical authority for Halloran. He could not avoid it washing through him. It brought with it even its own sensations, coming to him with the smell of dry pinewood coffins, tallow candles, the sad hearths of bereaved families. It was the *Trougha* wail, an old friend and demon from the awe-struck twilights of his childhood, when from kitchen corners, he eyed the willowy cleanliness of dead neighbours. He lifted his ear up to the old sound come all those miles to see him to his grave.

That is how to mourn the dead, he thought, proud of the wail, forgetting the dead was Ann. Then he remembered. He told his secret bride that he had left some silly flag or other flying on top of his tower of life. There was no time to climb the stairs and haul the thing down. He was sorry.

The word *sorry* went through his mind in shudders of meaning. Before it, his brain parted like the Red Sea, and through the cleft he saw and advanced into the crowd, and saw and leaned to a narrow bundle hung in sailcloth from the east of the gallows. Caught by rich draughts of the *Trougha*, the bundle turned softly. But it was, under the harsh modesty of canvas, a neck ravened by hemp and a face ballooning. He knew. He had seen these things. This was *their* funny justice.

He had been so passive. Now he moved like anger in the blood, past bug-eyed Mr Calverley. He screamed in a monotone, laid his shackled fists to the side of the Provost's head, and kneed the hard, proud, processional belly. They dragged him away and gagged him. 'Hell fry the balls off your damned Empire!' he tried to tell the Provost, but could not keep the words straight. And then they had him gagged.

The gag liberated him further still. He could speak aloud with Ann. They began to beat the drums. On he went, placid at the core. He was sure he was the worst of men, he saw it. It was because of his vanity. But there is serenity in knowing you are the worst man. You do not even have to ask for mercy.

The drums went stuttering but he still heard the *Trougha*. The slow circlings of its rhythm made him dizzy, its sad old arms kept rocking his secret bride. He was so dizzy he found he could no longer see a crowd or even a man as one thing. They were lozenges and dabs. The world was decomposing. Who sang the wail? He could never tell unless the morning colours cohered again. But the passion of the wailer was coherent, and the song went on and on.

The speed of everything then! Calverley gabbing at his side, Miles still reciting grace before meals. There was a brick-waggon beneath each noose, a man-drawn brick-waggon. The Provost touched the waggon closest to Ann, saying 'Miles!' and the further one, saying 'Halloran'! He was red in the face, and made too much of his intention of separating Halloran from his lady. 'Miles, Halloran,' he said three more times.

They rose like angels into the brick-waggons; Halloran had no sense of climbing. The drums gargled their pig's arse vengeance in his face, and someone, reassured by his stupor, took off the gag. 'Thank you, thank you,' he then said continuously to Calverley, knowing that he was interrupting all the man's delivery and earnestness. Halloran was happier when the parson nodded and touched his wrist, and climbed into Miles's cart.

'That's the end of all the vapourings,' said Halloran. In his short day, he had listened to a power of vapourings.

The hangman came into the waggon. He had a hood for Phelim.

'Listen old cock,' he said. 'You don't have to wear this. What do you say? It saves the mob seeing your face.'

'I lean upon the deep waters of a God who's owned by nobody,' said Halloran.

'I know, cock, but what about this thing?'

'Who is not recruited, and not spoken for by kings.'

'Listen, you're making a gawk of yourself. People are starting to look. Do you want the hood? The buggers down there want to see your eyes and tongue coming out. You'd better put it on.'

The man started to fit the black bag over Halloran's head. 'No!' Halloran called. 'If it's all the same,' he said, 'I won't.'

'I can promise you that, mate. It's all the same.'

Now he could see a dozen shrunken men by each shaft of his waggon. They were the brickyard teams. They would race the other waggon, and bet on Miles or on himself to strive longer, to twitch, double, poke out his tongue or urinate, this way or that or not at all. They were in the centre of his sight, they slewed but were visible, and their red wounds of eyes took him in.

Surely, the eyes said, *you know the secret of our daily sweat, and of our long closeting in the red earth, this year or next year, or some year close even to this honest morning.*

'How does that suit you?'

The hanging man was back. He had the hairy noose over

Halloran's head and tightened and arranged it with small tugs that could afford to be kindly.

'Good-bye,' he said simply. He was a stupid man, full of drama and business.

Halloran squinted out at all the brown scars of faces, luminously agog, aimed at him.

Snarl of drums. The Government House party arrived, His Excellency forbearing, with his right hand, to address the crowd.

The Provost-Marshal's sword rose and fell. The waggon-teams began pulling. He had to dance slowly as the waggon floor began to move without him. He could actually hear cheering.

It was as he had foretold. Every prayer, curse and snatch of song unleashed itself up the vent of his body. Oh, the yawning shriek of his breathlessness, above him like a massive bird, flogging him with its black wings; the loneliness ripping his belly up like paving-stones. On his almost closed lids, six-sided pillars of light came down with terrible hurtfulness. It was with such a surpassing crack that his head split open, he being borne presiding through so many constellations, that he asked himself, panic-stricken, 'Am I perhaps *God*?'

The Chant of Jimmie Blacksmith   Thomas Keneally

First published in 1972 this novel was the basis for the widely acclaimed film of the same title. Based on an actual event in Queensland in 1900 which drove a simple, hard-working Aborigine to the slaughter of white men, women and children. A story of racism written with compassion and sensitivity.

Three Cheers for the Paraclete   Thomas Keneally

From the moment he allows his young cousin and bride to spend the night in his room, Father Maitland causes raised eyebrows and dark mutterings amongst the brothers at St Peter's.

Time and again his efforts to do the right thing for his fellow men lead him into conflict with his superiors and the immutable laws of the church – a conflict which ultimately threatens to destroy him both as a priest and as a man . . .

Tirra Lirra by the River   Jessica Anderson

For Nora Porteous, life is a series of escapes. To escape her tightly knit smalltown family, she marries, only to find herself confined again, this time in a stifling Sydney suburb with a selfish, sanctimonious husband. With a courage born of desperation and sustained by a spirited sense of humour, Nora travels to London, and it is there that she becomes the woman she wants to be. Or does she?

Taking Shelter   Jessica Anderson

In a novel about and across the generations *Taking Shelter* has our attention from page one.

A group of people, young and old, are drawn together in their quests for permanence, tenderness and love in an era when there are no rules about the age, gender, or the faithfulness of lovers. Written with keen perception, wit and emotional honesty.

Hunting the Wild Pineapple   Thea Astley

Leverson the narrator, at the centre of these stories, calls himself a 'people freak'. Seduced by north Queensland's sultry beauty and unique strangeness, he is as fascinated by the invading hordes of misfits from the south as by the old-established Queenslanders. Leverson's ironical yet compassionate view makes every story, every incident, a pointed example of human weakness – or strength.

It's Raining in Mango   Thea Astley

Cornelius Laffey, an Irish-born journalist, wrests his family from the easy living of nineteenth-century Sydney and takes them to Cooktown in northern Queensland where thousands of diggers are searching for gold in the mud. The cycles of generations turn, one over the other. Full of powerful and independent characters, this is an unforgettable tale of the dark side of Australia's heritage.

To The Death, amic   John Bryson

The Civil War begins in Catalonia as a minor excitement for ten-year-old twins, Enric and Josep, up to the moment they become couriers for the Underground. Working alongside spies, arms traders, and document forgers, they watch an astonishing alliance mass to fight the fascist advance: the Los Solidarios bandits under sentence of death, the young Stalinist Ramon Mercader who later assassinates Trotsky, the smugglers from the Pyreness, the Basque priests, the young anarchist women of the bordellos, the nuns of Sant Pau, and the sidewalk tricksters.

Vibrant street-life – gaming, market-stalls, roadside theatre and dance – flourishes, but as Franco's forces isolate Barcelona, the city of a million refugees is bombed day and night by the squadrons of Hitler and Mussolini. Enric's mother prays to the saints and believes in the prophecies of cockroaches; his father deals in passports filched from the dead of the International Brigade; the starving city is barricaded for the siege.

This stunning novel is based on the life of a Catalan insurgent who quickly learns the first lesson of undercover intrigue; 'Mine is never the only game on the board.'

Turtle Beach   Blanche d'Alpuget

Judith Wilkes, an ambitious journalist, goes to Malaysia to report on an international refugee crisis.

Through her encounters with Minou, exotic, young French-Vietnamese wife of a high-ranking diplomat, the ambitious Ralph Hamilton and, ultimately with enigmatic Kanan who tries to liberate her, Judith is thrown into dramatic personal and professional conflicts.

It is on the East Malaysian coast, when turtles gather to breed, that the dilemma reaches its tragic, brutal climax.

White Eye   Blanche d'Alpuget

Diana Pembridge, bird lover and conservationist, finds the body of a genetic scientist on the foreshore of a lake in western New South Wales. Many people have a motive for killing Dr Carolyn Williams, and investigations into her murder put the high security research station where she worked under unwelcome scrutiny.

Blanche d'Alpuget weaves a suspenseful tale of twisted sexual and scientific morality, from which emerges a passionate and surprising love affair.

White Light   James McQueen

On 27 January 1945, Tony Caramia walked free from Auschwitz. More than forty years later, he is the tough and restless owner of a successful building business in Australia about to visit Thailand.

By chance, he sights a German guard from the wartime camp, reviving questions and feelings which have long haunted him. Issues of justice, responsibility and guilt emerge in the cat-and-mouse game that follows. Both men are forced to reckon with their past and their choices for the future against a backdrop of the people and landscape of Thailand.

The Kadaitcha Sung   Sam Watson

In his twentieth year, mixed-blood Aborigine Tommy Gubba is initiated in the eternal flames into an ancient clan of sorcerers – the Kadaitcha. He is sent into the mortal world to take revenge on the fair-skinned race who have plundered its wealth and laid waste to the chosen people. His fate has been ordained, and Tommy must race against time to confront a savage, evil foe.

When Nietzsche wept   Irvin D. Yalom

In 1882 while holidaying in Vienna, Dr Josef Breuer is approached by a beautiful, imperious young woman seeking help for her lover, Friedrich Nietzsche. His friends fear for his life but he refuses all aid.

So begins an intruiging battle of wills and intellect as Breuer sets out to unlock the mysteries of a tormented mind. As the story unfolds, we see a relationship begotten in duplicity and manipulation evolve into a friendship that becomes powerfully redemptive for both men. Yalom brings to life not only Nietzsche and Breuer but also 'Anna O.' and a young medical intern named Sigmund Freud.

Country Without Music   Nicholas Hasluck

The islands known once as the strangest penal colonies on earth are now seething with discontent and Jacqueline Villiers is torn between her uncle's determination to stay in power and the attraction of her Ilois friends. This is a country bedevilled by its past – a country without music.

The Law of the Land   Henry Reynolds

In this readable and dramatic book, Henry Reynolds reassesses the legal and political arguments used to justify the European settlement of Australia.

His conclusions form a compelling case for the belief that the British government conceded land rights to the Aborigines early in the nineteenth century.

With the White People   Henry Reynolds

Guides, linguists, diplomats, interpreters, trackers, troopers, servants, companions, labourers, concubines, nursemaids, cooks, stockworkers, porters, pearl-divers, mine-workers.

The fascinating story of Australia's black pioneers has been largely overlooked by both black and white commentators.

Henry Reynolds' book *The Other Side of the Frontier* was described as 'the most important book ever on Aboriginal-European contact'. *With the White People* now provides a challenging reinterpretation of the role of those blacks whose efforts were vital to the development of colonial Australia.